THE FABULOUS ENGLISHMAN

Robert McCrum has written four other novels: *In the Secret State*, which was made into a film starring Frank Finlay and Natasha Richardson, *A Loss of Heart*, *Mainland*, and *The Psychological Moment*. He also wrote the award-winning television series *The Story of English*. He lives in London.

Robert McCrum

THE FABULOUS ENGLISHMAN

PICADOR

First published 1984 by Hamish Hamilton Limited

This edition published 1994 by Picador
a division of Pan Macmillan Publishers Limited
Cavaye Place London SW10 9PG
and Basingstoke

Associated companies throughout the world

ISBN 0 330 33179 5

1 3 5 7 9 8 6 4 2

A CIP catalogue record for this book is available from
the British Library

Printed and bound in Great Britain by
Cox & Wyman Ltd, Reading, Berkshire

For Olivia

The author and publishers are grateful to the following people and organisations for allowing them to quote the song lyrics and extracts from published material which appear in this novel: Chappell Music Ltd for 'Time' by Roger Waters, David Gilmour, Nicholas Mason and Richard Wright, © 1973 Pink Floyd Music Publishers Ltd, and 'The Wall – Another Brick in the Wall Part II' by Roger Waters, © 1979 Pink Floyd Music Publishers Ltd; Fabulous Music Ltd for 'My Generation' by Pete Townshend, 1965; Faber & Faber Ltd and Doubleday Inc. for *The Making of a Counter Culture* by Theodore Roszak; Granada Publishing Ltd for *Bomb Culture* by Jeff Nuttall; Mayday Music/ Artemis/Intersong Music Ltd for 'American Pie' by Don McLean; Northern Songs Ltd at ATV Music Ltd for 'With a Little Help from my Friends', 'Strawberry Fields Forever', 'She Loves You', 'Sgt Pepper's Lonely Hearts Club Band', 'Lucy in the Sky with Diamonds', 'Hello, Goodbye' and 'When I'm Sixty-Four', all by John Lennon and Paul McCartney; Palach Press Ltd for 'Hundred Per Cent' by The Plastic People of the Universe; Penguin Books Ltd for Nevill Coghill's translation of the Prologue to *The Canterbury Tales* by Geoffrey Chaucer, © 1977 Nevill Coghill; Secker & Warburg Ltd for 'Fairy Tale' from *Notes of a Clay Pigeon* by Miroslav Holub; Schockon Books Inc. for the extract from Franz Kafka's *Diaries*, © 1948, 1949, renewed 1975, 1976; Warner Bros Music Ltd for 'Ballad of a Thin Man' by Bob Dylan; and Westminster Music Ltd/ABKCO Music Inc. for 'Let It Bleed' (1969), 'Mother's Little Helper' (1966), 'Let's Spend the Night Together' (1967) and 'The Last Time' (1965), all by Mick Jagger and Keith Richards.

THE FABULOUS ENGLISHMAN

Abroad

I saw a Peacock with a fiery tail,
I saw a blazing Comet drop down hail,
I saw a Cloud with ivy circled round,
I saw a sturdy Oak creep on the ground,
I saw a Pismire swallow up a whale,
I saw a raging Sea brim full of ale,
I saw a Venice Glass sixteen foot deep,
I saw a Well full of men's tears that weep,
I saw their Eyes all in a flame of fire,
I saw a House as big as the moon and higher,
I saw the Sun even in the midst of night,
I saw the Man that saw this wondrous sight.

Anon

One

This is a tale of a book, the story of my friend, Christopher Iles. Does that name ring a bell? Only to the *cognoscenti*, I suspect. If you've never heard of Christopher Iles, count yourself among millions. Once upon a time he was, in Andy Warhol's phrase, 'famous for fifteen minutes', noted for an achievement that is equally forgotten. Now he . . . well, in the pages that follow I am going to try, with his help, to make something of that missing time.

I say that Christopher is my friend, yet we have known each other for less than three years. In the beginning, when I wrote to him, I was simply offering a publisher's encouragement, the first for many moons. As time passed, and I lost count of the lunches and drinks we had together, I realized that, having given the stuff of his experience to one who has, candidly, led rather a sheltered existence, he wanted it stitched together into a seamless garment by someone he could trust not to make a balls of it, to use his own words. Now that my work is done, I hope that these do not seem like borrowed robes.

I want to make it clear that, professionally speaking, I have nothing to do with the publishers whose distinguished colophon appears on the title page. This is not an in-house job. In fact, my bread and butter comes from one of their rivals, for whom I work as an editorial dogsbody. It is, I suppose, natural to ask why I did not offer the story of Christopher Iles to my employers. After all, as some have commented, I could not have been unaware that it was they who first published his own book all those years ago.

That, of course, is the point. Both of us felt that it was a good idea to make a clean break with the past. Besides, until I took it upon myself to get in touch, they had neglected him for years, something they are now only too anxious to forget. For myself, I was keen not to have all my eggs in one basket. So, for all these reasons, we offered our immaculate typescript to this splendid imprint, and I'm proud to say that it was accepted without hesitation.

Needless to add, there were recriminations and threats about the so-called 'option clause'. Even before the ink was dry on the agreement, there was a vicious whispering campaign on the literary circuit to the effect that I had monopolized Christopher Iles for my own profit and sold his story to the highest bidder.

It's not hard to guess who would be likely to put around such insinuations and, for those readers who imagine that the book world is a society of fastidious bibliophiles whose taste is exceeded only by their erudition, let me insert a note of realism. This is a cut-throat business (I will not say 'profession') a million miles removed from the 'occupation for gentlemen' described in the trade's pompous handbooks.

For the record, then, I can state that I have a joint contract with Christopher Iles, reached by mutual agreement. I'm the first to admit that this is not all my own work: it has been a most rewarding collaboration, and I shall always be grateful for the lessons I have learned in the making of this narrative.

If, at first blush, it is an editor's role I'm playing here – scissors and paste and the blue pencil – my inspiration has been the knowledge that I can hear the sound of my own voice in these pages. Devising – I use the word advisedly – this narrative from the raw materials at my disposal has been an absorbing experience. I can use my editor's skills, but I can also make my tiny mark on the sand.

A word about that process is due here. Christopher Iles has given me access to all his books and papers, especially the letters of Peter Císař. In addition to the documents of the case, I have recorded hours of interview on tape with those who have played a significant part in his life. For their tolerance and co-operation I thank them.

All the facts are reproduced as they were reported to me. As my long-suffering wife, Jane, will testify, I have spent many hours transcribing every interview myself, and I have been scrupulous in my use of excerpt and quotation. In consultation with Christopher Iles I have, necessarily, taken some liberties with the presentation of the material, but if the book as a whole has its faults, then these are mine alone.

Perhaps my biggest anxiety is that, although the making of this book has depended on a certain dogged persistence on my part, I am nearly ten years Christopher's junior, a Me–decade man, mildy ambitious, happily married and quite without his kind of exceptional talent, a bookish Mr Average. I do believe I have a special sympathy for writers like Christopher, but all the sympathy (and all the slog) in the world cannot bridge the gap. As he enjoys reminding me, his experience is history as far as I'm concerned. That is part of its fascination. But history is not actuality: sometimes it seems impossible to do justice to the spirit of Christopher's age, those crazy years from Dallas to Prague. We've adopted a phrase for it: 'You can't get there from here.'

These are inherent difficulties. We have done our best to overcome them, a task that would have been well-nigh impossible without a number of important titles, many of which contain textual and footnote references to Christopher Iles himself. We acknowledge their help with gratitude:

The Young Meteors by Jonathan Aitken (Secker & Warburg, 1967); *The Neophiliacs* by Christopher Booker (William Collins, 1969); *August 21st* by Colin Chapman (Cassell, 1968), *Pop from the Beginning* by Nik Cohn (Weidenfeld & Nicolson, 1969); *Voices of Czechoslovak Socialists* edited by Tamara Deutscher *et al.* (Merlin Press, 1977); *Gates of Eden* by Morris Dickstein (Basic Books, 1977); *Bomb Culture* by Jeff Nuttall (MacGibbon & Kee, 1968); *From Dubček to Charter 77* by Vladimir V. Kusin (Q Press, 1978); *The Pendulum Years* by Bernard Levin (Jonathan Cape,

1970); *So Many Heroes* by Alan Levy (Jay Landesman, 1980); *The Czech Black Book* edited by Robert Littell (Pall Mall Press, 1969); *Revolt into Style* by George Melly (Penguin Books, 1972); *The Drama of the Gifted Child and the Search for the True Self* by Alice Miller (Basic Books, 1981); *Nightfrost in Prague* by Zdeněk Mlynář (Karz Publishers, 1980); *Born Under a Bad Sign* by Tony Palmer (William Kimber, 1970); *The Making of a Counter Culture* by Theodore Roszak (Faber & Faber, 1970); *Prague's Two Hundred Days* by Harry Schwartz (Pall Mall Press, 1969); *Why Dubček Fell* by Pavel Tigrid (Macdonald, 1971); *The Sixties* by Francis Wheen (Channel 4, 1982); *Prague Spring* by Z. A. B. Zeman (Penguin Books, 1969).

I have tried in this introductory note to be frank about *The Fabulous Englishman*, and so, in the same spirit, I must admit to one important omission. Despite prodigious efforts, I was unable to secure an interview with Dr Augustus Kuhn. If he should happen to read these words, on an aeroplane or in some hotel bedroom, I hope he will agree that this is a more or less faithful account of what took place. I hope, too, that he will find occasion for surprise.

So now, to begin at the beginning, I will reproduce Peter Císař's first letter, warts and all.

Praha
23rd September 1968

Dear Mr Iles,

Excuse me, please for writing to you. But as I suppose, that if you be so very kind, you can help me very much with my problem.

I'm 41 years old a czech bookseller, worked in the one of more bookshops in Praha. At the same time I lectured English and American literature in the special courses to our young booksellers and therefore I decide to write to you, because as I think, you can help very much with it.

Now I'm doing the first complete czechoslovak bibliography of English and American literature, written in English, as a textbook to our young booksellers and I'll be so very glad to include to this my work also your name and your words too, if it's possible. Therefore I'll be very glad, if you be so very kind and write to me, please, something about you, your work, what pseudonyms you use (if any) and be so very kind and send me, please, as well a complete list of your books with the date of first edition, if its possible of course.

I also hear more about your most beautiful and interesting book which you've published at this year. But I'm very sorry that to this date I'ven't any possibility to acquainted with this your most exciting book. And, therefore, I'll be very glad, if you be so very kind and advise me, please, how I be able to get this your most interesting book to read it, if it's possible, of course.

Thank you very much for your kindness and I believe that if you be so very kind, you certainly help to me with my problem. With all my best wishes and many good hopes your books.

Sincerely yours,
Peter Císař.

[2]

'Out of this world,' said Christopher Iles, speaking with a bursting heart to the wind and the sky and the sun on the water. 'Simply out of this world.'

Beyond the ensign fluttering in the onshore wind and the seabirds swooping round the stern, the ferry's wake bubbled and foamed, a broad highway stretching back to the white cliffs and the white Victorian promenade in the shadow of the Norman castle.

Iles breathed in deeply, as he had been taught as a child, and let out a shriek of impetuous joy.

He was sharing the taffrail with a solitary traveller like himself, a dumpy woman in a duffle coat and red woolly hat. The other passengers, the Japanese, French, Turks and Americans who had crowded aft to watch the ship navigate the harbour or snap each other against the famous view, were now inside, driven to the bars and cafeteria by the cold. His wild cry made her turn sharply, and he, who had imagined he was alone, met her eye with an embarrassed smile. 'Fantastic,' he murmured. The woman, who was of indefinite early middle age, beamed and said something, muted by the banging of the wind, that sounded like 'joys of spring'. Iles nodded back, and noted the sprouting Anglo-Saxon curls and the peachy glowing of her cheeks with a flutter of curiosity.

A tiny orange helicopter rotored choppa-choppa-choppa above the swinging radar. The perspex flashed and Iles glimpsed a pilot with a Robert Redford moustache. The small boy inside him might have waved. Two stewards appeared on the lower deck, heaving plastic dustbins, and tipped the rubbish from the previous crossing over the stern. Iles watched the trail of garbage tossing on the sparkling wavetops with astonishment. He looked sideways at the woman, who shook her head, apparently sharing his dismay.

He began to pace the deck, slightly exhilarated by the exchange of glance and words. Chance meetings, unexpected conversations, bizarre . . . He has this tendency to think like a thesaurus, but he was only too ready to recognize the traveller's sense of unreality and eager to step into the tradition of literary men who have taken the boat across the Channel in search of experiences unprovided for at home. He was glad to be feeling the symptoms, the true magical irresponsibility so often described. *But oh that magic feeling* . . .

Iles skipped against the pitching and rolling of the ferry as it breasted the Channel with the ease of a natural sailor. His white scarf, thrown across his shoulder, twitched behind him. (Later, the woman in the woolly hat will tell him that it was impossible to forget that distinctive walk: he had paced the gloomy corridors of

Bush House as if about to break into an unorthodox dance. Of course he did not recognize her. After all these years, why should he?) All his movements have this boyish zest, emphasized by the fact that he seems to be wearing exactly the same clothes as ten, even fifteen, years ago: scuffed boots, jeans, a stripy jersey, a plain white shirt and a jacket bulging with a notebook or a paperback. He has always looked like a quote-laden student.

'Who was it who said never take a job that involves a change of clothes?' Laughter from a studio audience fuddled with warm sherry. 'Well, that's one good reason for being a writer.' Laughter and applause.

Waves were breaking against the bow. Iles moved forward, craving the fine spray on his face. A party of Hasidic Jews was sheltering miserably by the bulwark, clumped together in their black coats. He crossed over to the port side. The white cliffs had become only a shadow dividing sea and sky, a peripheral intrusion on the life and movement of the water spreading all around.

When he reached the stern again, the woman was still leaning on the rail. He lost his thoughts in the maelstrom below. There was a time when he would have come straight to the point with her, charming, mad, talkative, winning. But he did not quite cut that sort of figure these days. His curls were greying; his 'mesmerizing brown eyes' (*Vogue*) were getting pouchy, dulled by cigarettes. There was, inescapably, his waistline, bulging with an infant paunch which summers of amateur cricket could no longer defeat. And then there was Helen and the children. He had come a long way from 'Christopher Iles is a member of a squat in Paddington.'

'Mr Iles, do you believe in the future of the hardback novel?'

'Who the fuck wants to read a novel in hardback anyway? Who does? Who reads them? Two thousand academics and the people who work in publishing houses. What's the point?'

Travellers are always darting glances, parrying and evading. Iles made a secret study of the snub-nosed profile to his left. A Home Counties girl, sensible and well-spoken, with the self-confidence of a private education; she was wearing court shoes and had a Sony Walkman round her neck like a stethoscope. She caught his eye again and Iles focused his attention provocatively. 'Good travelling weather,' he shouted, and moved one pace sideways.

She nodded keenly.

'Far to go?'

'Brussels.'

'Vienna.'

They watched a supertanker with a Greek flag churning low through the water behind them. The woman was rather short next to Iles; she looked up at him comically, with a disconcerting china-blue stare. 'Excuse me,' she said, in a voice that suggested great deliberation, 'but you are, aren't you?'

'I beg your pardon.'

'You're Christopher Iles, I mean the Christopher Iles.' She began to speak quickly. 'I spotted you on the train. You don't recognize me. It was years ago. An interview for the World Service.'

Iles said he had a bad memory, but looked at her with new interest.

'Please don't apologize,' she replied decisively. 'You must have given lots of interviews.' Her admiration was as wide as the sea. 'I've read your book dozens of times you know.'

He looked down with embarrassment and pride. 'Well, thank you very much.'

The tannoy crackled and a voice told the passengers in English, French, German and Italian that the shop, where cigarettes, spirits, perfumes and other items of luxury could be purchased at reasonable prices, was now open. Helen would expect a duty-free gift of some kind, preferably Chanel No. 5. He had also noticed a small furry lion that demanded a place in his children's menagerie.

He looked evasively at his watch.

'The boat was late leaving,' she said. 'As per usual.'

He sympathized. 'I'm getting cold out here. Would you like a drink?'

'I should love a drink.'

The ship plunged as they stepped into the warmth. A hard-drinking bridge four by the exit said, 'Oh-oh' in ragged unison. The woman gripped Iles to steady herself and laughed. He smiled, slightly distracted, and they found a place next to the Appeal on behalf of the Blind. He asked what she would like and ordered the same for himself, a double scotch.

The barman served with panache, as if mixing cocktails: at this time of the year it compensated for the shortage of custom.

'Cheers,' said Iles and, apologizing again for his memory, asked her name.

She pulled off her hat and shook out her curls, but the face triggered no memories and the name meant nothing to him. 'Doesn't it all seem such a long time ago?' he said.

'It is a long time ago.' She explained that a lot had happened to her since those days. She had left the BBC in the mid-seventies, having decided that she was getting nowhere fast. Instead she took a good job with the European Commission which at least paid real money. She was taking the boat because of her fear of flying. She was not looking forward to getting back to work on Monday and she was going to miss her fiancé whom she had left behind in London.

Iles has this way of encouraging talk. Now he wanted to know all about the wedding.

She laughed. 'Well, times have changed if Christopher Iles is getting interested in old-fashioned weddings.'

'Oh, I'm a married man myself these days.'

'Does it have your seal of approval?'

He seemed amused. 'You haven't lost the habit of interviewing people.'

'I'm sorry.' She tilted the last of her drink. 'My fiancé doesn't like my living alone in Brussels.'

He nodded but said nothing.

'It's not that he doesn't trust me.'

'No.'

'It's just that . . .'

'He doesn't trust you.' Laughter bubbled over between them and Iles said: 'The other half?'

She commented: 'You seem to be a pretty good sailor.'

'There's only one cure for seasickness.'

'What's that?'

'You've got to find a tree and sit under it.'

The barman handed him the fresh glasses like a conspirator. 'Here's to travel,' said Iles, sitting down again, sweeping a confident gaze across the empty bar. 'Doesn't it make you feel alive?'

She smiled and a silence came between them. The thump-thump-thump of the fruit machine and the unexplained rattling of the ship emphasized that they were nearly alone. The saloon was designed for cargoes of testy holidaymakers. Now it was a resort without the funfair. One or two business travellers were drowning the monotony of the crossing in brandy-and-ginger; an elderly woman with lipstick on her teeth was snoring open-mouthed on a bench seat under the window and there were a few sour-faced paperback readers hunched in anoraks and old sweaters. The barman himself was engrossed in conversation with a tall, bearded customer of Edwardian appearance and bearing, whose apparently irresistible flow of words was occasionally punctuated by deliberate stares in the direction of Iles and his new companion.

'Do you know,' she was very tactful, 'I can remember exactly when and where I first read your book.' She brightened with nostalgia. 'I associate it with strawberries.'

'I always was the flavour of the month.' He is not good at handling flattering curiosity.

'No,' she protested, 'it made a tremendous impression on me.'

He expressed a perfectly wonderful interest in this information and demanded to know all the circumstances: he has always liked to play a part, always adapts to fit the scenery. Perhaps the woman was surprised to find her neighbour's deep sympathetic eyes widen seriously before her and a stare of magnificent intentness peer, apparently into all the secret parts of her mind, but she never suspected for a moment that this was mocking.

Her nostalgic ramble ended and Iles confessed to having been spellbound. Commanding the stage for a moment, he explained how the manuscript had been completed in six short summer weeks, how it was written with a 2B pencil on the verso pages of a Letts five-year diary given him by a friend who worked in advertising, and how the title, which he could now never bring himself to repeat, had been inspired by reading R. D. Laing at a Rolling Stones concert.

'Would you say,' one interviewer has asked, 'that you are self-consciously trying to break down the conventional literary barriers between fact and fiction?'

'Let's just say that I'm, er, testing the boundaries of reality. That's all.'

'Do you see your work as a statement about contemporary culture? Are you making a protest, would you say?'

'We aren't really making it; it's kind of making itself.'

She said, 'I remember you told me you wrote it whenever you had a spare minute.'

'Oh, how boring. I'm still repeating myself.' Iles pressed two fingers to his right temple and blew his brains out. The woman laughed again and then looked down at her drink in the manner of one who thinks they are going too far with a stranger.

This version of his autobiography is a fairly faithful record of how things actually were, at least as the cuttings have it. In an interview he gave to the *Observer* for a profile of Alternative London, Iles is quoted as saying, 'I always carry pot with me, in my free state it's legal; but I write like I breathe: stoned or not.' Later in the same piece he is reported to have said: 'British Youth is treated like the American blacks are treated. From the very beginning they are given the idea that a lot that is going is not going to be for them.'

There was a short pause while they watched a waiter in a maroon jacket and black tie come into the bar from the restaurant and order four large brandies.

'One for the road?'

She drained her glass and put it down with a bump in front of her. The barman came over, temporarily deserting his fascinating customer. Iles met the stranger's gaze, eyes that seemed to echo his own sense of mischief. He winked back but then, turning to the woman, realized that the signal was not for him.

'I usually get fairly pissed on boats,' he confessed, hiding a momentary confusion.

'Only on boats?' Her voice squeaked out of register. 'I remember . . .' But she did not finish her sentence.

'Oh – I'm quite a reformed character, whatever you think.' Iles has had quite a susceptibility to fashion, especially where his body is concerned. He has progressed from Sit-In to Work-Out, swept away by a succession of health crazes. He has jogged with the joggers, eaten honey and oatcakes with his health food friends, practised yoga, joined a dance group (he still has his shrivelled leotards in the wardrobe), given up sugar, anathematized eggs and white bread, taken up swimming, and is now a member of an executives-only health club. 'I mean,' he said, searching for an example of his rehabilitation into bourgeois society. 'I play squash.'

A party of pink-haired teenagers, a youth club on an outing perhaps, came running into the bar, shouting and swearing. One or two began to work the Space Invaders; the rest crowded argumentatively round the juke box. Soon the beat of the disco joined the steady throb of the ship's screw. Iles asked the woman if she thought the music compared with the music of their own times.

'It all sounds pretty terrible to me,' she admitted, and expressed a preference for jazz.

'May I?' He took her headphones and eavesdropped a snatch of something cool.

'And what are you doing these days?' Her casual smile betrayed her curiosity. 'Living off your royalties, I suppose.'

He was unable to dissemble. 'I'm a has-been. My work is totally forgotten, a thing of the past. I've certainly made all the money I'm going to.' He sighed, fighting with a real preoccupation. Then he stood up as though put out by the turn of the conversation and walked over to the juke box. The stranger at the bar looked across with another frank stare. Iles, surrounded by bopping teenagers, studied the titles under the perspex, tossing the heavy British coinage in his hand.

'Would you like to dance?' he said coming back to the bar. The woman, not yet quite separated from her inhibitions, hesitated. He advertised his selection and took her hand. Leaning towards him, she put her lips close to his ear. 'Still crazy after all these years.' Out of the corner of one eye, he noticed that even the solitary commercial travellers were recognizing the music, exchanging nostalgic half-smiles.

On the dance floor, a slightly absurd circle of scuffed vinyl, Iles forgot about everything and surrendered to the rhythm, lost in a trance of memories. *Do you believe in rock'n'roll? Can music save your mortal soul? And can you teach me how to dance real slow?* The teenagers who had at first watched disdainfully, were now joining in, jerking and stomping, unfamiliar with the tune. The lurching of the ship in the spring sea made all their movements wilder. Slightly on the edge, two American girls in lumberjack shirts swayed to their own private tempo, like the celebrants of an obscure cult. The song ended and everyone in the bar, who had been watching with amused fascination, applauded. The bearded stranger shouted 'Bravo!' in a high-pitched voice. Iles found his partner looking at him with surprise. There was a line of sweat on her upper lip; his own temples were damp.

Catch sight of him in the mirror behind the bar as he sits down. He once told a newspaper, 'I have longish curly brown hair in a reasonably un-suave Jimi Hendrix cut,' a remark which, the interviewer noted, 'was about the most definite statement author Christopher Iles made in the course of a long conversation last week'.

Old songs arouse forgotten aspirations. For a moment, after the dancing, the original Iles, long-lashed eyes absorbing all around him with an amused and slightly quizzical expression of curiosity, is back again, and it does not seem to matter that the curls are stranded with silver or that his lean features are beginning, but only beginning, to dull and soften with middle age.

All at once there was another round of drinks in front of them. 'With the compliments of one who is too old to dance,' said the stranger, lying gallantly: even at a second glance he looked less than fifty. 'Bravissimo,' he toasted Iles and his partner, studying them keenly for an answering enthusiasm.

'Cheers.' They clinked glasses and chatted emptily about the crossing.

The stranger's clown-white features were full of mystery. His foxy copper beard was somehow cruel and even when he smiled his expression was strangely lacking in warmth. Iles mentally fingered the red notebook in his suitcase. It was for such encounters that he was travelling. 'What's your line of business?' he asked frankly.

The stranger frowned as though he was going to be offended. Then he gave a bleak smile. 'Ah, you English shopkeepers. We talk about life and all you want to know is my *shtik.*'

Iles hesitated, but did not riposte.

'You're wrong,' said his fan-club, quick in defence. 'He's a famous writer.'

He looked at her; he has forgotten that you can never really leave the land of fame.

The stranger considered the boyish, slightly defeated figure in front of him. As Iles will discover, he prides himself on his powers of identification. Now he was obviously decoding the casual, impecunious demeanour, interpreting the faded jeans and greying temples for himself. 'Indeed,' he murmured.

'Was,' Iles corrected. 'For fifteen seconds.' It was richly ironic that going abroad should put him on the map again. He had hoped to travel anonymously, making notes freely. He would have preferred to stay and listen to the squeaky-voiced stranger, but instead, with barely a nod to the woman, he made an excuse and went up on deck.

The French coast was in sight, a low-lying grey dune beneath an operatic sky. The sun was shining; out of the wind it was hot on his face. He turned towards the blinding warmth with a hum of satisfaction. Away from the office and the routine of his working life he felt like a truant. He pulled out the copy of *New Grub Street* he had picked up at the station that morning and settled down to read. Iles, whose own education was blown to smithereens by his notorious student career, has lately adopted a new course of self-education and has been known to become quite unstoppable on the virtues of *Clarissa* or *Nostromo*.

Despite the sun, it was too cold to sit still for long. He began to pace the ship again. Travel, which Iles has said is to do with fear and exhilaration, is also about boredom. A few passengers were leaning over the rail abjectly waiting to be sick; there were pink and yellow splashes on the planking. Hardier travellers, elderly couples especially, for whom a sea-crossing was the real thing, were strolling up and down, veterans on a promenade, pointing out ships to each other as if they were underwriters from Lloyd's.

Iles has decided to keep a diary throughout his trip, a maroon feint notebook with more than one hundred and fifty blank pages. Anyone can keep a diary, he told Helen. I've got to start again somewhere. For the moment it will remain in its chainstore wrapping: he is writing postcards to his family. Once he has completed messages to his mother and his wife, assuaging the sense of duty, he addresses a picture of the ferry to his three daughters, smiling inwardly, calculating what childish fantasy to spin for them.

He writes in the private zoo language they share.

This ship is not very crowded but there are two seals and a walrus on board. It's a lovely day, France is on the horizon and I'm missing you all. Look after Helen. See you soon. With lots of love from Christopher.

As he popped the cards into the postbox he visualized the three girls in a group portrait with a pang of happiness. Ruth, the eldest, already superior, would undoubtedly read out the message to her sisters. At times, how strange she seemed to her parents, the ex-world shakers. Recently, victimized by another girl at school, she had asked Christopher in the bath what to do. 'Tell her to bugger off,' he replied, rubbing soap on to his balls. She considered this. 'I can't say that,' she said, hesitating. 'I'll tell her to stop it.' Ruth has had the worst of her father's life and seen his career at its most chaotic. She has found safety in the conventions her parents scorned. Even at the age of ten, everything was so organized in her mind. Helen and Christopher, discussing their children in bed, always imagined that she would become a primary-school teacher, keep up an evening class kind of interest in a not-too-demanding classical instrument, marry a boy (probably called Geoff) from a good background, and have lots of well-brought-up children herself. Iles finds that some of his friends, those who do not understand the way his mind works, will occasionally point to his beautiful daughters and imply a future filled with abortions and heartbreak. He always refers to steadfast Ruth to confound their teasing.

Sometimes, in the words of Hal Strachan, his boss, it seemed that a whole generation was turning into retrospective virgins. Was nothing remembered, nothing valued? Was everything to be abandoned? When he considered his other daughters, precocious twins with a passion for Elvis and mascara, he was more at ease with himself. Emma and Rebecca promised to be the stuff of middle-class parental anxiety. Fascinated mothers at the local school were already predicting something called 'trouble'. He felt proud.

His thoughts returned to the letter in his pocket, his private anxiety about Helen (well, was she or wasn't she?), and his hopes that the children would not become too dependent on her sister, Sarah, who made up for the disappointments in her own life by devoting herself to the Iles family.

Now the afternoon light was fading and the seabirds that seemed to have followed the boat all the way across the Channel swooped blackly against the hard purple horizon. In the nearer distance, past the prow, he could see the high-rise waterfront buildings of Ostend and the fiery orange plumes where the refineries were burning off. He looked at his watch: nearly four-thirty. The Vienna train would surely not wait for the ferry if it was late.

He took the envelope out of his wallet. Tomorrow, after all these years, he would have a rendezvous at last, one that seemed to Hal Strachan perfectly rotten with mystery and romance, to use the ace publicist's words. If he missed the train, the mystery and romance would fly out of the window.

He strode anxiously up and down the deck, his head thrust forward, calculating their speed through the water. One of the deck cabins had a flickering television; he paused at the porthole, a child looking through a keyhole. A group of cooks was sitting in a semicircle watching soft-porn on the video.

His publisher all those years ago had written, 'This compelling, haunting and hilarious first novel has the dazzling impact of a collective hallucination', but the radio interviewer's question was different. 'Do you accept, Mr Iles, that your book is a manifesto for oral sex?'

'Oral sex has never needed any manifesto from me.'

He walked on; the ferry reverberated and the starboard beam drew level with the sea-front.

The rolling of the ship became a gentle rocking as it ghosted through the calm waters of the harbour. He went below to retrieve his things. There were still a few cadaverous executives clicking shut their briefcases and exchanging end-of-trip business cards. The music had stopped and the barman was clearing away the empties, wiping his formica tops with a deft wrist. 'No rest for the wicked,' he announced, catching sight of Iles. 'People are daft on boats,' he added, rolling his eyes. 'Just daft.' He threw his arms up and pulled down the bar-grille with a clatter. 'Ta-ta, sir.'

He wished him bon voyage and went to find the gangway. An announcement that passengers with cars should return to their vehicles on B Deck prompted another small migration, mainly among the Germans. Some of the foot-passengers began to gather where he was standing next to the roped-off exit. People on a long journey are so helpless. He studied his watch again. The train was timetabled to leave in exactly twenty minutes. Then, reassuringly, the ferry hit the wharf with a shriek. Everyone stumbled and a babble of apology began in several languages. The man next to him said, 'Thank God for the Navy.'

As they berthed Iles noticed the Edwardian stranger again. He was standing alone at the edge of the confusion, perfectly unmoved; in his checked tweeds, watch chain and brogues he looked like a minor part in a Shavian comedy. There was no sign of the woman from Brussels. His curiosity was cut short when, a moment later, the gang-plank was lowered and a Belgian customs-officer shouted, 'Landing cards ready if you please, ladies and gentlemen.'

Iles, who is certain that trains leave early, forgot all about the crossing and found himself almost running on to European tarmac in his determination not to miss the next chapter of his journey.

Two

[1]

Christopher Iles was on the move in the autumn of 1968, restlessly on the move. Ask him about it now and all he can remember is being mixed up on the fringes of a happening called 'The Alchemical Wedding'. Its theme: the revolution is over, and we have won! John Lennon and Yoko Ono made love in a white bag on the stage of the Royal Albert Hall.

David Frost, Ossie Clark, Lord Gnome, Alf Garnett, Twiggy and Malcolm Muggeridge were named in the *Observer Colour Magazine* as people 'the British look up to'.

Peter Císař's letter must have taken several weeks to find him. But when it arrived . . . A letter from Czechoslovakia! Of course he answered it at once.

Paddington
10 November 68

Dear Mr Císař,

Your letter was forwarded to me by the publishers and I've asked them to send you two copies of my book, which, by the way, is so far the only thing I've completed. It was written under my own name and has come out in Britain and the US, a genuine artefact of 1967. As far as your bibliography goes, I'll be happy to squeeze in between Huxley and Isherwood. For the moment.

All of us here in the West believe that the invasion of your country is a crime and, for reasons I don't want to talk about just

21

yet, I'd like to do all I can to help you. A lot of the people I live with are really interested in your letter and it would be great if we could all get something together and raise money or something. I know quite a bit about your country from friends and I would really love to help. Perhaps we could start an underground press for your booksellers. I've got dozens of ideas.

You ask me to tell you about myself. Well, I'm twenty-three and single. I'm not as good looking as the jacket photo suggests, but that doesn't stop me having fun. I live in this squat in Paddington so if you want to get in touch again it's probably best if you write to me c/o the publishers. They're slow with royalties but quick enough with letters. When the book first came out I had quite a fan-club, but never such a wonderful surprise as a letter from Czechoslovakia.

I hope this gives you some idea about me, and if you'd like to know more or want to tell me what you thought of the book, it would be great to hear from you again.

> Yours sincerely,
> Christopher Iles

The day after he wrote this letter, the lead story in *The Times* ran as follows:

Old guard communists were roughly handled by a crowd of 1,500 pro-Dubček supporters in Prague yesterday after a Czechoslovak–Soviet friendship rally. Many were chased, punched and beaten with umbrellas. Two girls on the arms of Soviet officers were dragged away, and their hair cut off ... The rally, used by Moscow loyalists to express opposition to the Dubček reform policies, was staged a week before the Communist Party Central Committee meeting at which the conservatives hope to mount a strong challenge.

Christopher Iles sat alone in an unreserved window seat on the Vienna express, apparently lulled by the rhythm of the train. To the stout ticket inspector working his way up the corridor and, one imagines, wishing that the job was like this all the year round (no football hooligans, no Americans), Iles was the picture of a traveller in a reverie, absorbed by the view from the tracks – pollarded willows and flat wet fields stretching towards a horizon flecked with spires. The sun, blazing on ditches of standing water, was sinking directly into his face, setting his hair on fire and puckering his expression into a satisfied smile that suggested a traveller with whom someone, getting on at, say, Bruges or Brussels, would be only too pleased to share a conversation about the pleasures of railway travel perhaps, or the monotony of the Belgian countryside.

The supposition that the man in the corner with a passport inscribed in the name of Christopher Iles (further identified by a not very good Photomat likeness) would be good company is one with which most of the published opinions on the subject concur. In his day, Iles has been described – in words that may do no more than suggest the shortcomings of journalism – as: spunky, fun-loving, selfish, drunk, witty, zestful, rangy, rude, vital, free-thinking, unkempt, worried, homespun, youthful, racy, anarchic, magnetic, monotonous, reckless, fast-talking, impetuous etc. etc. His friends would add that most of this makes him fun to be with. For Helen no one has ever presumed to speak.

The door of the carriage opened with a click and Iles was distracted from his reflections by the ticket inspector. Shortly afterwards, the train made its first stop, at Ghent.

It was the evening rush-hour. Gangs of schoolchildren were rioting up and down the platform. Iles spread out his books and suitcase across the seats and managed to stay solitary. Then the train slid noiselessly forward and gathered speed. A hard-hat in yellow overalls, stepping over the tracks, looked at his watch, spat once and hurried towards a lighted portakabin. It was nearly six o'clock and when a cloud passed over the sinking sun the land went into deep shadow.

A tuneless rattling in the corridor reminded him how little he had eaten all day. This mobile buffet turned out to be the only meal service. He ordered a can of Heineken, two ham sandwiches and a Mars bar. There was trouble when he proposed a twenty-mark note for change, but finally the trolley clattered away and Iles fixed his jaw into the first dry sandwich.

His thoughts returned to Helen and her note. She had pressed it into his hands with a perfunctory kiss as she swept the children off to school that morning. Now he flicked the crumbs from his fingers and took it out of safekeeping in his passport. It was barely twelve hours behind him, but family life in the big house on the edge of Wandsworth Common seemed extraordinarily remote. Temporarily he failed even to visualize his wife's expression. The conjunction of her features, what a passport would call her 'distinguishing marks', did not make an image he could focus on. At the end of a day's travelling he could only recall the occasional hint of garlic on her breath when she kissed him in the evening.

Her Britannic Majesty's Principal Secretary of State for Foreign and Commonwealth Affairs Requests and Requires in the Name of Her Majesty . . . What crap it was!

Occupation: writer, a lie. *Place of Birth*: Bexhill-on-Sea, but who cares? *Date of birth*: 10 May 1945. He always said VE Day, it sounded better. *Residence*: UK, shackled to the isles of despond. *Height*: six foot, the depth of a good grave. *Distinguishing marks*: none that show.

He tore open the envelope. Helen's italic script filled three pages.

Christopher darling . . . He read quickly down the page.

She was working over all that they had said to each other last night. She understood, she said, what his trip meant to him, and of course she wouldn't dream of stopping him.

'Thank you very much.' He associated rows with going to bed.

'Have I ever stopped you doing all the things you wanted to do?'

She knew exactly what he was referring to. It irritated her to feel vulnerable. She said the way he made a virtue out of indifference drove her crazy sometimes. She wanted to know, just as a matter of interest, if he understood the meaning of jealousy.

'There's been plenty of opportunity to do the research, but I'm obviously a slow learner.'

It was typical of him that all he could do was make flippant remarks.

'Well, if you would like me to hit you over the head with a brick. I happen to prefer jokes.'

'As a substitute for emotion?' Or was it, she wanted to know, that this was just another thing they never discussed together any more, they who had once talked about everything under the sun with a view to changing it the following morning? She was sure that his pen-friend wasn't a stranger to his feelings. It was typically English, the race he had once affected to despise, that he should come to be more at home with someone he had never met.

Iles said something about lack of sympathy at home, cramming his shirt into the Ali Baba basket and catching sight of his podgy white torso in the wardrobe mirror.

'Who was it who always wanted an open relationship?' She paced up and down, pulling off her jewellery and thumping angrily over the carpet in her bare feet. Lounging on the bed, Iles had a particularly good view of her scarlet toenails. Helen was always an impressive figure, tall and well-made, with fierce dark ringlets (he was remembering again) and bold determined features, not a woman, he told his friends, to argue with if you were out of training.

In that case, he said, he couldn't understand why she objected to his trip.

'I don't object to your trip: it's just the way you go about it. You seem to be more interested in this refugee than in your own family.' He suppressed a number of provocative replies and Helen went on without interruptions. 'You do see, don't you, that after all these years without a foreign holiday it's a bit hard on me and the children to see you whizz off on your own to Vienna without us?'

He said he was sorry she didn't want to help someone who was presumably in distress.

'Oh of course I want to help whatshisname. Bring him home. Let him stay as long as he likes. There are plenty of spare sofas: after Prague, that will seem like luxury I'm sure.'

As quickly as it began, the exchange ended. Helen came and sat beside him on the bed. 'Don't you see, darling, that the thing I find hard to take is the way you've always kept this man to yourself? I'm sure you tell him things you never tell me. Really, it would be nice to have him here, then perhaps I could begin to observe this – this special relationship.'

She used the same phrase in the letter which was as full of her personality as the flamboyant royal blue signature at the bottom of the third page. The Iles family address was spaced in fourteen-point Perpetua across the top: there was a time when he could not contemplate such evidence of domestic stability without wanting to catch the next flight out.

'Would you describe yourself, Mr Iles, as a restless person?' The interviewer looked over her clipboard in a way that suggested she already knew the answer. 'I like to travel – yes.' The cigarette smoke curled upwards. On the small screen, his off-camera smouldering contributed to an air of sardonic contempt for the programme.

'Can you be a little more specific about your . . . yen for foreign parts?' Researchers had told her that Christopher Iles had been all over America, Europe and the Far East. 'I'm sure viewers –'

'I see.' Slow inhalation. 'You mean: do I like to screw around?'

Helen's approach was always a volatile mixture of arrogance and humility, one moment expressing her love, the next lecturing her husband about his family responsibilities. When she was only his current girlfriend, Helen McPhee, as she preferred to be known, was once described – in *The Queen* – as 'a slim, passion-ate-looking Celt, Scotland's answer to swinging London'. She was a cradle-to-grave reporter in those days, angling to make the move South, blowing all her money on fashion and parties.

Now, when they have people round for dinner, she and her husband tease each other about their first meeting. An old joke between them has hardened into a discreet conduit for currents of private bitterness.

'Chris,' she says, in the mild Morningside accent that gave away her family background, 'thought he was so-o fashionable.'

'Well, darling, to be fair, I was.'

Everyone usually laughs.

'He had this disgusting tee-shirt with "Superstar" stencilled across his chest.'

'I was stoned.'

'He was always stoned. And so I said, "Hello I'm Helen McPhee from the *Scotsman*." And he said –' pointing to Iles – ' "How nice for you." '

'Both playing hard to get.'

'That's not what I remember.'

'Well,' appealing to their audience, 'she badly needed to be given a hard time.' To those who know him well he is not entirely at ease. 'As you can imagine.'

Someone will ask what year that was and he will say, 'The year of *Suck*.' He never expected it to last; after what had gone before it was . . . How could he put it? *We all need someone we can cream on*.

He has a note somewhere: Some people look back at those times and say that we, the former love-and-peaceniks, have softened with the years. Look, they comment, black and white has turned to grey, the bright, intransigent dreams of youth have been replaced by cynicism and indifference. Trusting worldliness, they choose not to see the emptiness and pain. If only they knew . . .

The carriage skated sideways with a lurch across the points and Iles with the letter safely in his pocket moved on to the Mars bar. The wrapping crackled like fire: A Mars a Day Helps You Work Rest and Play. He nibbled carefully, a man with bad teeth.

27

The train was slowing down. Out of the window, there was a city, amber in the gathering darkness. The voice of the guard sounded incomprehensibly at the end of the corridor. Iles continued to negotiate the dental hazards of the chocolate and pressed his face against the chilly glass. Brussels. He saw the woman from the boat taking a taxi to her high-rise apartment and making a long-distance call to her fiancé in London. Would she mention the meeting with Iles, or admit to getting more than slightly tipsy with a charming stranger? Or would she, already turning to evasion, talk about the heavy seas? The minute hand of the station clock jumped two minutes forward to 6.17.

Iles pulled out his new notebook and jotted down some of the things he could see. Then a soldier with a childish moustache, and his girlfriend, both incredibly young-looking, came down the platform arm in arm and, as if to satisfy the writer's curiosity, stopped in front of the carriage and began to kiss goodbye with longing. Iles, watching, identified the tender movement of the girl's hand over her lover's cheek as they kissed. Such high windows, he scribbled, and then, self-conscious, crossed it out.

A door banged and he looked up from his writing to find that the platform was empty. Outside a whistle shrieked. Heavy feet and a suitcase thumped down the corridor. All at once the door of the carriage was wrenched open and the Edwardian stranger barged in without apology or preamble, throwing a large, much travelled briefcase with many labels on to the seat. He looked at Iles with a calculating, deranged stare. In the harsh overhead light his hair was carroty and unattractive; his face seemed, as before, almost unnaturally white. '*Oy vey*,' he said. 'You again.' They jerked forward; he sat down heavily as though he did not have the energy to move on. 'The bloody train is full of journalists.' He waved at the notebook. 'If you don't mind, off the record, please, while I get my breath back.' Then, to emphasize his uneasiness, he reached up and switched off the light.

On 16 January 1969, Jan Palach, a philosophy student at Charles University, became the first martyr of the Russian invasion of Czechoslovakia by setting fire to himself in Wenceslas Square. He died four days later with the words 'My act has fulfilled its purpose.' Half a million Czechs transformed his funeral into a statement of national solidarity.

This was the event which prompted Iles to write again to Prague enclosing a newspaper article about himself, a letter which has been lost. Looking back, he says, it was the shock of Palach's sacrifice that persuaded him to unfold his own story to the unknown bookseller. To his amazement, he received encouragement almost by return of post.

Praha
4th February 1969

Dear Mr Iles,

Thank you so very kindly for your most interesting letter but the newspaper article is not inside. Your book has come to me. It is very beautiful and I hope to acquainted with this very soon.

Please, excuse me, your photograph is saying you are nice person. So I ask to you some questions. If you be so very kind, you will help me very much. I lectured to our young booksellers and when to them I tell your interesting book I like to tell them about you, Mr Iles. What is Paddington? I had old map of London city here. Paddington is railway station to it. Is this your house? I am not understanding squat (SQUAT?) at all. I have good English dictionary. Does you know what one I say? It is edit by H. W. Fowler and F. G. Fowler, from Oxford at the Clarendon Press, Fourth Edition. But it say squat is: 'Sit on ground etc with knees drawn up and heels close to or touching hams; crouching with hams resting on backs of heels.' This I am not understanding. Hams is pigs, no?

I ask to you how I write English. My wife and I have study of same book. It is a czech textbook and we say it is good. Also from it we are teaching our little daughter Hana. At Spring in last year I had talk with young English journalist and he say I talk very good. You tell me, please, where I make big mistake. I have not trouble to read English books but writing was not a like to me.

You write me about your very nice friend in Praha. I am so sorry with your news of this.

With all my best wishes and thanking for your nice letters and the book.

Sincerely Yours,

Peter Císař

P.S. I find newspaper article in goddam envelope, excuse me.

Christopher says, probably quoting, that the most important thing about a book is what you leave out. That's my problem – in spades. There's enough material in the newspapers alone to fill a whole series.

At the risk of over-egging the Palach business, I think it's right to report that, a few weeks later, on 25 February, Jan Zajíc, a nineteen-year-old engineering student, swallowed heavy sedation and then, having poured cleaning fluid on to his clothes, set fire to himself and rushed blazing from the door of a house into Wenceslas Square. He died soon afterwards. 'Human Torch No. 2' said he had decided to take his life to force the government to act on the demands of Jan Palach. Similar suicides took place throughout Czechoslovakia, and were hushed up.

Three

[1]

As the train gathered speed through the Brussels suburbs, Iles studied the stranger from the privacy of the shadows. He seemed to have vanished into himself, leaving only the outward form of a whiskery man of leisure dressed up for a day in the country. The chalk-white face was a mask, as impenetrable as his secret eyes. His hands betrayed movement only when the ring on the little finger of his left hand glinted in the pale light from the corridor. The writer scrutinized his subject greedily as though he might never get another chance: the imposing blankness of the expression opposite suggested that this was not someone to stare at freely in plain daylight.

An electronic beep-beep broke the stranger's composure. He reached automatically into his waistcoat pocket for a small, fancy pillbox and took a capsule, almost without swallowing. Then he pressed his watch; the digital face glowed in the dark. His lips moved and, in that surprisingly high-pitched voice, using an old English formula that only underlined his alien manner, he said, 'Allow me to introduce myself, Dr Augustus Kuhn.'

They shook hands.

'Christopher Iles. I'm not a journalist,' he added quickly. 'That girl was right. I was – I am – a writer.'

Kuhn brushed aside the disclaimer. 'No worries. You, I trust.' He shook his head. 'Back there was a reporter asking us all questions about who we are and why are we taking the bloody train. For a travel article, he claimed. You know, this world of ours, it is like a rotten French cheese with too many nibbling

31

maggoty journalists, asking questions, questions, questions.' He sat up proudly. 'I said, if you don't mind, I like to keep myself to myself. I do not give interviews to every Dick, Tom and Harry. One must be a little prudent. There are people who will use my name to capitalize on the market. Sure, among business associates you can trust a handshake in a coffee-shop. A deal is a deal. But journalists . . . *Yentas*. So, I move carriages. What do I find? A man all alone with a typewriter. Tap, tap, tap. Another one. Crikey! If I am going to be put in a book, I will choose who puts me in it, *ja*. I can tell you a few stories about the newspapers, no kidding.'

To avoid controversy, Iles changed the subject. 'And where are you heading?'

He seemed evasive again. 'Nürnberg.'

Did he have an office there?

Kuhn looked at him seriously. 'Mr Iles, I am in business. You are not. Let me tell you that in my line of country, as the expression goes, you have to be confidential. Questions like yours make me nervous. When people are nervous they become irrational.' He paused and then added, 'Europeans like you and I have seen what the irrational can do to our society. So –' He seemed pleased to have demonstrated this equation, but his fist was closed tight and the skin showed white next to the gold band on his wedding finger.

'I beg your pardon.'

He held up an appeasing palm. 'No problem, squire.' It was as though he had picked up his English from sit. coms. Now contempt came into his voice as he turned away to consider the even blackness outside. 'Belgium,' he said with scorn.

They looked out. There was a floodlit factory yard with crates of Stella Artois piled up like children's building bricks. 'Piss,' said Kuhn, and stood up to take off his overcoat, switching on the light as he did so. Everything about him betrayed a determination to look rich. Iles noted an awkward newness in his Scottish tweeds, his silk handkerchief and his chocolate brogues that suggested a credit-card spree rather than a quarterly account. He lacked the discreet self-confidence of the truly wealthy.

'Why is it,' he went on, sitting down again, 'that women are so much more attractive abroad?' The question was obviously puzzling him. He ran his hand thoughtfully over his beard. There was a heavy gold bracelet on his wrist. 'You live in a place like Paris or New York, and all the women look hysterical. Then you take a little trip away and everywhere you find delightful girls. Yes, I feel like a new man.'

Iles heard himself asking about the girl on the boat.

'On the high seas she was fine and dandy. We have a nice chit-chat. But,' he raised a finger and his ring flashed, 'on trains? No. I have papers to read. Look, I am in business.' He flicked a piece of fluff off his sleeve. 'Of course, even business has its women, if you luck out. There's a bank I know in Luxembourg keeps a suite of rooms in this hotel. You are invited to spend the weekend there as its guest. There's a different woman in six bedrooms. Oh boy! The vice-president is with you and if you're a drinking man he'll get into the sauce too, take you out to dinner, you know what I mean? By Sunday you're a little wiped out – how do you say? – snookered.'

'Amazing.'

'You don't believe me, Mr Iles. It's true, I promise you. This fact can be verified by Scotland Yard.'

Iles protested: he had not meant to sound sceptical. 'I've led a quiet life far too long.'

'Are you married, Mr Iles?'

'Nearly ten years.'

'A writer too?'

He hesitated. 'A journalist.' Kuhn did not react. 'She writes occasional pieces for the Sunday papers and looks after our three daughters.'

'You have daughters?' His eyes were like liquorice. 'I have a daughter – but she does not know me.' He was enjoying the enigma he presented. 'I have not seen her mother for nearly thirty years.' He clicked his perfect teeth with pleasure. 'Listen, Mr Iles. I will tell you a story.'

Iles left his notebook unopened beside him and listened. Later, when there was time to write it up, this is what he recorded. (Most of it is what Kuhn actually said; but most of that is at best only half true.)

Kuhn took out a packet of the smallest cigarettes Iles had ever seen. You could, he explained, find them only in Switzerland; buying Beedies was almost the only reason to go to Geneva. 'The Swiss, *ach*, they get up my wick.' He sprang his gold lighter ('a grateful client in the Gulf') and the air filled with the aromatic smoke: it was to become indistinguishable from the figure of Kuhn himself.

'Look at me, Mr Iles. I am almost fifty. *Unglaublich*, no? It's true. A passport need not lie. I was born in the year Hitler came into the Rhineland. My father was a Dane, a fine-looking man from his photographs, and a member of the *corps diplomatique*. Top drawer, you know. His name was –'

'Kuhn is not . . . ?'

'I will come to that. *Ecoutez*.'

His mother was an Austrian Jewess who had fled to Paris when the Nazis came to power. His parents met when his father was posted to France. He was born soon after. When the war came they were caught in the city. He could remember being taken for walks by the Arc de Triomphe and seeing the Germans racing past in jeeps. Later, his father made his way back to Denmark to fight in the Resistance, but he was betrayed and disappeared. The Occupation became a nightmare; his mother was deported. He never saw her again. When the war ended he was sent back to Austria to stay in the house of his uncle, Herr Otto Kuhn, a man he had never met, a merchant in leather.

'Strange origins,' said Iles.

'Sometimes I think to myself: I have no parents, no home, no roots. I ask myself: who am I?' He lit another cigarette. 'Then I make a new deal, and I know.'

34

As might have been expected, Kuhn said, he hated leaving France, hated his uncle, hated Austria. He rebelled. No school could hold him. By the time he was shaving he was out, living by his wits. It was a strange time. Austria was just part of the West again. He teamed up with a young adventurer like himself. 'A perverted cheat from Pécs. Never trust a Hungarian.' If the margins were right, they would sell anything, chocolates, nylons, paraffin, penicillin. 'Boom times, the fifties,' said Kuhn. 'We were lucky.' He seemed surprised by his own modesty.

'You obviously had flair.'

'At that age there is no fear. I was not yet twenty-one,' he added with pride. 'Wet behind the ears, as you say.'

His audience laughed and Kuhn said gravely, 'I like you ... Christopher. I like to talk with someone who understands.'

Iles returned the compliment. He has always had a gift for bringing out the best in people. Kuhn proceeded. This is the conversation as it appears in the writer's notebook.

'But money is not everything, you know.' His face crinkled with a dead smile. 'Almost but not quite.' He weighed the effect of his words. 'I was young and hot-headed. It is nineteen-fifty-six: that's a year to remember. I had a grand passion for this girl from Budapest. Marisa, she was ravishing. Blonde as snow, legs like a Venus, a smile to open your heart to, and a great line in blow-jobs. Soon I am in love with her country too. So much excitement in the air. Sitting up all night in talk. You know how it is.'

Iles knows only too well. He said, 'Sometimes I feel I'm getting younger all the time. The older the world gets the more irresponsible I feel.' He yawned. 'And the more pessimistic.'

Kuhn was amused. 'Like me, you have too much heart. You and I, we are the romantics. Out there,' he waved at the roaring blackness, 'they do not want us just now.'

'And so Marisa was the mother of your daughter?'

When Kuhn was serious the whiteness of his face was like a death mask, his carrot-red hair a tasteless joke. 'She carried the baby throughout the days of freedom. In November I was forced to flee across the border to Vienna. The child was born the following month. That was the message. But I have never seen them since.'

Iles hesitated. 'One day perhaps . . .'

Kuhn raised his eyebrows. 'Let me tell you, I have spent tens of thousands of marks, but I have never traced them. In nineteen-seventy-three . . .' He had this way of pinning his talk to dates, as though he saw himself in the spotlight of history.

'That's a very sad story,' said Iles when he had finished. A short silence came between them. The sound of ragged singing broke in on them from down the corridor.

She loves you, yeh yeh yeh
She loves you, yeh yeh yeh

'You know something,' said Kuhn, striking an elegiac note. 'If I had my time again, I would not change a minute. I accept my fate. Up there somewhere is a God.'

The train was pulling out of Liège. The singing turned out to come from a group of French students. One of the boys had a cluster of gas balloons on a string. He had his arm round a girl in pink dungarees. She was holding a bottle of champagne. Bubbles spurted through her fingers and her friends were laughing and joking.

'Why is it,' Iles observed, 'that real life supplies caricatures that no fiction could tolerate?'

'Well then . . .' Kuhn challenged. For a moment he seemed about to take the remark personally. 'Are you the perfidious Englishman? Should I, after all, not trust you?'

'That's for you to say,' he laughed with relief. 'I'm a chameleon. I take colour from my surroundings.'

'To spy?'

'If you like. I make notes and observations. I watch the world like an outsider.' Iles became untypically sombre. 'A writer has to be willing to betray anything for his story.'

Kuhn was strangely impressed. 'It's true. You English are good at disguises when you want to be. Once, the English abroad were a joke; they used to wrap their Englishness round them like – like a flag. But now I must watch out. Today the Englishman can be anyone, anyone at all. Perhaps,' he went on, 'it is no accident that you have the best actors in the world.'

'And the best spies.'

Kuhn became egotistical again. 'Well, if I am honest, I too will betray anything for my work.' His eyelid fluttered in a sickly wink. 'So, what notes will you be making about Dr Augustus Kuhn?'

The carriage door jerked open. Two German officers in pea-green uniforms carrying short-wave radios came in.

'Passport control,' said Kuhn automatically, and produced his own documents from his inside pocket with a guilty, practised gesture. To his surprise, Iles saw that he was travelling as an American citizen.

[2]

History has its rhythms. The attack on the 'counter-revolutionaries' of the Prague Spring came within the year. These are the words of a certain Dr Gustáv Husák. It is, Christopher says, the voice of Orwell's Squealer throughout the century.

> Those people, whose mouths are full of democracy, are so deeply undemocratic that they will not recognize the elementary rights of citizens, workers, peasants and technicians. They do this so that they can become the élite which they already imagine themselves to be. We need no élite . . . The anti-socialist and various opportunist forces strove to crush and destroy the political power of the working people in this state, and loosen the leading role of the Communist Party . . .

Shortly after Iles wrote his next letter, Husák replaced his old friend Alexander Dubček as the First Secretary of the

Communist Party of Czechoslovakia, and became the subject of a leader in *The Times*.

> The romance and the romantics are going out of Czechoslovak politics. The fact of the occupation will now be more squarely faced. The sadness will be greater but the emotional stress will be less. Things could have been worse.

Paddington
12 April 1969

Dear Mr Císař,

It was wonderful to have your reply. I'm glad the books made it across the frontier. Would you like some more? Just let me know. It's impossible for me to imagine what real political repression etc. is really like. The West is so corrupt and cynical you wouldn't believe it. Vietnam, Chicago, Paris, and now Prague – it's all the same. Victories for Respectable Man. It's ironic, isn't it, that capitalists and communists behave in exactly the same way when the chips are down, exercising their own kind of violence to maintain something called 'law and order'?

I'm still at the same address. Paddington is full of these huge, decaying Victorian mansions which unscrupulous landlords leave empty, hoping to exploit the next property boom. At least you don't have that kind of thing under socialism. With so many homeless here it's a scandal. That's why we've occupied this one. It's called a 'squat', a word that certainly won't be in the Oxbridge English Dictionary. Most of the words we use aren't in the dictionary yet. Language imperialism is just another way Respectable Man keeps the prisoners in their cells.

Just now I'm involved in this anti-American theatre event. When you read about the billions they're spending on the Apollo moonshots and the millions of tons of bombs they're dropping on North Vietnam, it's all you can do. It's being put on at a place called the Arts Lab, an alternative theatre in Drury Lane run by this guy called Jim Haynes. The theatre is a good way to get a message across. Jim is really into the miracles of life – children, flowers, trees, women – but he's political as well. He wants PEACE like the rest of us. That's what it's all about in the end. Sorry this is a bit rambling; I'm stoned I think. Your English is fine. It will get better if you write me another letter.

Your friend,

Christopher

(Later) P.S. Thank you for your kind words about Milena. You probably can't understand, but it makes it more bearable to have someone to share it with, someone who knows what those days were all about.

The first time Christopher showed me his collection of Císař's letters, I was tempted to blue-pencil the old bookseller's atrocious English for the reader's benefit (how typical it was, *en passant*, that such a serious amateur scholar and bibliophile should have such a struggle with the day-to-day realities of our language). As it was, Christopher dissuaded me from taking a Bowdler's course. He was right, of course: the authenticity is all.

Four

'Stone bottoms,' said Kuhn as the carriage door closed. He pocketed the passport with a flourish. 'These Krauts – police, dogs, computers, the whole *schmeer*. You never know what they will do next with your papers. But at the moment,' he added, flattering him with another confidence, 'I have no viable alternative.'

Iles has a good line in provocative indifference and merely said, 'I could use a drink. Shall we find the bar?'

'This, of course, is the disadvantage of trains,' Kuhn expounded as they swayed down the corridor. 'The frontier control problem. Third-rate *klutzes* with too much time on their hands.'

They passed the customs men lounging heavily against an open doorway. A German girl in an anorak was answering questions. Iles caught her eye and saw through to the fears in her mind. Kuhn was still speaking, launching into another of his stories, and Iles saw with a flash of inspiration that he was in the grip of an autobiography. Checking the flood of reminiscence for a moment, he asked tentatively if he was a naturalized American.

For once Kuhn did not parry the direct inquiry. 'When I was nineteen I was a father, a wanted man and a dollar millionaire. I fled to Vienna. For a while I lived quietly. Then like a berk I got married. Soon enough I was divorced. It is the beginning of the sixties and I am nearly thirty. That is a moment in a man's life for decisions. So – I emigrated to the United States. From the moment I landed I knew I would be at home. And that is where my problems began.'

Iles, intrigued, said he could not imagine what these might be.

40

'Listen,' said Kuhn. 'I came from nowhere. Out of emptiness comes fantasy. That is the States for you. In America I learned one thing: you are what you say you are. All at once I discovered the big lesson of capitalism – how to lie. No, no – it's true. I have to tell you these things.'

A junction. The story was swallowed by the roar of the train. Iles is fascinated by Kuhn's walk, as though he has gold bars strapped to his thighs. Later, he discovers that the travelling doctor is plagued by haemorrhoids.

They crossed into another carriage; first-class, blue plush and shaded lights. Iles caught the familiar sound of a typewriter. A hunched, stubbly, cigar-smoking figure in bottle-green corduroy sat alone with a portable on his knees; as Kuhn passed he looked up and scowled, tossed a rug of lank grey hair out of his face and bent furiously over his keys again.

'Journalists . . .' murmured Kuhn and strode on like a robot.

There was no bar. The empty restaurant car presented an unswept, inattentive air. They sat by the window. Each table was covered by a paper cloth with 'At your service' stencilled in several languages. The waiter, a humdrum teenager with a smeared-on moustache, offered them a menu.

'Côte du Rhône, Blanc de blanc, Muscadet.' Kuhn became satirical. 'Is this what you call a wine list? Do you realize, young man, that you are in the employment of a once-great railway enterprise, the Compagnie Internationale des Wagon-Lits, yet you present us with the kind of *dreck* that would disgrace a Frankfurt *gasthaus?*' The waiter, confused, spoke quickly in German. 'He says the Champagne is quite good,' Kuhn translated. 'Quite good is not good enough; I think we shall risk the Muscadet.'

The boy shook his head and lowered his voice apologetically. Kuhn waved indignantly at the food-stained menu. 'This nebbishy-looking pipsqueaker tells me there is no wine. There is only beer and second-rate bubbly. We shall have to bow to our fate.

Two cans of Skol.' He dismissed the waiter. 'Tourism,' he lamented, 'has corrupted our civilization.'

For a few minutes he could only mourn the end of elegance, finding fault with the plastic carnations and the polystyrene beakers. In due course his irritation faded and they began to converse again.

'When I was a young man I dreamed of being an artist like yourself. I have made a million, I said, and now I will retire into the green countryside and write a great book.' The aromatic smoke curled dreamily about him. 'It did not happen of course.' His rueful expression was strangely winning. 'But now it's your turn, Christopher. You tell me, please, about your writing.'

'What can I say? I write letters to my friends and tell fairy stories to my children. I write publicity copy. Everything else seems . . . impossible.'

Kuhn responded with schmaltzy grandiloquence. 'The artist, he is something. Sisyphus rolling his stone uphill. That I understand, the constant search for self-expression.'

Iles says he was worrying away in his mind at Kuhn's half-begun life story. 'Perhaps,' he commented with an encouraging smile, 'the business instinct is not so very different. Words, money – they are only the means.'

Kuhn's attention sharpened. 'There you go again, prying into my business affairs.' Iles protested, then realized that this time the rebuke was playful. 'I see,' Kuhn went on, 'that you are what you English call a nosy-parker. Of course we all have skeletons in the broom cupboard. But I wonder if you would like me to put such questions to you.' He watched shrewdly. 'I think not.'

The doctor is wrong. There was a time when Iles was only too happy to indulge quite a flair for self-promotion. You will find his photograph, grainy, tousled and astonishingly youthful, in the colour magazines of those years, sandwiched between advertisements for the new British Overseas Airways Corporation VC–10, High Speed Gas, Barclaycard and the Triumph Herald 13/60.

He looks surprised by it all, but he handles the questions – especially the personal questions – with the greatest of ease.

'Mr Iles, do you feel any inconsistency in your views and your life-style? You are known to have left-wing opinions, yet you drive an Aston Martin.'

'I don't remember Marx saying socialists shouldn't drive fast cars.'

Now, when Iles pulls out his wallet in the shabby restaurant car of the Vienna express in a way that says I'm about to take you into my confidence (a quite different confidentiality from Kuhn's: Iles means what he says), it's not out of character. In fact, it has all the spontaneous charm of himself at his best.

'Here's something that may intrigue you,' he said.

It is not difficult to imagine Kuhn watching his fine, thoughtful features as he fingered through photographs, luncheon vouchers, addresses and credit cards. The Englishman's skin had an almost girlish softness, even where a day's faint stubble was greying on his jaw. On close examination, Kuhn would find nothing to challenge his first impression that this was someone you could trust and, better, with whom you would have a good time. Here was a face that had maturity. It had experienced people, places, emotions; it knew things. But it was still eager for more, still inquisitive, not yet marked by cynicism, the mask that some people take for personality. It was too vulnerable to be threatening; an intelligent face, modest, open, alert and amusing.

Iles had found the letter. He passed it over.

Kuhn took out a pair of tiny pince-nez to study the message. 'Dear Christopher. I will be at the Franz Josef–bahnhof in Vienna, platform number eleven at 7.28 in the evening of Saturday 2nd April. Please, is it possible you are there to meet me? In haste, Sincerely, Peter.' He read the words aloud slowly, like a man reading a lesson in church. 'And this is out of the blue, as you say?'

He nodded.

Kuhn handed the letter back, full of admiration. 'Well done, Christopher. You have my curiosity aroused. Who is this Peter?'

Iles hesitated, noticing that their beakers were empty. Kuhn saw this and, with perfect timing, hailed the waiter. '*Noch einmal.*' Iles poured his drink with exasperating care. Finally, Kuhn gave way to his impatience. 'So you are going to Vienna to meet this Peter – a writer from Prague, no?'

'I'm deciding where to begin.'

Kuhn approved. 'Good.'

'Once upon a time,' he began, enjoying the conventions of the storyteller. A faraway look came into his eyes. 'Once upon a time there was a young Englishman, a child of his generation.'

'Those were the days.'

'If you were to meet this man now, the father of children, the company dogsbody, the slave of his overdraft ...' he made a gesture to accommodate a spasm of verbal paraplegia, 'you would be astonished to be told that in those days he was – well, he was given free lunches in practically any London restaurant you can think of.'

The Iles Restaurant Index is one of his inventions, the infallible guide to social and cultural consequence. When he was in the swim he was known at Parks, Trattoo and Mr Chow. He was on personal terms with the chef at Bianchi's, had tried all the hors d'oeuvres at the Brasserie, enjoyed the *coq au vin* at Quo Vadis, and, on one memorable occasion, to the scandal of his publisher, a bread-spitting geriatric with large feet, a limited supply of anecdote and a habit of forgetting to button his flies, he had sent back the quails at the Garrick. His own best score on the Iles Restaurant Index was the day he was invited to lunch at the White Tower by the Minister for the Arts to endure a patronizing interrogation on the subject of 'what the youth of Britain are thinking today'. Now, he is lucky to get to Bertorelli's once a month. Nothing, he will say to his friends with melancholy pleasure, recedes like success.

(Where are they now? Sixties trendy and pop novelist Christopher Iles was spotted yesterday with an unidentified escort at the bar of Langan's. Quizzed about his situation he quipped, 'Heady

cocktail overtures have not become post-prandial symphonies.'
Quite so, Mr Iles. *Standard*.)

'When I was in London in those days,' said Kuhn, 'there was a
riot of students.' He spoke as though it was all his doing. 'About
the Vietnam war.'

Iles has a theory that for many of his contemporaries the
excitement was always happening just around the corner, to other
people. (Even he, an Aeolian harp, as he was once described,
through whom the winds of change had blown, was aware only in
retrospect of all that had happened.) But he is still touchingly
self-assertive about his hey-day. 'I'm sure I was there,' he
said.

'It was very amusing.' Kuhn's voice cracked again and he gave
his chilly smile. 'Now here we are again, drinking Skol in cans,
travelling in the same train across Europe.'

'I still believe in the things we used to demonstrate for. I would
hate to think it was all just fashion.'

'Just fashion? What?'

'Our commitment.' He put his drink down. 'History has been
cruel to my generation. Once we wanted to change the world, now
we put the world on the video. My children cannot understand
what we thought was so exciting.'

'You talk about those times – how shall I say? – like a woman
you have lost.'

He was taken aback. 'If only you knew.' He could sometimes
wound himself with candour. 'What's that line? Something happened to me yesterday. At first, it all seemed easy; I thought I was
immortal, perhaps because none of us expected to last that long.
Then we were older and nothing was easy any more, and finally
nothing was possible. Yet for most people I've never grown up.
I'm remembered as a survivor, a left-over, a Peter Pan if you like.'
He looked directly at Kuhn. 'It's a terrible thing to be just what
you're cracked up to be.'

His meaning did not register and he added, compassionately,
'I'm telling you things, by the way, I wouldn't say at home.'

'I prefer travelling,' Kuhn admitted. 'It has a special kind of truthfulness. My life is as open or as closed as I choose. I have no friends from whom I have to hide myself. Sometimes I stay for days in my hotel, living off room service, just reading and reading.'

'What do you read?'

'I like a book that knows what it's doing and with a bit of a mystery. When you live in aeroplanes and Hiltons your brain is only fit for bestsellers.'

Iles bridled involuntarily. 'I like to think that what I did was not completely without merit, despite its popularity.'

'I beg your pardon. I did not mean –'

'Please don't apologize.' He found a curious satisfaction in Kuhn's embarrassment. 'That person no longer exists, regardless of outward appearances.'

'But I do not understand, Christopher. You are young, obviously gifted.' Kuhn sat forward with his elbows on the table, confidential again. The veins stood out on the back of his clasped-together hands. 'Look, I make a deal. It goes wrong. I lose a small fortune. I try again.' Gesturing, he lowered his guard. 'You are a writer – write! In my country we have a saying: the dogs howl, the caravan moves on.'

Iles has often said that he never really discovered Kuhn's nationality; he was, like his accent, impossible to place. At times he sounded American, at other times German, occasionally Scandinavian, even, once or twice, Australian. The phrase, of course, is familiar to him; he has heard it appropriated by half a dozen speakers from as many countries. He managed to stay polite. 'Well, this caravan got stuck in the sand, that's all.'

'And now,' Kuhn pointed to the letter on the table, 'you are going to meet this mysterious Peter.'

When the envelope arrived a week ago, Iles had come home to find it among the pile of bills and circulars. The laconic signal from across the border inspired his imagination. Like all those literary travellers before him, he would take the express; he would stay in Vienna. He would allow his journey time to get interesting. This, he explained to Helen (who couldn't understand why he didn't take the morning plane), was probably Cisař's intention; the old bookseller knew that his correspondent would relish a railway adventure.

Moody with alcohol, he resented Kuhn's intrusion into this private world of make-believe. Very matter-of-fact he said, 'There's no mystery about Peter,' and began to sketch the origins of their relationship.

'And of course,' Kuhn interrupted, 'you wrote back.'

'There were many reasons for answering that letter,' said Iles simply.

'And so now you are friends, *ja?*' He was absorbed.

'We've exchanged lots of letters, one way and another. But, in all these years, we've never met.'

Kuhn studied him intently, digesting the story. He lit another Beedie; his bits of gold twinkled in the flame. 'In my mind I am thinking that this Peter is perhaps not a bookseller.'

Iles was taken aback. 'What are you suggesting?' There was no disguising the irritation in his voice.

Kuhn was not discomposed. He swirled the herbal smoke expansively. 'I must tell you that I know all about Prague. In my experience, there is usually more in such matters than is meeting the eye.'

'I do not understand.'

'A spooky city, my friend. Full of lies.'

While he was speaking the carriage had filled with an unmistakable stink. Iles wrinkled his nose with embarrassed amusement.

'No,' Kuhn instructed, 'it is not farting. It is German industry.' He pointed at the fires in the darkness. 'Aachen. The bloody Krauts don't bother with pollution at night. *Typisch.*'

Iles reconsidered his companion's suspicions. Finally, he said, 'You may be right about Peter. I ask you to believe that I at least

47

have told you the truth. I'm going to help someone who's asked me to. What more can I say?'

It is characteristic of him to be generous towards all suggestions and receptive to all ideas, though it would be wrong to imagine that he is naïve. It is just that he always believes in the fullest expression of things, in anyone's right to their own opinion.

'As my old grandmother used to say, Christopher: there will be complications. Especially in Prague. The apparatchiks must know all about your letters.' His expression darkened; he seemed to relish the prospect of difficulty. 'Císař . . . Císař . . . It is, of course, a common name.'

Kuhn came out with some memories of Czechoslovakia, and the conversation took another turn.

The writer listened: Prague could never lose its power over his imagination. 'You've certainly been about,' he commented.

'I still do,' Kuhn replied, repeating the sentence two or three times. He seemed to fear silence, as if it might turn out to be an ambush for a tricky question.

He called again for more lager. Refreshed, he began to elaborate on his travels. Iles came to understand that this was a conversational arpeggio he could practise with any stranger.

The train was slowing down. 'Cologne,' said Kuhn, glancing past his reflection. 'My dear Christopher,' he continued, 'I hope I will astound you when I say that last year I travelled more than one-hundred-and-seventy-five-thousand miles in the air alone. Several times around the world. I keep a record in my diary. You name it, I've been there. Hong Kong, Tokyo, Sydney – there is a fine city – Calcutta, Rome, Oslo, Rio, Paris.'

'I love Paris.'

'Paris,' he pronounced with scorn, 'is a city looking at itself in a mirror. But take Prague –' He became rhapsodic. 'Golden Prague, raped by those Ukrainian pigs.'

The train pulled out across the glittering Rhine. Iles looked at his watch. It was nearly nine-thirty; another twelve hours to

48

Vienna. A barge with a red lamp was moving upstream on the dark water; between the girders of the bridge he could see an ensign fluttering at the stern. Behind them Cologne cathedral was lit up like a prison.

He found parts of the conversation reverberating in his mind. He pulled out his wallet again and handed over a dog-eared passport photograph. 'Do you recognize that face?'

Kuhn betrayed nothing. 'Should I?' His eyes were glassy marbles as he studied the smudged print, a snapshot of a head tilted back; flattened features, a plastic smile, pupils dilated by the flash.

'That is my friend Peter.'

'How do you know?'

'What do you mean?'

Kuhn wore an expression of wicked satisfaction. 'A few minutes ago you are telling me you have never met.'

Iles found himself looking at the snapshot as if for the first time. 'Can't you take some things on trust?' he countered. The tiny image showed an ordinary-looking man with small close-set eyes, cropped hair and a receding chin, someone, an observer might say, whose enjoyment of life was modest, bookish and secluded. 'I've corresponded on and off for fifteen years with a man called Peter Císař. Some years ago one of his replies included a photograph. The face seemed to fit the personality in the letters, that's all.'

He was entitled, Kuhn said, to make that assumption. Why was it, he inquired, that they had not been able to meet?

'We've often discussed it.' He was not inclined to be more specific.

The train, which had been racing through the darkness, began to brake hard. Kuhn's elbow slipped and he recovered himself with difficulty. 'So – you have never thought of your friend in this way,' he said with an intuitive glimmer.

Iles stood up, knowing he had drunk too much. 'Excuse me.' He was offended and disturbed. 'I suppose I should be grateful to you for your rather novel suggestion, but if you don't mind, I'll go back to the compartment now.'

Kuhn faced him on his feet. His cold smile became an unexpected laugh that Iles had not heard before, a mad hilarious braying that seemed to bring a temporary colour to his face – or was it merely the reflection of the plush red drapes? 'So you are afraid of fiction after all,' he said cruelly. 'Perhaps you should stick to real stories from real life,' he added. 'Facts are so much safer, are they not?' His words went through the writer like a curse but he was already hurrying away down the corridor and did not turn back.

[2]

Soon – within a few months of their first letters – Iles and Císař had discovered a common interest in chess. Or rather, since I have to say that my friend is not naturally the silent analyst of statuesque ivory, it was the bookseller who asked, Do you play chess? and his correspondent, anxious to find points of contact, decided that he did, even if it meant relying on some dullish acquaintances to answer gambits and manoeuvres.

Here is a letter, dated 7 July 1969, in Peter Císař's meticulous hand:

Dear Mr Iles,

I'm very kindly thanking you for your postcard. My move is Queen's Knight's Pawn to Queen's Knight 5. This is famous beginning.

Please, there is nothing to be doing now. I can work as bookseller in the shop and I write very interesting English authors, and that is all to do. If I do not have wife and daughter and very many interesting nice friends I think I leave, but that is no good. I am czech and I must be staying where I live.

I like very much what you are saying from your country. My wife is telling me you write very good and it is nice to have English letters. It is hope of us that you write nice new book very soon. I am sending you in this letter the picture of River Vltava. It goes to River Elbe, on to Dresden and Magdeburg, and then to Hamburg estuary and the North Sea. I like to walk there by the side of Vltava. The water in the river is free, I think. It is going to the other side of the border. When I look at Vltava I am happy man.

With all my best wishes and thanks for your nice letter. Hoping for your next move.

Sincerely yours,
Peter Císař

As Christopher has pointed out, this letter is something of a rarity: Císař usually avoids any political comment, even of an oblique kind. That's simply the way he is, a man of caution (right down to his precise, crabbed handwriting), essentially a bookman, not a dissident. Besides, the penalties of activism are serious.

Within a year of the Soviet invasion, the first arrests began, and with the first arrests, the big freeze. Dubček and his colleagues were urged by the new men 'to speak frankly' about the events of the previous summer. This, it was reported, 'is important because, if certain circumstances are not clarified, it will be difficult to overcome the view held by the general public that "the Russians are to blame for everything".'

Five

Dr Augustus Kuhn was drunk when he returned to the carriage, but he was not one to be socially inhibited by the effects of a disinhibitant. Instead, he became majestic: his large-boned frame seemed even more stately and his fluting syllables (Iles, with half an ear open, heard him apologizing to the carriages he mistakenly invaded), acquired.a temporary resonance from the effort of articulation.

When, finally, he pulled open the door of his own compartment, he found his drinking partner apparently asleep, lolling upright next to the window. There was now another passenger by the door, an elderly woman in puritan tweeds knitting baby clothes with pink wool. Kuhn acknowledged her traditional courtesy and said in English, 'Time for a bit of a kip.' Then he took off his jacket, stretched full length beneath it on the opposite seat and fell asleep.

Iles came to as the train rattled over the points into Frankfurt. He had an ache in his shoulder; his left leg had gone to sleep and his mouth was a scrapheap. Kuhn was snoring his head off in front of him. The woman by the door was collecting her things. As she pulled her suitcase off the rack, it slipped from her fingers and landed on Kuhn, who sat up with a grunt. Iles, anxious to smooth over their former contretemps, interrupted her apologies.

'Sleep well?' he asked playfully.

'Until this silly old cow dropped her sausages on my tits.' He directed a think-nothing-of-it gesture at the departing spinster. '*Gute Nacht, Fraulein. Auf wiedersehen.*' He preened his beard, cryptic with pleasure. 'Over the years one acquires a certain politesse with the small investor.'

'So nice Doctor Kuhn has a way with little old ladies.' Iles has the knack of saying things that from other lips would give offence.

'*Eh bien*,' he was making up his mind to tell another story, picking up where they had left off as though nothing had happened. 'A few years ago I was in gold. A very kooky market, let me tell you. I was acting as principal for a number of important clients –' He broke off, as if a stranger had come into the carriage. Outside there were lights, shouting, a platform, one or two bleary travellers and a bell ringing pointlessly in an empty office. 'So here we are in Frankfurt, the anus of Krautland.'

'There was a concentration camp here.' Iles used to pride himself on this sort of knowledge.

'You know Frankfurt?' Kuhn was impressed. It was as though they had discovered a friend in common.

'Every year there is a book fair. I went once.'

That was the season his own book came out. The trip lasted two days and a night. He was introduced to publishers from all over the world, Holland, Finland, Germany, Norway, France, Japan, Sweden, Brazil . . . Harassed, well-lunched, shiny-suited men whose minds buzzed with international telephone codes and percentages. Although they took a polite interest in his work, he could only smell their curiosity. Was this, they were saying to themselves as they tried to penetrate his spaced-out indifference, was this the face of the future? He will tell you now, if you get him on to the subject, that they all carried little black notebooks in which they made obscure, memo-to-self-type jottings. He felt like a mule at a bloodstock fair. The books themselves, thousands upon thousands, shelf on shelf, row on row, seemed faintly irrelevant, a colourful furnishing for the drab concrete hangars they were housed in. He got stoned, had a one-night stand with the publicity girl, and flew home exhausted and disillusioned.

'Frankfurt,' the thought seemed to depress Kuhn as well. 'I made a bad contract here – in gold.'

The Vienna express was moving again, accelerating through darkened suburbs. The rhythm of the carriages over the track distracted their thoughts for a while and they both stared out into the night, lost in reverie.

'Gold.' Kuhn's speculative murmur broke the silence between them. 'They say that Jesus Christ himself was run by gold.' Iles ignored the challenge to disbelieve. 'The theory goes that he was a member of this sect, the Essenes. Okay, so the smart money says that the operation was funded from a store of gold hidden in the hills. I was told this by a chap on a plane. He was on this treasure hunt for the stuff. Sure as hell was he convinced by the story.'

Iles, who is a keen conspiracy theorist, observed that there was probably more in heaven and earth than was dreamt of in his philosophy, a remark that was lost on Kuhn.

'You have to admit that it takes care of one hell of a big problem.'

'What's that?'

'The whole Jesus movement's campaign costs. Look at it: three years on the road. That's almost as long as the bloody Presidency. That kind of show doesn't come cheap, even for the Son of God. He must have had money from somewhere.'

'It's a nice theory.' Iles made no attempt to disguise his disbelief.

'Well then, my friend, since we speak of fairy-tales, tell me how long you will spend with your –' he winked '– *soi-disant* bookseller in Vienna?'

Iles, unruffled, explained that he had taken a week's holiday, though the plan was to return home as quickly as possible. His boss, the diminutive but obsessive Hal Strachan, was not delighted to have a sudden holiday request just before an important conference.

An interview between Iles and his immediate superior was always something of an ordeal. Strachan, the smallest person in the office, smaller even than Germaine, the token black, suffered from the delusion that he was of average height. The begging of favours from a man who only came up to his collar-bone was made worse by the fact that Strachan was a great admirer of his work.

'And over there,' he would say to visitors, 'we have Christopher Iles,' his voice dropping to a stage whisper, 'the writer, you know.'

Iles always played on Strachan's weakness for his reputation. On this occasion, he took him into his confidence, unfolding an enthralling narrative to which Strachan listened in the spirit of one tuning into a rare broadcast from radio archives, only breaking in now and then to murmur, 'Great', 'Super', 'Fabulous', or 'Terrific'.

Once he had shown Strachan the letter, whose mysterious authenticity had the little man pacing up and down with excitement, the necessity of saying more was removed by the anticipated response.

'Well, of course, Chris dear boy, you absolutely must go. When's the first flight?'

Iles said he thought he would take the train, it would be more, as it were, in keeping.

'But of course. That Rhine journey. The *Schlösser*. Such interesting people on trains. Yes of course you must go. How long do you need?'

He had already made up his mind to ask for a week.

'A whole week.' Strachan could not hide his dismay. 'That's, well, that's quite a little suggestion. Now, I really ought to have had notice of that sort of plan, but –' waving the letter '– I suppose you couldn't – no, I do see – wonderful story – great trip – can't leave him stranded – no, quite – all right Chris dear, but this must be an exception – only out of the highest regard – Germaine, pet, that phone's driving me bananas.' Strachan snapped his fingers. 'Errol. Here, boy.' He strode ridiculously back to his glass office, followed by his favourite Afghan.

Iles rang the travel agent to fix arrangements. As he explained to Kuhn, his boss could always be relied upon to rise to the occasion.

'Vienna is a ghost town,' Kuhn observed, breaking the hungover silence. 'A week will be more than enough.'

They looked at each other across the carriage with a conspiratorial benevolence.

'Only another ten minutes to my destination,' said the travelling doctor. 'Let me give you my card.'

The express was clattering between light suburbs. Through the windows they could see deserted avenues stretching away into the darkness, linden trees punctuated by a chain of sickly sodium street lights.

'It would be nice to stay in touch.' The writer studied two addresses, a well-known club in Pall Mall and an apartment off the Wahringerstrasse.

'London,' Kuhn explained, 'is perhaps one of the last great civilized cities. Vienna used to be another. Built for empires, they satisfy a man's most exotic needs.'

Iles tore a page out of his notebook and began to write. 'Wandsworth Common is not exactly the Ringstrasse,' he said diffidently.

'Thank you,' Kuhn indicated his wallet, 'but I have it already.'

He was taken aback. 'I – you didn't –?'

'My dear Christopher,' he had that expression of ·his, the nearest he ever came to obvious pleasure. 'I can read, can't I?' He pointed to the luggage rack and the large labels childishly stencilled by the efficient Ruth.

'Oh, very good.' He hesitated. 'Well, it's been very enjoyable.'

'For me, too,' the courteous central European to the last.

How difficult, he says now, it was to articulate a carefully laid plan. 'You know,' he began, stammering slightly as he always does under pressure. 'Earlier, in the restaurant car – I think I owe you an apology – I mean you were right.'

'Come on, my friend, what is it you want to ask me?'

'You said I should stick to real stories from the real world. I know you don't trust writers but – well, I'd love to work with you . . . on . . . your story. We could go fifty-fifty. It would be a terrific seller, and we'd both make a bit of money. I told you I'm looking for a new subject. How about it?'

Kuhn was obviously enjoying the expression on the Englishman's face. He lit another Beedie with an air of triumph. 'I knew it,' was all he said. The smoke bloomed between them. 'You are,' he added after a moment's thought, 'one of the most suggestible people I have ever met.' He delivered this verdict like an accolade.

'I find it hard to resist a story, that's all.'

'Quite so.'

Iles did not know how to go on. Was his offer snubbed?

'So –' Kuhn put out his hand, 'we shall meet again. I shall visit your city in the course of the next few weeks. We must talk some more about this most interesting proposition.'

'You mean –?'

'Now then.' Kuhn was teasing again. 'Not too many questions just now. It is my rule never to discuss business after midnight.'

The train was snaking and groaning under the net of overhead cables. The platform was moving fast at their feet. The train stopped with a jerk and they both staggered forward. It was after three in the morning. Nuremberg station was a cave of echoing shadows, blue and cold.

The Englishman felt a tap on his shoulder, and started nervously. The guard was pointing to his notebook; it had fallen out of his pocket on to the platform. He bent down to pick it up, eager, possessive. 'Thank you – I mean, *danke schön*,' he said. '*Danke schön*,' he repeated loudly, smiling and nodding to the guard in a pantomime of gratitude.

'Well,' he said, turning back to Kuhn, 'nearly lost all my raw material there –'

But his fellow traveller had already disappeared, and he was left staring stupidly at the names on the plate by the door BRÜSSEL – AACHEN – KÖLN – FRANKFURT – NÜRNBERG – WIEN.

[2]

The exchange of letters during the second half of 1969 was interrupted, Iles says, by the kind of life he was leading at that time, never in one place for long, living out of two suitcases – he can't remember all the moves, but he's sure that some letters were lost.

Among his writings from this time, there is his report on the second Isle of Wight Pop festival for the *International Times*:

A 2000 watt PA system of exceptional clarity enabled the music to be heard not only by the festival but also by the prisoners in Parkhurst and the monks in the Quarr monastery who hadn't heard music since the war . . . Huge crowds of fans listened to the Nice, the Who, the Rolling Stones, Françoise Hardy, and Tom Paxton singing 'Talking Vietnam Blues'. *Something is happening here, But you don't know what it is, Do you, Mister Jones?*

He came back from the festival with a spaced-out American flower child from UCLA and for three mad weeks camped in a conservatory in Fulham, almost suffocating among the rubber plants and busy lizzies, and smoking amazing quantities of marijuana.

Just before Christmas, he went to stay with his mother in Bexhill, and it was here, five minutes from the sea front, with gulls swooping in the white winter sky, that he sat down one morning to write to Prague, a letter which has survived.

3 The Colonnade
Bexhill-on-Sea
Sussex
10th December 1969

Dear Peter,

I'm afraid we've lost contact recently. I have been all over the place these last few months and I imagine that your letters will have gone astray. I'm having a row with my lousy publishers about my royalties, and I can well believe that they aren't as scrupulous about forwarding my mail as they were when I was pet of the month. Hardly two years! It's humiliating the way those people lose interest. They have simply no idea how long it takes to write a good book.

So what have I been up to? Writing occasional pieces for magazines to keep my hand in. I spent two months on a film script of my book for a guy who turned out to be a total loser. I'm now working on a couple of short stories, staying with my mother here by the sea.

You must meet my old lady one day, an amazing woman, the most wonderful, loving, tolerant person I've ever met. She used to be on the stage and when I was living with Milena, we used to have a great time together. She's the only oldster I know who's not bothered by drugs etc., so I sit around on the long boring evenings here rolling joints and watching the Wednesday Play on the television, while she criticises the director.

My friends come and stay here and do what they like. She's great that way and they all love her too. Last week I had this Scots girl called Helen staying for two or three days and she brought us breakfast in bed every morning. 'What would the neighbours say?' has become this great joke between us.

It's nearly Christmas. I'm going to stay here and write, and then hope to move back to London in the New Year with some work to sell. I've still got quite a bit coming in from the book and I know how to live cheaply, so there's no problem.

Mother has just come in and says she would like to meet you one day. She's read one or two of your letters. She remembers the Czech refugees here during the last war. So, from both of us, very best wishes for Xmas and the New Year.

Christopher

That's a typical letter from Christopher: when he writes it's as though he's chatting to you on the phone. (Ironic, really, that he should be so fluent and natural when it doesn't, so to speak, matter.)

And that was all those years ago, in the festive season of 1969. Words, for him have only become more problematic with the passage of time. Why else would he turn to me, Mr Scrivener-in-Chief?

It's a funny relationship we have – he's the first to admit it. He likes to poke fun at what he calls my 'March of Time' paragraphs. Though when, after a good burrow through the cuttings, I remind him of things he's forgotten, he's always grateful to be surprised and intrigued.

For instance: on December 15 that year it was announced that President Svoboda had nominated Alexander Dubček as Czechoslovak ambassador to Ankara, and shortly afterwards the Central Committee plenum 'accepted the resignation' of the former First Secretary. The new ambassador left for Turkey in January of the new decade. A hostess with Czechoslovak airlines who handed him a bouquet of flowers as he departed from Ruzyně Airport was sacked immediately.

Six

[1]

Iles had the compartment to himself as far as Linz and slept well enough to feel, on waking in broad day at last, that he had not been travelling all night. The Vienna express was less resilient to the journey: the lavatory was now blocked, a heap of paper towels blossomed in the waste bin. He splashed cold water on his face but had to dry himself with his shirt and returned to find the carriage crowded. A mother and her small son were sitting opposite, knitting and nose-picking respectively. There was an open-pored man with cropped hair reading a Jacqueline Susann by the door. From his anorak and running shoes he took him to be a US serviceman in mufti. Finally, a woman in faultless *Loden* and tiny polished shoes, wearing her hair like a hat, came in, sat down and started to go through her handbag. Iles opened his notebook to record his impressions of Kuhn.

His beard is red like tobacco, or a conker, or beech trees in winter, or even madeira. In bright light it turns slightly orange. His lips are wet and fleshy and when he tells you a story they take on a life of their own. He watches you from behind his eyes. It's a face for an artist or a sculptor's model. He reminds me of Mother's repertory friends, self-consciously theatrical, convinced that they are always in the limelight. He's one of those types, sometimes called 'real characters', who seem to transform people, situations. You live more vividly in his presence and find yourself talking better than you know.

There was a metallic rattle in the corridor; the buffet car attendant was selling hot coffee which came in plastic jugs that went to two cups. For a moment, the train glimpsed its former transcontinental glory.

It was eight o'clock, an hour ahead of London. Soon Helen (or would it have to be faithful Sarah?) will be getting the children to their Saturday painting class. Ruth, quiet and grave, with a satchel full of paper and felt pens, her pale oval face lost in its own thoughts, usually had to help with the intractable twins. She was at the age when she asked disconcerting questions like: 'Do you think the Russians will destroy the world?' Ruth probably remembered her father when he was still slightly in demand to join a panel or give a lecture to sixth formers, even though, as far as she was concerned, the sixties and the Second World War were equally historical. Sometimes her inquisitive barrage – 'Who was Hitler?' or 'What was the British Empire?' – left her parents wondering about their choice of school, even though they knew they could never afford to run for cover to the private system like so many of their acquaintances.

Emma and Rebecca, born five years later, knew nothing of those early days. They were ignorant of the reasons why the Iles family no longer lived in a four-storey Victorian mansion in Islington. In some ways, he hoped they would never find out. The past was a lost and faintly ridiculous society, and how could he ever explain it, the shattered dream? He would hate to become a bore on the subject; instead he would prefer to boast of his children, trade en-prints like any parent and admit they were popular: the house was always invaded after class and in the holidays with schoolfriends who came to watch TV or make fudge and egg-box brontosauruses. Sometimes, looking at these animated faces, absorbed in painting a strip of blue sky, or playing in the small leafy garden, sometimes that seemed like the best thing he had ever done and he felt tears of pride pricking in his eyes.

Now the train swayed across an Austrian plain. The earth was waking up in the spring sunshine. There were willows misted with green and birds swooping in the warm. The track ran alongside a

municipal sports ground. A team of red-and-white-shirted football players was stamping in the shade of a row of aspens. Then
there were sidings, a goods train, and a convoy of ten, twenty,
thirty tanks loaded on to rolling-stock. He looked at his map:
they were less than fifty miles from the Iron Curtain.

The Austrian lady was trying to say something to him, pointing
insistently at the plastic coffee jug. 'That, I would like please.'

'But I'm sorry. It's finished.' He turned it upside down. 'No
more.'

'Please, I am liking it, sir.' She pulled it away from his fingers.
'See – with it, I fill with, what do you say, *bonbons?*'

'Sweets.'

'Thank you. *Switz.* Then I tie a ribbon, so.' She gave a
kindergarten teacher's demonstration. 'A nice present, no? The
children of my cousin like it the most.' She turned the jug in her
hands, sizing it up professionally, a woman for whom the experiences of war and liberation had taught that everything has its uses.

Iles complimented her English.

'Thank you, sir.' She stiffened like a cadet on parade. 'Some
years ago I have been in London.' She stowed the jug efficiently in
her bag. 'Oxford Road.'

'Oxford Street,' he corrected with an encouraging smile.

The serviceman chipped in. 'Let me tell you something, sir. I
was mugged real bad in Oxford Street.'

Iles found himself answering on behalf of Her Majesty's
Government, but the American was not pacified. 'It's a fact, sir.
Your cops are the lousiest law enforcement officers in the world.
They don't carry guns and they don't give a damn.'

'The Force is not what it was,' he admitted pleasantly.

'Are you kidding me?' The dough-faced soldier coloured with
anger. 'Let me tell you, sir. I don't come here for what I can get at
home. I visit Europe,' he concluded, 'for her culture.' He glanced
round the carriage definitively and, emphasizing his claims,
returned to his reading.

Iles closed his notebook and went to find the dining car which

63

was now quite crowded, like the train. He ordered more coffee and went back to his writing:

The Austrian countryside is beautiful. There's a broad river by the track, a sickly-yellow sluggish creature winding past a vine-covered escarpment. Why did Kuhn automatically suspect Peter's identity? Could he possibly know something I don't? I have that feeling with him, that he will always be better informed in ways I do not understand.

The more our acquaintance has grown, the more I have discovered Christopher's tendency to favour conspiracy theories. Visitors to his house will find his bookshelves crowded with paperbacks about the assassination of President Kennedy, the activities of the CIA in Latin America and Indo-China, the collusion of multinationals and fascist juntas, the machinations of Henry Kissinger, the exploitation of the Third World by the pharmaceutical companies, the true story of Watergate, etc., etc. Quiz him carefully, and you will find that Christopher accepts it is unlikely that Lee Harvey Oswald was a hired gun for Texas oil barons in league with Cuban revanchists, or that the British secret service plotted to overthrow Harold Wilson, but he will argue that his fascination is with stories, with the psychology of plots.

There are plenty of other books on Christopher's DIY shelves to scan: *The Double Helix, The Last Whole Earth Catalogue, Language and Silence, Up Is A Nice Place To Be, Zen and the Art of Motorcycle Maintenance, The Greening of America, The Last Words of Dutch Schultz, The Armies of the Night, A Clockwork Orange, Understanding Media, The Little Red Schoolbook, Journey to the East, The Third Policeman, Fear and Loathing in Las Vegas, The Fat Man in History, A Spaniard in the Works, A Dying Colonialism . . .*

A tall, high-cheeked girl, with tight blue jeans tucked into Spanish boots, strode into the dining car from nowhere and joined the queue. She had fjord-blue eyes and piles of hair the colour of sunflowers; she stood with a model's poise, conscious of her looks. Like everyone else, he watched her surreptitiously, jotting a few words of description as a distraction . . . Unbelievable luck, she was bringing her coffee to his table. He became modestly engrossed in his writing. The voice above him asked, in English, if there was a free seat.

He looked up expectantly: but it was another passenger, stepping awkwardly to one side of the gangway to let the Rhine goddess stride past to a table at the far end.

He nodded, 'Sure.'

This was a boyish-looking woman in jeans and a heavy knitted sweater with an anti-nuke badge. She had short, chewed hair and a slight scar on her pale forehead, possibly from a long-forgotten car crash.

He watched her drink her coffee for a few moments and then, curious, asked, 'How do you know I am English?'

The girl laughed. 'But of course you are English.' She seemed to find the idea that he could be anything else amusing.

'And what is your country?'

She was shy with her answer, as though she did not trust herself to get into conversation. 'I am from Denmark.'

England, Germany, Turkey, Hungary, France, Norway, Denmark: divisions, frontiers and borders scored across old Europe like wrinkles on a face. 'I would like to have a holiday on the Baltic,' he said, articulating one of Helen's cherished dreams. He looked clearly into her eyes. 'They say it is very beautiful.'

Her lips parted slightly and she gave him a patriotic, midsummer-morning smile. 'You are a journalist?' she hazarded, pointing at the notebook.

'Yes. Well, a writer.'

'Once I was in love with a writer.' She looked out of the window. 'It did not last long. He was very selfish.' She put her hand to her throat, adjusting her tight orange-flowered scarf; she wore a thin silver ring, her only jewellery, on the middle finger of her right hand.

They talked; he praised her English. She was still learning all the time, she said. So he showed her how *ghotio* pronounces as *fish*.

'. . . and *tio* as in station.'

'That's very good.' She was full of admiration. 'I will tell my teacher this.'

He gave her the scrap of paper. He was pleased and it showed. He loves language games. At home he is known to be a keen Scrabble player these days, mining the Compact Oxford English Dictionary for three-letter words beginning with X. His maddening favourite is *Xel, an obsolete form of Shall, v.* In his better days he bought every new dictionary as it was published. He likes to experiment with transatlantic coinings like *schlepp, gofer, honcho* and *frag.* He also invents words in his head, *indefagnable, gloop, glucid, elegate, pompify, stupendid, broozle.*

The train was slowing again. He yawned.

'Excuse me,' said the girl. 'I am going off now. It's been nice talking to you.'

He was taken unawares. 'Oh. I enjoyed it. I hope . . . See you later then.'

'Have a nice day,' she said.

This was the last stop before Vienna. The train clanked across an iron bridge. There was a town piled up like a wedding cake on the banks of a river. Sunshine touched golden cupolas. The atmosphere of quiet bustle on the platform seemed typically Austrian. A painter on a ladder was laying creamy brush-strokes on the Tyrolean roof.

As he returned to his compartment he recognized one or two passengers from the long journey strolling in the corridor. They exchanged smiles, obviously satisfied that the trip was drawing to a close.

When he looked at his watch again it was exactly a quarter to ten and the Vienna express was pulling into the Ostbahnhof, punctual to the minute.

He walked slowly down the platform, enjoying the new sense of freedom in a foreign place. The air was cool and carried the smells of the station. At the barrier, families waited for aunts and grannies, lovers kissed, taxi drivers held up cards, 'Sony', 'Bell', 'AEG', and Christopher Iles, who needed somewhere to stay, went to look for the Information desk.

[2]

The reply to Christopher's Christmas letter came almost at once.

Praha
3rd January 1970

Dear Christopher,

It is being so nice to have your letter from your mother's house. I imagine you are very happy by the seaside. I have friends here with very nice things to say about kind English people.

Would you do something for me please? I will tell you a story. After the invasion of the Nazis, some of my friends came to England, where they stayed until war is finished. Karel Hodek is one of these people. He knows me now a very long time. I tell him about you and he asks me to say when he was eighteen years he stayed in English town called Saint Leonards Town. He say the people called him Charly Czech! The family is named Bailly he says. He not remember very much more about their house. They were very nice to him and have music concerts with friends. He would like to know if you can write to Mr and Mrs Bailly and say hello from Charly. Perhaps it is too difficult, but he say people in England never leave their house in their life!

This has just been Christmas-time. In good days before it is very nice for all of us. Snow is here and all the people are on the river in ice skates. It is very pretty picture. Do you still

67

have goose for Christmas dinner? In Czechoslovakia we have carp. He is very nice with children. I know your English Christmas-time from Charles Dickens. Do you like *Christmas Carol*? I have very nice collected edition, London: Chapman & Hall, 1894. It is sent me from London, but I have missing *Nicholas Nickleby*. These books have been in red bindings and look very nice on shelves. I have hoped one day I am finding the missing one.

Is chess game okay now? I make move with Queen to King's Bishop 2.

Sincerely,
Peter

I wrote earlier that Christopher has dissuaded me from many of my normal editorial practices (it may surprise you to know that, faced with the more timid kind of writer, I can come on pretty strong with my 'Deletes' and 'Over the tops') but there has been one exception, one alteration. We did agree, after much agonising, to anglicise Petr to Peter. Looks better, doesn't it? We try to please.

Some more 'March of Time', from 1970 again. On 16 January, Mrs Caroline Heller, her daughter Zoë and a group of sympathizers placed a wreath in memory of Jan Palach at the entrance to the Czechoslovak embassy in London. Speaking to the press afterwards, she said she was 'appalled at what had happened to a hopeful looking society after the invasion'. She urged people to 'Remember Jan Palach. Remember Czechoslovakia'.

Then, as though he had forgotten something, Císař wrote once more.

Praha

Dear Christopher,

I am thinking you try look for *Nicholas Nickleby*. Please it is not a worry. I get books from the world all the time. Not always they are arriving here. In Czechoslovakia we have special post office. I go to Maxim Gorky Square and I have to sign. One day I have copy of *Animal Farm* by George Orwell. They say at post office I cannot have Orwell. He is enemy propaganda they say. But they know me well there and we are friends. When I promise I never lend books, just read myself, that is okay they say. A book is a friend, very precious. Of course I look after very carefully.

Now, please, I must say to you about your friend Milena. I am very sorry I am not saying this very much before, but it is difficult. She was known to me, and that is why I was writing you. So now perhaps I can help you. It will be very nice and kind of you if you tell me about when she is in your country. I hope I am hearing from you again.

With all my best wishes,
Sincerely
Peter

This letter arrived in Bexhill after Iles had returned to London. He asked his mother to read it over the telephone. He says that when she had finished there was a long silence. She was perfectly understanding but also perfectly firm. He had to answer those questions, she said. The more you try to forget, the more you remember. He had to write back. Now, in retrospect, he wonders whether his mother saw the letters to Prague as a way of coming to terms with what had happened.

Seven

[1]

Towards the end of the afternoon, when the light reflected in the wardrobe mirror was full of shadow, Iles woke up. For a moment, before he caught sight of his suitcase still unopened on the floor, he suffered the traveller's amnesia. Slowly he began to pick up reassuring signals: voices in the street, the returning memory of the manageress in her turquoise overalls, and the mock-imperial chandelier chiming faintly in the draught from the window. He was in Vienna. He rolled over and lifted his watch off the bedside table. It was exactly six o'clock.

The station was deserted. Iles was ahead of time. He went across to the news stand. There was a surprisingly wide choice of English and American newspapers: Thursday's *Daily Telegraph* and *Guardian*, Friday's *Daily Express* and *Herald Tribune*. A copy of *Time* seemed to be the best value. Turning over the pages, he walked slowly back towards platform eleven.

A gipsy woman selling sprigs of white heather stopped in his path. He pushed a twenty-schilling note into her hand, an act of charity that gave him a diffuse sense of well-being. He fastened the buttonhole jauntily in his jacket; it complemented his white scarf. He might have been on his way to a party. *What a drag it is getting old, what a drag it is* . . . His tuneless humming is a habit his daughters love to mimic.

He has never explained Císař to his children. They are still too young to grasp the significance of his airmail correspondence. There have even been Czechs at the dinner table, but these probably mean little either. They would only be vaguely aware of occasional visitors from abroad coming to the house, bringing wine, chocolates, a book of cartoons perhaps, asking strange questions in words they can hardly understand.

One day, when they were all older, then perhaps he would explain in painful detail why years of letter-writing have filled a decade of silence, would open the bottom drawer of his desk upstairs and pull out the half- and quarter-finished typescripts: a novel, abandoned after fifty pages, an incomplete play (in truth, barely begun), and some short stories. In the early days a few of these were published in magazines, advertised as 'By the author of'. Read them today and they seem inferior stuff, trading on a reputation. Some are still attached to their rejection letters: 'Dear Mr Iles, Thank you for sending us your short story which the Fiction Editor has read with great interest. I regret to have to tell you that owing to the recent pressure of space . . .' (I can now reveal that he's decided to sell these unfinished manuscripts, as a tax dodge, to an American university library. As he remarked to me the other day, he might as well cash in on 'his decade' while it's good box office.)

A long time ago, in the days of his self-confidence, he had occasionally raised a smile by quoting Dr Johnson, 'Your manuscript is both good and original. Unfortunately, the part that is good is not original, and the part that is original is not good.'

He's told me that in his experience Grub Street was quite as brutal but nothing like as elegant, and I'm not inclined to disagree. It's not difficult to understand why he became discouraged by the pain of watching other writers, friends and rivals, produce work in an apparently effortless rhythm. Study the letters and you'll see that, as time passed, rejection became blunter. I've seen sharp, dictated-but-not-read kinds of replies in which he was told plainly that he was no longer in tune with the mood of the times. Discordance – once his unique selling point – escaped him. More simply, he drifted towards middle age. Injured pride (the making of the Scots, as he teased Helen) did not fuel creativity. He was, instead, stunned into silence, a profound inarticulacy from which his correspondence was the only escape.

The loudspeaker came to life. He turned to look up the track curving away beyond the end of the platform. On the station clock it was 7.30. But there was no train. From the shaking of heads around him he realized it was late and plunged back into his magazine.

When it came, a huge combat-green locomotive pulling half a dozen carriages, people began hopping off and running for the exit long before it had stopped. Doors swung back on their hinges and the engine gave a loud conclusive hoot. Behind the first wave, there was a handful of weary passengers, old women, fathers, soldiers, a party of nuns and a class of schoolchildren. Iles turned his attention jumpily from face to face, bright, confused expressions of travel-weariness. His mind's eye became a jumble of human features, lips, eyes, beards and noses. Everyone was laden with baggage. Some were greeted by friends and relatives, with kisses or handshakes, rich smiles and cries of happiness. A few were obviously coming over for good.

Slowly the crowd began to thin out. The stragglers came down the long platform, deep in conversation. There was no sign of Peter Císař. Apart from a sweeper and a drunk, the platform was deserted.

He became like a man who has had his pocket picked in a crowded street, a case study of indecision. Finally, he went up to the great engine itself. The driver and his mate were climbing out of the cabin. He pointed up the line. 'Praha? You come from Praha?' he demanded, rude with anxiety. The driver nodded, indifferent.

He turned away. People were coming on to the platform for the next departure. He ran past the barrier and made his way to the timetable. The next Prague train was not due until the early morning.

At the information desk there was a young woman with watery eyes who spoke English, smiling proudly at the end of each sentence. 'I can make an announcement if that is what you will like.'

'Please. I am most grateful.' His own English was turning pidgin.

'Not at all. It is my pleasure.'

He went out and stood in the concourse, beating the rolled-up *Time* against his thigh. The loudspeaker crackled and a woman's voice began to speak in German. The announcement was repeated in English; he imagined the girl was showing off to her colleagues. 'Will Mister Císař-sař-sař go please to information-ation-ation. Will-ill-ill Mister Císař-sař-sař go please-ease-ease to information.'

The old station seemed more deserted than ever. Outside it was dark.

'Perhaps your friend is travelling on the next train,' the information clerk suggested. 'Or perhaps I shall try again.'

'No. Thank you.' He was sorry, he said, to have caused the trouble.

'It's no problem,' said the girl.

Iles went back to the platform. The Chopin express was gone. As he watched, another train, empty, inched forward with roaring diesels, and began to pick up new passengers. They climbed on board with shouts of excitement and much door banging.

He noticed a small crop-haired figure in a long leather overcoat, smoking a roll-up cigarette, also pacing up and down, and recognized him, in the way that is common on stations, from his earlier wait. Conversation started easily.

'You too,' said the man. He had something of the look of a Nazi war criminal. 'You are looking for someone?'

Still watching over the man's shoulder for a glimpse of Císař, he explained that he was supposed to be meeting a friend from Prague. 'I don't quite know what to do now.'

'This is a sad place,' said the man. He took the cigarette out of his mouth and threw it onto the track. The tiny cinders glowed in the dark. 'You know, refugees come from the East, day by day.

73

Poland, Hungary, Czechoslovakia.' The thought seemed to make his restless. Iles walked alongside the discontented stranger.

'Perhaps they are happy to be free.'

'No one likes to leave their homeland.'

'Are you waiting for someone yourself?'

The man was deftly rolling another cigarette. He smiled sourly, a scarred veteran weighing up a question about a forgotten war. Later, Iles faithfully recorded his story in his notebook.

His name, he said, was Alexander. Many years ago, long before the invasion, he had lived in Prague, working for the Party. As a young man he had made the decision in 1948, when the communists came to power, that if life was to be bearable, he would have to compromise. He was a good and faithful servant of the state, rose in the hierarchy and, towards the end of the sixties, backed the reformist movement. For a few heady months it seemed like a dream come true. In retrospect, it was of course a fatal miscalculation. When disgrace was imminent he and his sister loaded everything into his Škoda and drove through the night to the Austrian border. Fortunately, they were not alone. Many others were leaving. There was no difficulty in getting out. The Russians were probably glad to see the back of them. In fact, there was a funny story. The Škoda actually broke down at the frontier and a couple of Czech border guards helped him push it across into the West. It was amusing to remember that, he said, but he didn't smile. Now he lived in Vienna and earned a living as a translator, and occasionally by playing his cello in a Palm Court sextet. Every weekend, he told Iles, he would come and wait for the express from Prague, watch it arrive at the Franz Josef-bahnhof in the hope of spotting old friends, and for the secret pleasure of seeing a few Czech faces among the crowds. 'I cannot tell you,' he concluded, 'how much I look forward to my Saturday evening at the station.'

'Do you ever correspond with your old friends?' asked Iles, the letter-writer. He found himself being considered with great seriousness. 'I can never do that,' said Alexander. 'Think, please, what might happen to them.' A memory surfaced. 'Once – there was a letter.' He paused. 'From a friend.' His jaw went weak. 'But I did not reply.'

'Zlatá Praha,' Iles murmured, thinking aloud.

'Very good.' There was surprise in his admiration. 'How do you know this, please?'

'Once,' said Iles with the recklessness that comes in talk with strangers, 'I was in love with a beautiful girl from Prague.'

When Alexander smiled a momentary warmth came into his yellow features. 'Love,' he replied. 'That is the way to learn a language.'

'I'm a bit rusty,' Iles confessed. 'It was a while ago.'

Snow-haired Milena, woman of his dreams: there are nights when, close to Helen, the emotion strays in his mind to the past; there are days when he will see her face in a crowd, or walking down the street will quicken his pace to draw level with an English look-alike. He has shown me her picture; he has shown me what he lost. He says I'm privileged. In the past he's been very secret about her memory. He admits that's been part of the problem.

Now he was being offered a cigarette, and countered with one of his own.

'So you have visited my city?'

He heard himself evade the fact that he had never actually crossed the border. 'Look,' he said impulsively, 'I want something to drink. Will you join me for a beer?'

'*Prosím.*'

Iles almost clapped his hands together, and followed his latest acquaintance towards the station restaurant and its long American bar.

[2]

By the time Christopher found what he calls 'the necessary madness' to reply to Císař's last letters it was March – this is

75

1970 – and he'd just moved in with Helen McPhee. He thought he was in love again. The new emotional security in his life should have made it easier for him to write about Milena, but it has to be admitted that his first effort was not a success.

Dear Peter,

I have your letter, forwarded from Bexhill. It's taken a while to get round to a reply, mainly because this is going to be a difficult one to write.

You cannot know how painful I've found your questions about Milena. Of course it's simple, really; in one way she was just someone with whom I started this brief affair at the end of 1967, but that leaves out everything we felt for each other and the crisis in my life when she decided to return home. It also leaves out the reason why your first letter to me was so important. If it had come from Budapest or Warsaw I would have been intrigued, might even have replied as I did, but I would not, frankly, have had the same incentive to keep writing. I have to admit that I have been answering your letters as a way of staying in touch, so to speak, with the memory of someone I loved, adored really, more than anyone else in the world. Even though time has passed now and there are many distractions, sometimes I wonder if I will ever get over what happened to her.

In an odd way I'm glad to know that your writing was not simply a coincidence. I'm quite a superstitious person; your letter, arriving when it did, came to me as a sign. Don't misunderstand me. I've been grateful for the chance to correspond. I have had some painful moments these last two years and they have been easier to bear thanks to you.

Honestly, it would be easier to talk about Milena than to write about her. I think I would like to visit Prague, despite what has happened. Then we could meet and talk and I could explain everything. Now it's my turn to ask questions. Is she a family friend? Someone who worked for you? I'd love to know more.

For now I'd like to end by saying that she was someone very special. I still cannot believe I shall never see her again. If I come to Prague it will be a kind of pilgrimage. I'm sorry, I must stop now.

  Yours,
  Christopher

Oddly enough he kept a copy of this letter (a first draft?) and Císař's reply is clipped to it:

           Praha
        April 16th 1970

Dear Christopher,
  Milena Hamplová was my daughter.
    Your friend,
    Peter

Eight

[1]

Alexander had exquisite hands, long white tapering fingers, perfectly manicured. This was the first observation Iles made in his notebook when he wrote up their encounter the following morning. The distant chiming of church bells emphasized the Sunday silence. It seemed appropriate to write about Alexander in the faded Viennese splendour of his hotel room. For all that he had been a loyal communist for half his life, Alexander sustained an air of Habsburg gentility, the slightly dilapidated look of a character from Chekhov. His waxy, well-preserved features, the hint of French perfume and the frayed but well-cut suit all spoke of a man who, despite everything, had not forgotten the pleasures of vanity.

I talked freely about Milena, Iles wrote, prompted by his undisguised curiosity. There is also, his notes continue, the joy of telling stories to a stranger, someone to whom you can unburden everything with the certainty that your circle – family, friends, and enemies – can never know your secrets. I like the idea that my words may be passed on by Alexander to people I'll never meet; what we say together will live on, like a Chinese whisper.

So we sit in the station bar, each with a soapy Austrian lager. Alexander is a familiar customer here; from time to time people stop by to exchange greetings and chat, or even to arrange bookings for the sextet. Despite these attentions, he is a lonely person, a sad old queen not fully out of the closet, an exile pining for his homeland. He questioned me as though he wanted to unearth a misery to match his own. I don't know whether he

78

succeeded, but it's true we talked of things I've not dared discuss for years. This is roughly how the conversation went.

'Tell me please, what is your profession?'

The habits of the official mind were still there; I suppose it was to be expected that an ex-career man should consider this a necessary opening.

'I work in advertising.'

'I see. And your Czech girl – what is her name?'

'Milena Hamplová.'

I found it impossible to say more. He repeated 'Hamplová' to himself a few times, the way the English do when they are trying to get a fix on you. Milena always said the Czechs and the English were surprisingly similar. He seemed disappointed that he did not recognize the name.

He inquired how we met. This was easier for me, a good memory. I asked if he knew London. Only from Sherlock Holmes he said. So I explained that I once lived in a district called Notting Hill. The house was being leased by this band I used to write lyrics for. 'They let me have a small room at the top.' After some of the places I'd been it felt like luxury. I didn't tell him about the book or the publicity. 'And there was this girl you see. Beautiful. Tiny. Vivacious. A fantastic dresser.'

I stopped myself in time. I was about to run away with my description and tell him about Milena's surprised, almost child-ish, wide-awake expression I always found so winning. But no, I just said, 'She used to go to the corner shop every day.'

I looked at him as I spoke. I could see that he was translating out loud in his head, getting stuck on the colloquial bits. He was interested in Milena in the way that the kind of men who used to be known as confirmed bachelors often are with good-looking young women. I found it rather touching to see his thin lips show their appreciation when I mentioned the stylish way she used to dress.

'Milena Hamplová.' I could see he was questioning himself again and regretfully finding no answer.

'She was a student.' I told him how she had come to England with friends – and how she had decided to stay behind. In those days that sort of thing was easy. I explained how she wanted to make it as an actress. She had done a bit of theatre work at home and hoped to make her way on the Fringe. She had gone up to the Edinburgh Festival, made a few contacts and come back to London full of crazy expectations. 'And that,' I concluded, 'is how she came to be living in this ground-floor flat in Notting Hill Gate with another English girl and four cats.'

'Cats!' Alexander's excitement surprised me; it seemed out of character. 'I love cats. In my room I have three beautiful cats. Siamese.' He looked at me shyly. 'What you call moggies, yes?' He was thrilled to try out a bit of English idiom.

'Moggies, yes. Likewise, puss, pussy, tom, kitty, tabby and so on.'

I don't think he followed that and I didn't feel inclined to parse it for him. He said, 'My favourite poet is T. S. Eliot.'

'*Practical Cats*.'

'Exactly.' Alexander's eyes began to show real animation. 'How nice it is to talk to a man of culture.'

What can I say? We talk about Macavity, Growltiger and Mr Mistoffelees for a few minutes, quoting lines at each other. Finally, when these feline raptures are over, and I've decided not to remind him that the great man's name is an anagram of toilets, I go on where I left off, with Milena.

'So every day I see this girl, buying a newspaper, or some teabags or cat litter. She appeared to live very frugally. We used to smile at each other. Once, when it was dark, I followed her at a safe distance, just to see where she lived.'

'Ah,' said Alexander sadly. 'A romantic.'

If only he knew: the excitement I get with strange women, with the sight of a bare torso in a lighted window, even with the scent of a woman's body at a crowded party . . . Anyway, he seemed pleased with his observation. I smiled and went on to explain how, after this, I used to walk back home from the Underground via

Milena's street, just in case. Then I told him about the day we first spoke properly, outside the corner shop, of course.

'I saw you on telly last night,' she said. Her accent was good. 'I liked the programme.'

I could see Alexander was dying to know why I should have been on television, but I decided not to give him that satisfaction. There is an art to a good story and I went on with it, knowing that his interest was sharpened.

It was, I remember, a brilliant autumn day and I said so.

She replied that it made her homesick for the golden colours of her native Prague. She was trying to tell me about herself, where she came from etc., but none of it was a surprise. I'd already chatted up Pedro, the shopkeeper, and knew all about her. Now we were walking away from the corner with our modest groceries. The freedom of the West was wonderful, she said, but sometimes she was nostalgic for Czechoslovakia.

Alexander nodded with approval and I told him how we talked, how she came back to the house, drank tea, smoked some dope, and how, quite quickly, we became lovers. (If only it was always that easy.) When I think of the few months we had together, I think of the Stones, *Let's spend the night together, Now I need you more than ever* . . . That season it seemed to be playing at all the parties we went to. Of course, I did not tell Alexander that sometimes I ache for her body, even now. (I have to confess it.)

I wrote earlier that one can speak with amazing freedom to someone you know you will never see again. But now, when I think about it, I am conscious of the things I didn't talk about, private memories I preferred to keep to myself, thank you very much.

What comes back to me most vividly after all these years? Milena with flowers in her hair, Milena in a mini-skirt, her excitement shopping in Granny-Takes-a-Trip, Milena throwing snowballs in Kensington Gardens on Christmas Day, Milena sitting at mother's piano playing *Hello Dolly* and *Penny Lane*, Milena in my ears and in my eyes, Milena with the whole earth people at Glastonbury, Milena scoring from that weird pusher in Brixton whose only ambition was to set up shop in Saigon, Milena swimming in the Thames at midnight after the band's gig at Windsor. I suppose that's the worst. I still remember thinking: how can she be so mad and happy the day before she leaves?

Those things are the easy memories, the ones from the scrapbook. The small things, the way she did her hair, answered the phone, talked to Pedro (who thought he'd invented our relationship), stroked the cats on her knee, the way she breathed, moved, spoke, smiled . . . how we belonged to each other! I'll never be able to explain the charm of all this to anyone, except perhaps to say there was a quality of innocence and wickedness about everything she did. When we were together, she took over my life completely.

I don't think mother, who can't see the point of politics, ever understood why Milena had to go home. It was inevitable that she should become fascinated by events in Prague. Perhaps if we had met at any other time she would have stayed. I'm ashamed now to think I tried to stop her going back. It was selfish – and counterproductive. She only became more determined.

Student friends were giving her the impression that at last they were getting what they wanted. Stuck in London, she thought she was missing something important. I shall never forget her frustration when she read about the May Day celebrations that year, the spontaneous crowds, the happy excitement. I mentioned all this to Alexander: I knew he would have things to say.

'It's true,' he replied. 'It was incredible. Dubček was Goethe's Fool, the Sorcerer's Apprentice, you know? He didn't know how to break his own spell. Students, intellectuals, writers, reformists – we were all swept away. We never believed they would do it: invade. It is my custom to work late. After the first phone call, my sister came into my study. "That idiot Jiří, he says the Russians are here." Her reaction was the same as mine. No, that was unthinkable.' He was aware that he had intruded his own predicament into my story and asked about Milena again. 'What happened to her?'

What could I say? It was too complicated; the truth is still so painful. 'I never saw her again,' I replied.

I suppose he made the obvious inference. 'So now at last you are meeting her here.' He shook his head. 'But she does not come.'

No, I said, it was someone else, another old friend . . .

This time he saw the Do Not Trespass signs and, nodding gravely, went over to the bar and ordered two large brandies. We toasted each other. I noticed that he drained his glass in one fiery gulp. 'To our friendship.' In his official days, he must have been a good comrade.

I could see he was longing to know more about Milena, but now he switched the talk and turned to flattery, praising my charm and intelligence, and finally my appearance. 'That is a fine jewel,' he commented, almost patting my hand.

I had noticed, soon after we met, that he was eyeing my father's signet ring. I assumed this was part of the game. I found myself beginning to think about ways of escape.

'Look at that crest,' I said, taking off the ring and placing it in his moist pink palm. He turned it over like a Hatton Garden con-man. 'Old French,' I went on in my antique-dealer voice. 'According to the documents, Domesday Book and all that, my ancestors came to England with William the Conqueror. Family legend has it that we carried spears at Hastings . . .' I realized he was not following the historical excursus. 'Yes,' I repeated, providing a handy subtitle to the conversation. 'It's an old crest.'

He was impressed; as I've said, he was basically an *ancien régime* type. I would have liked to explain our impoverished gentry heritage, but after a large brandy and a long day that was going to be taxing. I settled for a few words about 'an old English family' in a way that hinted nicely at decent coverage in *Burke's*, then a quick change to a sincere, God-slot vibration. 'The ring belonged to my father.'

'He is dead?'

I might have guessed: he was going to ask about everything. 'It was a flying accident. Christmas, 1944. Father was in aerial camouflage. Before the war he was in the theatre on the repertory circuit. Ipswich, Coventry, Warwick, Salisbury.'

Alexander repeated the place names like a tourist.

'He met my mother in a production of *French Without Tears*. He was married at the time. It was a great romance, greatly disapproved of by my mother's family. By the time his divorce came through, he'd been drafted into the RAF. They weren't married until 1943. Less than two years later, he was killed. And I was born, oddly enough, on VE day – an only son.' I can look quite tragic when I need to. 'When I came of age, mother gave me his ring.' I put out my hand. 'Thank you,' I said, taking it back briskly.

That silenced him for a bit. If his hopes were dashed, it was as I intended. He got up, rather unsteadily I thought, said 'Excuse please,' and disappeared, presumably into the Gents.

While he was gone I found myself thinking about mother and my early life in Bexhill. I sometimes wonder: would it have been better if I had never been born? She was only twenty-five at the time. She could have made her peace with the family, remarried, moved away and known something better. Instead, she devoted herself to my education. That typing school she ran! I feel ashamed when I think about the sacrifice. What can she have thought when I came down from Oxford two years early? I suppose there have been compensations. She was so proud when the book came out. That was her triumph too. When the film deal happened, how I hoped to make enough for her to give up then and there. But by the time the middlemen had taken their cut, and I'd paid my tax bills, and put some money into that dump in Islington, there was less than I'd expected. At least she was able to retire in the end, sell her share in the business to a younger woman and enjoy some leisure. Actually, I can't imagine her retiring. She will always be making plans for some little trip abroad, or giving an illustrated talk on anything from fruit fly to the Pyramids, or inviting herself to stay and spoiling her grand-children.

At this point I realized I had been sitting alone for several minutes and was wondering, in the way you do when you're slightly pissed, where my friend had got to (perhaps he was tossing off a porter in the loo), when he reappeared as suddenly as he'd departed.

'Goodbye,' he said. 'I go home now.' It sounded like part of a ritual.

I walked with him to the front of the station. We shook hands and he went off down the Strasse, shuffling slightly, the way the elderly do when they're tired.

I stood there, holding my copy of *Time*. I was alone again, watching the taxi drivers leaning against their cabs and gossiping in the chilly shadows.

Thinking about it now, I cannot disguise the sense I have of wondering what the hell it is that's keeping me here. . .

Iles pushed back his chair and stretched his arms above his head with a yawn. He had been writing all morning, ever since he had returned from meeting the early train from Prague, another fruitless expedition. There was only the prospect of a solitary Sunday in Vienna, a walk in the Prater followed by dinner, a meal dominated, if Saturday was any advertisement, by the hotel's micro-heated *Wiener Schnitzel*.

He closed the notebook, now looking quite lived-in, with a snap and put the cap on his biro. (How quickly, he noticed, these slight but meaningful habits reassert themselves.) Then he stood up and went over to the dark mirror on the wardrobe.

He was proud of the fact that he did not look nearly forty. 'Youthful' is a word people often use about him in conversation. 'Vain boy,' he said aloud, using the words that Helen might have said if she had been there.

After a few moments, lazy with boredom, he flopped on to the hard Austrian bed. Perhaps he should ring Helen?

'Mr Iles, your book is very frank about the women in your life.'

'It's all true. I like to make my girlfriends come on the phone.'

Does it worry you to be alone? Do you need anybody? Would you believe in love at first sight?

Perhaps he should ring Helen? Or perhaps he should not. Helen is standing in the shower at home, her daughters safely dispatched for the day to friends in Highgate, having her breasts soaped by her lover, both of them slightly drunk from a bottle of Moët.

[2]

You'll remember my admission on page 4 that part of my satisfaction with this work has come from finding a voice that's my own. For an editor, let me tell you, that is a rare opportunity, a luxury. Of course, I realise that such power has its responsibilities. Did I, for instance, go too far in that last paragraph? Christopher says not: he is determined that everything should be included.

Besides, I'm afraid to say that it happens to be true. It's my proud boast that everything in these pages has been double-checked for accuracy, relying on what the Americans call 'oral testimony'.

My obsession with verification has compelled me to discuss everything with Helen (who rather likes the idea of being in a book) and, once I was accepted, with her lover himself. I have kept his role to a minimum and have made him anonymous. His story is unimportant.

So, before you decide that I am taking unpardonable liberties with Christopher's story (people are so touchy about dramatised reconstructions, aren't they?), let me remind you that all the participants have seen and approved these words: all except

Augustus Kuhn, as we shall see. I, for my part, am now no longer surprised that most people's vanity outruns their discretion.

I consider it a duty to dig up the truth. My wife says I'm one of nature's Boswells. Who can forget the indefatigable Scotsman calling on the dying Hume to discover if the celebrated aetheist was showing signs of fear at the approach of eternity?

I digress.

After Císař's April confession, the correspondence faltered. At first, Iles could find nothing to say. Gradually, contact was resumed, the conversation taken up again. Sharing gossip about his daughters, Iles discovered that 'little Hana' was the only child of a second marriage. Milena's mother had apparently died many years before. They played chess: there are several postcards about the game (and also the Fischer–Spassky championship) in Christopher's possession.

In the course of that silent spring, about nine hundred scholars and scientists were dismissed from colleges all over Czechoslovakia. A questionnaire was issued to schoolteachers.

Question One How do you evaluate developments in 1968 in view of information now available?

Question Four What is your attitude to proletarian international ism? Do you rectify incorrect political views which your pupils bring to school from their homes? How?

Question Eight How do you propose to prove your attitude to the socialist motherland and to socialism in general?

In May, Dubček was summoned home from Ankara on the pretext that his mother was ill. In June, he was dismissed as ambassador and expelled from the Communist Party. He returned to his home town, Bratislava. For a couple of years, he was allowed to work as chief of the Regional Forestry Administration's car pool, commuting to work by tram in his green forester's uniform. He lived quietly in a two-bedroom house on Mouse Street, tending the garden and doing the family shopping from time to time. The address was always guarded by soldiers with sub-machine guns.

Towards the end of 1970, through the good offices of a friend in the book trade, Iles sent Císař a signed copy of *The French Lieutenant's Woman*, and was answered with a wall calendar, mossy-green and yellow reproductions of famous Czech landscapes. He wrote a rather formal thank-you letter and received this reply.

Praha
February 12th, 1971

Dear Christopher,

I have finish reading the John Fowles novel. I thank you very much for such interesting English writer. My bibliography goes very nice. One day I hope you will see. You should come here to Praha please in summertime. It is beautiful city and I will look after you very much.

I know you do not like this. You say to yourself (please forgive me), This is Milena's city. It will be bad memories for me. But I, your friend, promise this is not so. If you are liking, you are welcome to stay with me.

Please, I understand very well how you feel. If I can speak a little of myself (which I do not like) I can tell you that when I was young man I was in love too. I lost the woman I love. I have very much sympathy for what you are saying.

The situation now is not so good. I am old bookseller who hurts no body but I must be careful.

Please come.

Your friend,
Peter

When Peter Císař wrote that 'the situation now is not so good' he was describing the gradual process whereby Dr Husák reasserted state control. The taste of freedom faded. The reformist activists in the Czechoslovak Communist Party were driven underground and became like any clandestine movement in a police state.

In March 1971, a group of nineteen young people was sentenced to prison terms of up to four years for what the state prosecutor termed 'anti-state activity'. The indictment alleged that the defendants had co-operated closely with New Left groups in the West, formed 'resistance cells' and distributed 'tens of thousands' of anti-régime pamphlets and leaflets based on the works of Trotsky and Milovan Djilas.

This was to be the pattern for the rest of the decade. The State Security police, keeping a watchful eye, subjected their enemies to petty annoyances and humiliations, taking away telephones and driving licences, breaking windscreens, making random arrests and dumping people in the countryside to find their own way home. Small groups using smuggled duplicating machines did what they could to keep the flame alive.

Some of the co-ordination of this effort came from émigrés living in Rome, Paris and London. Iles himself played a small part on the very fringes of this movement; in due course he found himself writing occasional pieces for the magazines that sustain an opposition from the West.

Meanwhile, he continued to send a stream of letters and books to Peter Císař, as if filling the universe with words would make up for the silence in his heart.

Nine

Literature nowadays is a trade. Putting aside men of genius, who may succeed by mere cosmic force, your successful man of letters is your skilful tradesman. He thinks first and foremost of the markets; when one kind of goods begins to go off slackly, he is ready with something new and appetising. He knows perfectly all the possible sources of income. Whatever he has to sell he'll get payment for it from all sorts of various quarters; none of your unpractical selling for a lump sum to a middleman who will make six distinct profits.

Iles did not get up on Monday morning until, reading quickly, he had finished *New Grub Street*. The happy sensation of lying in bed with a long novel, while the rest of the world was going to work, was not completely spoilt by Gissing's painfully accurate portrait of the literary purlieu in which pathetic hopes battle with penurious expedients.

There came a day [he read] when Edwin Reardon found himself regularly at work once more, ticking off his stipulated quantum of manuscript each four-and-twenty hours. He wrote a very small hand; sixty written slips of the kind of paper he habitually used would represent – thanks to the astonishing system which prevails in such matters: large type, wide spacing, frequency of blank pages – a passable three-hundred-page volume. On an average he could write four such slips a day; so here we have fifteen days for the volume, and forty-five for the completed book.

Could he write up the Kuhn story in forty-five days? He'd have to find out a lot more, of course. What he knew at the moment barely amounted to a sneak-preview of the first chapter. But what he did know was, he felt, a tantalising appetizer. Should he, like Reardon, announce to his friends, 'If I had to choose between a glorious reputation with poverty and a contemptible popularity with wealth, I should choose the latter'? Should he follow Gissing's advice: 'Go to work methodically, so many pages a day. There's no question of the divine afflatus; that belongs to another sphere of life. We talk of literature as a trade, not of Homer, Dante and Shakespeare'? You will find these, and other passages, carefully marked in the margins of his pocket-crumpled Penguin.

Not since the days when he and Helen were living together in Islington in the months after his miraculous film deal had he felt so privileged and carefree. Everything was new then: his work, her magazine, their relationship, their house. That building, part of an imposing Victorian terrace, was said to offer, in the estate agent's phrase, 'bags of potential'. At the time, the same could have been said of Iles himself.

Watch him today as he leaves his hotel. It's about eleven o'clock. Everything seems perfect. He has indulged that almost-forgotten taste for late rising; he has had a perfect Viennese breakfast. Instead of climbing on to the airport bus as he had planned, he has extended his booking for twenty-four hours and sets out into the city with his passport, his traveller's cheques, a map of Vienna and Kuhn's business card. He is, as the phrase goes, feeling on top of the world.

See him walking along the Ringstrasse in the sunshine and it is not difficult to imagine him ten years ago, striding across Soho Square from the Tottenham Court Road tube station on his way to a pub or restaurant.

Often he did not get home until the following morning. And if he did not go out (with or without Helen), it was then that he wrote, working his biro across the pages of Croxley Script in the circle of white light, as the evening closed in and grew still, until the darkness was roaring and he was totally absorbed in the rhythm of his words.

But the words were no good. He hated everything he did. Some nights the writing would be too strong, others too thin. For a while, when he thought he was suffering from hallucinations, he found that every sentence formed a perfect iambic pentameter. He tried writing under the influence of drugs; he tried writing drunk, and sober, and even, for a mad week one January, with all the windows open.

At first, the house itself, conceived as a future dream palace, seemed to offer a way of escape. If he could not write, at least he could rewire, and in the spirit of self-help he bought a DIY manual from *Reader's Digest*. This electrifying diversion turned out to be only a temporary relief because, in the end, the place outwitted him, ate up all his money and forced him to sell out, everything unfinished, to a smug-cheeked merchant banker.

That defeat was the first of many, often more wounding. But now, at last, Calliope had touched him on the shoulder, put ink in his pen, ribbon in his Olivetti. The years of letter-writing to Prague were doubly over, could indeed be set aside and forgotten. The fallow decade was past, it was time once again to resume his trade. Gissing was right, of course he was. All his powers should be devoted forthwith to the opportunities suggested by Dr Augustus Kuhn's business card.

Research: that was what writers did these days. If their hero was an airman, they learned to fly; if he ran a garage, they manned the pumps. And when imagination ran dry they put a publisher's contract in their knapsacks and trotted the globe, took trains, motorcycles, riverboats and Greyhounds across bits of the planet not generally known to their readers – the East Asia railway network, Mark Twain's river, the islands of the South Seas, and the distant fastnesses of China and Tibet. Back at the typewriter in Kentish Town, they claimed that the books they made from these travels were not travel books after all, but actually a new kind of fiction. If that made him a novelist again, so be it: he looked up at the street sign – Wahringerstrasse – and made a careful note.

The passing tram was green and yellow and crowded with

Viennese commuters. The Josephine mansion across the street had a wrought-iron gate, bitter gravel paths flanked by low, boxed privet, and several red and white Austrian flags clustered limply over the doorway. These were easy notes. Now – turning into a side street – he must start researching Kuhn, a more demanding proposition perhaps.

The building, when he found the address, was like all the others in the street. A heavy tall door opened into a small dark courtyard full of litter, like the bottom of an old well. There were doors on both sides leading to two clammy stone staircases, running up five or six storeys. As Iles stood there wondering which side to visit first, a stocky, bearded man carrying a music case came hurrying out. Iles stopped him and asked in his strip-cartoon German if this was the house of a certain Dr Kuhn.

The man murmured, '*Ach*, Kuhn,' and pointed to his right, and disappeared.

At the foot of the staircase was a row of rusty aluminium letter boxes, with names and numbers. At the end of the row was No. 21, very faintly marked in pencil, A. Kuhn.

He climbed slowly; the sound of a tenor saxophone provided a solo backing to his footsteps. The apartment was on the top floor. There was a skylight and up here the smell of urine and boiled vegetables was less insistent.

Kuhn was away, of course. Iles pressed the bell for the last time and again heard a distant pealing. He imagined long corridors, high ceilings and a parquet floor. Then he sat on the top step and made some more notes in his book.

The sun filtered opaque and warm through the overhead glass. He jotted down a few little details, then he paused and wrote, 'I am thirty-nine and tired of being forgotten. It's time to grow up, sell out and make a come-back. I wonder what Helen will say?'

At Home

International Times favours Design Revolution, Spiritual Evolution, Ying-Yang Uprising, Inner Space Adventure, Work Democracy, a Release of Man's Extraordinary Potential and the Transformation in the Myths that direct Life and Thought.

If you really want to travel why can't you just transfer yourself – by changing your matter into energy and back again? Why can't you? What's stopping you from doing it? The answer is in your head!

International Times

One

Christopher makes no bones about the fact that the home life of the Iles family is not going to be his favourite reading. It's perfectly clear from a thousand comments he's made to me that he has always been indifferent to the issues of the hearth. His home, for him, is an unruly state, full of discontents: a broken window, a blocked drain, a mouse in the kitchen. Shopping is not his forte; he is bored by queues and when he goes to the butcher, the deli, the grocer and especially the market he knows he is being ripped off. He doesn't exactly like to be reminded of this (am I being too manipulative?), but the catalogue of his other homely worries and irritations includes: his children, their schooling, his overdraft, the neighbours, their dog, its bark, the police, his squash partners (a shortage of), the family Volvo, the rate bill, the television (unlicensed), *Private Eye* (shouldn't he take the *New Yorker* or the *TLS*?), his wife . . .

As your narrator, these are the subjects I shall be treating in the next several pages. It is my duty as a reporter; though, as I've admitted to Christopher, I am diffident about the rather personal nature of the material. He replies that I have no choice: our collaboration has to function at all levels. I suppose I'm proud to have his trust, just anxious about fulfilling his hopes. Anyway, as he says, what's a secret? Something you repeat to only one person at a time. Fortunately for everyone perhaps, the bizarre figure of Dr Augustus Kuhn will rather overshadow the mundane intrusions of family life.

But first, another of Christopher's letters.

Wandsworth
3rd April 1974

Dear Peter,

I'm giving this to a journalist friend who will be passing through Prague on his way to Budapest. It seems a good opportunity to write.

Note the new address. I've just moved here with Helen and the baby. It's a large, sunny Edwardian pile on the edge of Wandsworth Common and, because this is not exactly the most fashionable part of town, it's at a price we can afford. It will need a lot of work, but it's structurally sound they say and I'll enjoy the distraction of painting and papering.

Did I tell you that I'm now working for an advertising agency? I really wasn't making ends meet as a freelance, and so, thanks to a distant cousin, I fixed myself up with this copywriting job. At least it pays the mortgage.

Sometimes I think I'm copping out all round, but so is everyone else I know. I suppose the main thing is the attitude, and I know I'm not waving goodbye to my ideals just because I'm selling beer and hamburgers to the Great British Public. In a way, I hope I can help to change things from within, the quiet revolution if you know what I mean.

My other latest news (which I wanted you to be the first to hear) is that we've decided to get married. I never thought I would find myself doing this (nor did Helen), and I'm sure some of our friends will be a bit surprised. But we've been living together for nearly four years and now that Ruth is on the scene and we've got this place, it seems in some strange way I can't explain the right thing to do. It will be a very quiet affair, just for close friends, the way I prefer it.

I feel you've always encouraged me to live without regrets. Of course this is going to be a very big step for me, but I hope you will understand.

I'm sending some books in a separate parcel.*

As ever,

Christopher

P.S. I enclose a copy of the game so far. It's your move I think!

A rejected version of this letter, still in his possession, has this sentence, 'I was sorry to read about S.'s death. I know you don't like my references to the past, so I shall not say any more.'

S. was Josef Smrkovský, one of the most popular and influential members of Dubček's government, who died on 14 January that year. The régime took complicated steps to prevent the funeral from becoming a demonstration of resistance like Jan Palach's. In the event, over a thousand people turned out, with workers' delegations standing alongside friends, acquaintances and members of the family at the graveside.

Two months later, in March, the police informed Smrkovský's widow that the urn with her husband's ashes had been stolen from the grave in Prague, presumably, they said, so that the enemies of socialism could smuggle it out to the West. As if to corroborate this bizarre theory, the police then reported that they had found the urn in the men's lavatory of a Bohemian railway station while the Berlin–Vienna express was passing. Two journalists from Prague were interrogated, but this was only a ploy.

The real purpose of the episode, surreal even by the standards of the State Security police, became clear when Mrs Smrkovský was told by the authorities that they could not keep watch indefinitely over the urn in the cemetery. It would be better, they said, to have it buried in her husband's home village, far away

---

* For some reason he remembers the selection: *In A Free State* by V. S. Naipaul, *The Black Prince* by Iris Murdoch and Graham Greene's *The Honorary Consul*. He also remembers making a conscious decision not to send the latest Solzhenitsyn, knowing that it would jeopardize the whole package.

from the capital. In this way the people of Czechoslovakia were encouraged to forget about the awkward past.

[2]

'Are you really going to write a book about this man?' The bedroom curtain was only half drawn, and through the window Helen Iles, the Helen McPhee of the by-line but not the bank account, lying on her back in the afternoon sunlight, could glimpse birds swooping in the spring air, and occasionally a silvery aeroplane, circling to land at Heathrow, passing across the blue suburban skies. When the jets were quiet she could hear the shouts of children bicycling furiously up and down the street. She stretched out a long white arm and made shadow creatures on the wall, a rabbit, a camel, a bird. Sex in the afternoon made you feel free. The gold on her wedding-ring glinted darkly; she was getting ironical pleasure from these hours in bed with her husband. Her face has a natural, moulded beauty, strong lines and clear, slightly yellow skin. A twist of hair, greying, was limply coiled on her forehead, but in the half-light of the pillow there was no other hint of tiredness or approaching middle age.

Helen and Christopher had slept in this small, cluttered room ever since their move. There was still a bald patch on the carpet where Ruth, barely one, had slept in a cot by the bed. The wallpaper, too, now showed wear and tear, but they could not afford to do anything about it. Probably they did not mind. The photographs propped on the mantelpiece, the heaps of clothes and piles of books by the bedside, even the stains on the floor, all made a nest of memories.

Iles stretched across and kissed her on the cheek. 'I haven't made up my mind yet,' he lied.

'What will you do about Peter Císař?'

To Christopher's way of thinking, Helen has this knack of putting her finger on rotten teeth: ever since his departure from

Vienna he has worried despondently about his obligations to the old bookseller. 'I've written.' He frowned. 'What else can I do?' He would never admit to her suspicions and say it: I'm in a terrible quandary.

As usual after sex, they were drifting apart again.

'You feel let down.' Helen's conversation always said: I think I know you better than you think.

'I don't know what I feel.'

'Except you're thinking of becoming a ghost.'

To her annoyance, he remained patient, explaining that no, he would not dream of getting involved in an agreement on such conditions; that yes, he would like to consider writing Kuhn's autobiography; that no, he didn't mind following fashion if the material was promising; and that yes, he would make sure he did all this on her own terms. 'Happy?'

Coming home was often like this, a return to a foreign country. In Vienna, Iles says that even while he was enjoying his exploration of the city, he imagined how nice it would be to be with his family again. Similarly, when he rang Helen from the airport she was obviously excited. She made her own call. 'He's back,' she said, and was accused of pleasure. After the anticipation, they always lapsed into a series of small but irritating disagreements. Alone, they had asserted independence; together there was the difficulty of living in sync. The moment she thanked him for his postcard, the pattern of his homecoming merged into the pattern of their daily lives.

'Are you saying I should have phoned?'

'I'm just saying it was nice to have some news from you.'

'Actually, I did ring. But you were out.'

'What are you saying?'

'I wasn't aware that I was saying anything. What's the matter with you?'

This is the way they are, have been and always will be. Their friends will look at Helen and Christopher and their three beautiful daughters and discuss, they think, a successful marriage. A few of them, the ones with whom Helen or Christopher have had transitory encounters, will know of the need that both husband and wife have felt, over many years, to renew their relationship by rebelling against it.

Now Helen wanted to know about Kuhn. What was he like? A cloud passed over the sun and the room darkened, softening their faces to each other.

He tried to remember everything he had been told. 'He wears as much gold as I've seen on a man. And he really is into deals.' To fill the gaps, he began to invent. It seemed the appropriate thing to do. 'The idea would be to ask him over the next time he's in London and talk it through properly. I know he's got an amazing story to tell.'

'He sounds revolting.' Helen has always taken a firm line against capitalist profiteers, against male chauvinism, in society as well as in the media, and, less out of principle than self-preservation, against anyone she suspects of manipulating her husband's weakness for business adventure, quick routes to a self-sufficiency that will set the writer free. Over the years, she has torpedoed several such schemes, ranging from a 'bar-to-door' cocktail courier service speculatively entitled Interbooze, to *Laid, My Fairy!*, a gay revue loosely based on *Pygmalion*. A transcontinental entrepreneur selling the story of his life and loves in the bar of a European express train was simply the latest manifestation of all her oldest and deepest phobias.

Iles, who is proud of what he calls his optimism, was aware of the likely condition of his wife's views and feelings. 'I know what you're thinking.'

She protested.

'No, I do. I just ask you to accept that Kuhn is different.'

There is, if his sincerity needs objective corroboration, a grandiose note, written about this time, which suggests the tenor of his own thinking:

In my mind, Kuhn stands for post-war Europe. He is the

archetype of all those displaced persons: a survivor by his wits. A man of commerce, culture and experience. A sophisticated jack-of-all-trades who has too much originality to settle for the thin-blooded collectivism of the Eastern bloc, but also too much *savoir-vivre* to swallow the sickly pill of American materialism.

'It will be pure faction,' Helen complained. 'It's not serious.'

He made a lavish gesture. 'When I've finished . . .' He crowded into her arms. 'He has this extraordinary white face, as though his blood is still. He demands to be written about.'

It would only be worth doing, Helen commented, shifting her ground, if he had complete control, and no one in Kuhn's position would allow that. 'He must have an ulterior motive.'

'Perhaps he just wants to make some money. Nothing wrong with that, surely. We will – we would go fifty-fifty.'

She said she understood he was rich already.

'The rich always want more.' A vision of Kuhn the classical patron swelled in his mind. 'Or perhaps his motives are truly altruistic.'

'It's a bit improbable. You hardly know the man.'

'There's always impulse. Some of the best businessmen work on that basis.'

She commented wryly on the history of his own impulse decisions.

And so they talked. Gradually, the advantages of her husband's newest enthusiasm took root in Helen's mind. If he was actually busy, actually writing, after all these years of anguish, rejection and prevarication, actually at work on something, she would find greater freedom in her own life, a ready-made opportunity to leave him with Sarah and the children, and to enjoy herself a bit. After all, as she has observed on more than one occasion, a girl must have some fun from time to time.

They had discussed the idea of open relationships endlessly with their friends, sitting on the floor late into the night, passing

The Fabulous Englishman

joints and listening to Pink Floyd and Steely Dan, letting the midnight mood draw out the lost candour in their lives. *Nothing is real*. Disloyalty, Helen had once said, was her credo, the only true form of self-assertion. The boasts and evasions added up to a statement that they did what they wanted and built their relationships around the consequence. Emotionally they were happier in the shanty town than the big city.

And then one day you find ten years have got behind you. Especially when Helen was pregnant, sleeping around was, for Christopher, a way of staying in touch with his fading youth and its fading ideals. At least that was what he used to say when, in the spirit of openness, he described his adventures afterwards. 'Star-fuckers,' she said, not minding it seemed. Privately, she was relieved that Ruth was obviously Christopher's child.

In marriage, neither expected to take their vows seriously. Their life-style (a word which made its first dictionary appearance in Volume II of the Supplement to the *Oxford English Dictionary* in 1976) was not significantly affected. After the ceremony, one of the guests had mimicked the registrar and they had all laughed.

'So how does it feel?' someone asked.

Christopher looked at Helen; their eyes danced and they squeezed hands. 'Just the same.' The cameras flashed; the photograph is still there on the mantelshelf. They parked the baby Ruth with Mrs Iles and flew to America the next day. For three weeks they toured around, staying with friends, spending money they didn't have, enjoying the vast, persuasive luxuries of American city life. When they stepped back into No. 7 again, the baby howling in the carrycot, both knowing that the escape was over, Iles looked about. 'Well,' he repeated, dropping on to a dusty beanbag, 'how does it feel?' Helen looked at him as though he had just crossed her palm with silver and told her she was going on a long journey. 'I don't know,' she said, 'I honestly don't know.'

Helen Iles, who is at this moment watching her husband light a cigarette as he lies next to her in the conjugal bed, was a disappointed woman. Her star had turned out to be a meteor. Worse, she had compromised her feminism by agreeing to the marriage contract. Her daughters, whom she loved, loved much more than she expected, were the source of another disappointment: the limitation of Helen McPhee. It was impossible to deny that Christopher, in his broken-reed sort of way, was the bread-winner.

Her escapes from this tight circle of frustration made the mother feel like a woman again. Although she never really imagined that she would leave her husband, she sustained a sort of half-life in out-of-the-way picture galleries, unfashionable winebars and, from time to time, the tourist hotels of King's Cross and Bloomsbury. The main thing about affairs, she will say with a bitter laugh, is not to fall in love.

She is the first to agree that her search for happiness leaves her divided, wretched and uncertain, tortured by self-doubt and misery. It has, for me, been one of the incidental pleasures of working on this narrative that it has, in an almost cathartic way, brought Helen closer to her husband than she has been for many years.

Christopher's Marlboro glowed next to her, illuminating his features in the shadows.

'The girls will be home soon,' she said, looking at her watch.

He stubbed out his cigarette in the heart-shaped ash-tray. His daughters were very severe about smoking.

The front door banged. Helen, half-dressed, went to the top of the stairs. 'Christopher's back.'

There were shouts of excitement, feet thumping upwards. Iles pulled the duvet over his head and pretended to be invisible.

Two

[1]

Throughout these years, Christopher followed the news from Czechoslovakia closely and my work has benefited greatly from the folders of magazines and cuttings stacked in the basement of No. 7. The story of Dr Husák's repression made very few headlines.

Other events dominated the world stage. The Arabs and Israelis fought another war; Charlie Chaplin and P. G. Wodehouse were knighted; Pompidou died; the Symbionese Liberation Army kidnapped Patty Hearst; Edward Heath lost two elections; Nixon resigned; the Americans pulled out of South Vietnam; and Karpov and Korchnoi battled to determine which of them would challenge Bobby Fischer, the reigning chess champion.

To everyone's surprise, Dubček, who was finally shunted to a desk job in the planting section of the Regional Forestry Administration, was not imprisoned, perhaps because he kept silent.

Then, on 28 October 1974, the anniversary of the founding of the Czech Republic, spurred on by Smrkovský's death, he wrote a long letter of protest to the Federal Assembly in Prague. He described his life under constant surveillance, how cars followed him everywhere and how the most mundane human contact was accorded elaborate political significance. Then he attacked the leadership and its policies.

Husák reacted furiously, publicly announcing – when the letter reached the West – that the disgraced First Secretary now held 'the position of a traitor . . . He can pack his bags tomorrow and move to any bourgeois state.' The letter, he claimed, was 'a falsification of history'.

But Dubček, for all the harassment, remained free.

It was at this time, in the autumn of 1974, that the postman brought a reply to Christopher's last letter. It came as a shock.

Praha
5th September

Dear Christopher,

Excuse me please that I don't answered your letter sooner, because I am a long time in hospital with a heart attack and now I shall be in bed for a very long time at home.

I am glad to hear about you and Helen. It is nice to share live with other people. We wish you good fortune for future and in many years to come. I know my daughter would also.

Your books have just been here. At the moment I do not want reading, but soon I hope I will be better again. Still I am weary after heart attack. Perhaps I am getting typewriter for a friend to write for me soon.

Thank you very much for your kindness and I hope to hear from you again. Perhaps you bring wife Helen to see us in the new summer.

With all my best wishes,
Peter

Iles, who was relieved to have the old bookseller's blessing, says he was disturbed by the deterioration of Císař's handwriting and English. He wrote back at once, sending another parcel, asking if he could help in any way. There was no reply.

Several times in the past there had been gaps and silences, but he never doubted that in due course he would get a letter or a postcard. On this occasion, he had a premonition that the correspondence was finally on the point of collapse. It was a realisation, he tells me, that brought home to him how little he really knew about his shadowy pen-pal, how much he had exploited Císař's sympathy. Selfish? Well, so was Císař: if he wanted a book, there was no stopping him. Christopher reckoned the score was even.

[2]

Hal Strachan's first reaction to his favourite employee's aborted expedition was to suspect the worst. Nothing, of course, could provide a more satisfying compound of apprehensions. Strachan's life was one apparently confronted with a series of appalling problems (always thorny), tough nuts (to be cracked) and, worst of all, dilemmas (on whose horns he was inevitably impaled).

He paced about his glass office, a diminutive worrier in cowboy boots and polka-dot handkerchief, chewing unsuccessfully at his moustache, while the writer sat in the canvas chair marked Director. Strachan's two Afghans, Errol and Samantha, drowsed like hearthrugs in the warmth by the radiator, oblivious to their master's concern.

His second reaction was, 'Are you free for lunch today?' Now Iles knew for certain that his boss was taken with the problem: it was generally held that on the outbreak of the Third World War Strachan's immediate response would be to invite the office to lunch. He was, as Iles had once observed, a legend in his own lunchtime.

Lunch would resolve every difficulty, smooth every path, oil every wheel, lunch was the universal balm. And when lunch failed, there were tranquillizers. Strachan always carried a selection in his briefcase. 'Anyone for a mother's little helper?' was a familiar question during a late meeting.

Iles was strangely fond of Strachan, was grateful to him as well, even though he often found the little man cynical, offensive and opportunistic in a vague indefinable way that was probably to do with his cosmic indifference to people outside the circle of his self-interest. But today he was touched by his concern and said of course he'd be delighted.

Strachan suggested his favourite restaurant, a quiet table in the corner. 'They've got some excellent Stony Hill Chardonnay at the moment. Napa Valley.' He sounded like a doctor recommending a prescription.

'So tell me, Chris,' he began, as the waiter withdrew with their order (vichyssoise and sole for Iles; Parma ham and Scottish salmon for Strachan; a bottle of the favoured vintage in the ice bucket), 'tell me why your great mission into the unknown was – was –' He pulled out a large white handkerchief and, pre-empting a sneeze, carefully blew his nose, one nostril at a time, as though servicing the constituent parts of a valuable machine. Iles started to explain what had happened in Vienna.

Strachan was intrigued. He is a former account executive, easily distracted by persuasive clichés, one of those successful failures who has had an expense-account career with long lunches and no prospects. On first meeting he is, frankly, unattractive, affecting a callous haughtiness, 'a little shit who doesn't give a shit', in the words of a colleague. In conversation with total strangers he will manage to make a boast out of his former jobs, the people he knows and his last year's holiday. Know him a little better, and he will soften, launching into any number of dirty stories. It is only those like Iles who attract the rare attentions of his sympathy and know another Strachan, a good cook, a generous friend, and a keen Wagnerian. He is also a devotee of spy thrillers. The idea of Christopher's Czech coming into the West is meat and drink to his imagination. In the absence of a watertight explanation, he now speculated freely, composing a number of high-temperature narratives.

His guest sat opposite, listening to suggestions of double and triple bluff, playing his own private word game, alphabetical descriptions of his boss: *arriviste, beady, cowardly, devious, eclectic* . . . He was being asked a question. He apologized.

'You were miles away.'

'I was remembering what this place was like in the old days.'

Strachan, who is five years his senior, concealed one great regret. He had passed from a sheltered childhood to a suburban maturity almost overnight. While the youthful Iles was laying waste his powers with all-night parties at Sibylla's, the eager meritocrat was living at home experimenting with his sideburns, commuting on the Northern Line and devoting his income to the upkeep of a cantankerous old step-mother. Naturally, our hero never hesitates to remind his boss how seriously he has missed out.

At this point the hors d'oeuvres arrived and Strachan, in his own words, put the conversation on hold while he quizzed the waiter about the freshness of the ham and insisted on two kinds of pepper. 'It's all monopoly money here and no one gives a hoot, but one has one's standards, don't you think? Now do tell me, Chris, what did you make of the *Schlösser*?'

As Iles had got to know him he discovered that Strachan had the fixed tastes of the self-educated. Culture was German. With only the mildest provocation, he would enthuse about Bach or Beethoven, Brecht and the Bavarian baroque. His managerial mind admired the entente between state and industry. In his more ludicrous moments, he would confess to feeling rewarded and encouraged by the seriousness with which German intellectuals confronted the human situation.

It would be amusing to admit that he had travelled down the Rhine in the dark, distracted from the famous view by the conversation of a talkative stranger, but he settled on a lie. 'Oh yes, the *schlosses*,' he replied casually. 'Well, they were rather magnificent.'

Iles says he has a fantasy in which Strachan, overcoming his

absurdly small proportions, wanders up and down his beloved
Rhine valley conducting a hopeless but chivalric quest for flaxen-
haired virgins in the *Weinstuben* and *Bierkeller* of Bonn and
Cologne. This is a cruel reference to Strachan's chief problem,
viz. that most people take him for a homosexual (though he
himself has a strong preference for teenage girls). His other
solace is Wagner whose operas in a dozen different recordings fill
the bookshelves in his tiny South Kensington flat. Every summer,
when the rain poured down and his girls went to Wimbledon or
Cannes with other beaux and Strachan became depressed, he
would lock himself away for solitary weekends and play the Ring
cycle at full blast on his quadrophonic stereo, driving the rest of
the mews wild with irritation and curiosity.

'One day,' said Iles, who can play his boss's conversation like
a fly fisherman, 'I'd like to take a holiday in Germany. On a
barge.'

'Magic.' His enthusiasm is Teutonic; he has no inkling of the
writer's game. 'So it wasn't a wasted trip. For someone who's
been let down, you're amazingly cheerful.'

'But that,' said Iles, casting again, 'is only because you have not
yet heard the real story.'

'It's a funny thing, Chris, but the moment I saw you this
morning I knew there was something special on your mind.'

Iles admitted he was preoccupied; he described his meeting
with Kuhn. Strachan listened, temporarily neglecting his pen-
chant for celebrity-spotting. 'This chap sounds like a walking
melodrama,' was his comment when the waiter came to clear away
their plates.

'Gold, furs, drugs, arms,' Iles found himself exaggerating
again. 'He's into everything.'

'AC/DC?'

'He was taking pills for something he picked up in the Gulf. We
both got fairly pissed. And when he left the train at Nuremberg we
made this strange sort of pact.'

As he began to explain, he watched his boss grasp the

implications. 'But, Chris, this is what you've been looking for. The big break.' Strachan's expression became childish with pleasure. He filled their glasses. 'We must drink to this.'

'You don't think it's something I shouldn't do?'

'I don't understand what you're saying.'

'Helen says if I do a deal with Kuhn, I will compromise my integrity as a writer.'

Strachan looked astonished. 'Sometimes –' He stopped. He was conscious of straying into a marital no-man's-land and was afraid to get caught in the crossfire.

'Sometimes what?'

He seemed to find a sudden, rare courage. He had special feelings for Iles. 'If you don't mind my saying so, Chris, sometimes I think Helen's off her head.'

'You mean you think it's a good thing to do?'

'I think it's the opportunity of a lifetime. I don't know what she's talking about. You've done much worse things in the past. Think of that Time-Life business. From what you've said, this guy's probably got material in him for a shelf of novels. You'll never have to work again.'

Iles laughed painfully. He had a slight headache. 'After I'd written them all.'

'There is that, of course. But it's not the writing, it's the material. Isn't that it?' Strachan was vague about the process.

'Sometimes. It certainly helps if you have something to say.'

'So what you do is sit him down in front of a tape-recorder and pump the stuff out of him. If he's on a percentage, he'll talk. Strachan's Third Law.'

'That's what you'd do?'

'Sure. It'll probably come rolling out in ready-made paragraphs and chapters. Cross out the ers and ums, number the pages from one to three hundred, and Bob's your uncle.'

Iles looked despondent. It was the foreign-country syndrome again. Everything about his return home was so unfamiliar. It disturbed him that someone who took himself so seriously should have such a breezy attitude to a colleague's self-esteem.

Coffee arrived, together with two exquisite chocolate snails in silver green paper which he put on one side for the twins. He wished he could exploit Strachan's enthusiasm to brush aside Helen's objections, but his wife has reservations about the pocket publicist, despite her daughters' attachment to the man they called Hal-pal.

Now Strachan was pouring a final glass of wine. 'Look at any great writer. Look at Shakespeare. He wrote for money. They all do. Don't be so ashamed of your luck.' He was beginning to sound impatient, which is the way that most people encounter him. 'As long as I've known you, Chris, you've been waiting for a break. As soon as the real thing turns up on a plate, you run away. Are you afraid or something?'

An elongated man with black, go-to-hell glasses and a very large, well-groomed head came over to their table. He was wearing a faultless dove-grey suit, he was carrying a large brown envelope in one hand, a cigar in the other, and he appeared to be slightly drunk.

'It's Christopher Iles, isn't it?'

He looked up in bewilderment, that out-of-contact sensation again. He has not been accosted in a restaurant for years.

'You probably don't remember.' He gave his name in a voice cultured at Winchester and Balliol. 'I was in the publicity department when your book –'

'Of course. Hello. Nice to see you again.' He looked riskily at Strachan. 'This is my bank manager, Mr Bottoms.'

'How do you do?'

Strachan played his part and shook hands. There was an awkward pause and then Iles asked, 'What are you up to these days?'

'Same old thing I'm afraid. Of course,' he was very smug. 'I'm the boss these days.'

Iles supplied indefinite noises of congratulation.

'Perhaps,' Strachan interrupted, 'you'll soon be doing business together again. My client has been telling me that he is hard at work on a new book.'

'Oh really.' The publisher seemed extremely doubtful about the value of this information. There was another uneasy silence. 'Well, that's marvellous news. We must have lunch. I'll get my girl to give you a call. Still at the old address?'

'Actually we moved about ten years ago. But we're in the book.'

'Splendid.' The publisher moved on to escort his guest, a fashionably dressed American woman with fishy eyes, towards the staircase. 'We must set something up. Good to see you again after all these years. Bye.'

Strachan waved cheerfully and they both returned to their conversation. 'Now all you have to do is write the bloody thing,' he said quietly as the tall grey figure stooped out of sight. 'Don't look now, but isn't that Omar Sharif?'

Three

[1]

In the New Year, having heard nothing from Císař over Christmas for the first time ever, Iles wrote again with the strong sense, he says, that this would be his last contact with Prague.

Wandsworth
6th January 1975

Dear Peter,

I wrote immediately after your last letter but perhaps my reply did not reach you. Did you get the Christmas parcel? I do hope that you are now safely out of hospital and on the road to a full recovery. If you are not yet well enough to write, do ask your wife to send a postcard. We should both like to know that you are okay. Please forgive my interference but we have got to know each other so well these last few years and your silence in these recent months has disturbed me.

Apropos your suggestion that we should come to Prague this summer. It is difficult to make such a plan with the baby so small, but perhaps I could come on my own for a few days. Even if I took the train it would be an expense we can barely afford. And there is still that other problem you know about. Finding the courage to come to Milena's city. I've been thinking about her a lot recently; I know you say I shouldn't, but I can't help myself. Looking back, it is still the worst moment in my life, and I'm sure that it has a lot to do with the difficulties I've had with my work.

Since I'm on that subject, I really must thank you for giving me what has frankly been a lifeline. If there had been nothing to write, not even a letter, I think I would have cracked up completely, as we say. You've kept me sane: I'll always be grateful for that in ways you'll never know.

Please, please write.

As ever,
Christopher

Iles held his breath. No reply. Still no reply. He says the tension was killing. Then, just as he had decided that Císař would be silent for ever, an answer came from Prague. Yes, it was from his old friend! Unexpectedly, it was typewritten – badly.

Praha
21st March 1975

Dear Christopher,

I hope you like my typewriter. It is a new present I have given me from my wife to make me better. Yes, I have not been well. I am sorry to have not replied to your very nice letters and thanked you for the books.

But now, please, I am going to write you about Milena. You are good person to have trust of me. I think it is many years now since the days you write about and now I do not think they will come again. You will listen to an old man and love your wife. This is for the best.

I do not think you should come here just now. It is very sad. One day perhaps when the future is better I would like to see you and talk about all these things, but understand please that it is not well here just for the moment.

My wife has taken photograph of me just now and I send one which I do not like but she says I must give you it.

I am your very nice friend.
With best wishes,
Sincerely,
Peter

P.S. My next move is Q to QB5.

He added the letter to his collection. He could not make sense of Císař's move on his chessboard and wrote to suggest a new game. You cannot imagine, he recalls, what a relief it was to be in touch with Prague again.

From time to time I have these fears that Christopher has had enough of my questions. I arrange for us to have a breather. But he is always the one who wants to get down to business again. He will write to me with a clipping or a photograph, or phone me up with an idea. (He's so enthusiastic!)

Here's something he found in a back number of *The Times* about Husák's reaction to Dubček's October protest. Presumably in self-justification, Husák lashed out publicly. He revealed that after Dubček's fall, six years before, he had broken down and cried, saying, 'Now there will be trials, arrests, and executions.' But, Husák boasted, 'We chose the political solution, even though administrative solutions existed . . .'

'Husák's comment,' Christopher scribbled in his covering note, 'reminds me of the mental disorder – I can't remember the Latin – in which the patient is convinced that by giving something an entirely new name he can change its nature.'

[2]

'You're pissed,' said Helen, kissing him coldly. She was preparing a salad in the kitchen, a large airy room with a conservatory roof and glass doors leading into the garden. They had pulled down three walls to make this space. It was an informal museum for half a generation of taste, a 'farmhouse' table bought years ago from Junk City, Art Nouveau posters and commemorative china from Camden Lock, the chair that Helen had rescued from a skip down the road, and then all those unconscious tributes to a month of Sunday magazines: designer lighting, ceramic hob units, cork floor tiles, white pine fittings, a Kenwood Chef, a Hoovermatic in the peninsula, a Swedish wine rack, several Penguin cookery books, a forest of indestructible house plants by the garden door and a couple of peasant rugs hanging on the wall by the louvred windows. 'Very aesthetic,' said the man from the building society when Iles negotiated a second mortage to tame his mounting debts.

'Not as pissed as I was.' He bowled an imaginary fast ball and tried, unsuccessfully, to kiss her again. 'Hal gave me lunch. Then I had a few drinks with some blokes on the way home. We have to plan our fixtures for the season.'

'You're pissed,' she repeated with distaste. 'I don't suppose you'll want anything to eat.'

He did his Jagger. 'I am the little red rooster,' he sang.

'Christopher. Will you be quiet, please. The girls are trying to do their homework. I don't want them distracted.' She pushed him towards the stairs. 'Go and sober up in the bath.'

He lay down on their bed and fell asleep in his clothes.

'Wake up, wake up.' The twins were jumping on him; they were getting heavy. 'It's supper time.'

He yawned and pushed them across the bed. 'So what have you two been up to today?'

'What have we been up to today, dear?' said Rebecca in her Jane-Austen voice.

'Well,' said Emma, badly short of teeth, 'in the morning we had English, then we had Maths, and then we had science, yuk. And then we had PE in the afternoon. Miss Drewitt got cross with Ruth, and Rebecca had a piano lesson. Stephen has a crush on Ruth and asked her back to his house. Ruth didn't want to and we all went shopping with Helen. And then we did our homework, yuk.'

'And then Emma did a big fart,' Rebecca added.

'No I didn't.'

'You did so.'

'She who smelt it dealt it.'

He tried to explain that grown-ups are not interested in farts.

'And then you came back,' said Rebecca. 'And now you're going to tell us a story.'

He protested. He was tired. He had a hangover.

'You shouldn't drink at lunchtime,' said Emma.

'And you smoke too much,' said Rebecca.

'Tell us a story,' Emma demanded.

Rebecca pulled his nose. 'What's white and flies across the Irish Sea at a hundred miles an hour?'

'I don't know.'

'Lord Mountbatten's plimsolls.'

'Who was Lord Mountbatten?' Emma was curious.

'An old sod.'

'What's a sod Christopher?'

Rebecca was pulling his nose again. 'Why won't you tell us a story?'

He yawned again. 'Once upon a time,' he began, a magic formula. The twins rolled next to him like kittens. 'Once upon a time there was a snail called Sammy.' He paused. 'Sammy lived in a smelly old drain next door to a huge motorway. One day Sammy said to himself, I've had enough of living in smelly old drains. I'm going to give myself a good time. I'm going to explore the wide wide world.' He looked at his daughters; Emma had her thumb in her mouth. 'So Sammy the snail crawled very, very slowly to the top of the drain. Up, up, up he crawled. And there was the world in front of him. The sun was shining and there were cars and buses whizzing in all directions. Now, said Sammy, now my life can begin. Then he crawled on to the motorway and was squashed flat by a passing lorry.'

There were shrieks of horror and excitement from the twins.

'End of story and end of Sammy,' said Iles. 'I want something to eat.' He jumped up and they all went downstairs.

Ruth was helping Helen with the supper, spooning home-made tomato chutney out of a jar.

'Christopher has just told us a really horrid story,' said Rebecca proudly to her elder sister.

'All Christopher's stories are horrid,' said Ruth.

'Tomorrow,' he said, 'I'll tell you a story about a beautiful princess and her love for a handsome young shepherd.'

'Male chauvinist stereotyping again,' Helen commented, only half joking. She is serving cottage pie; fresh from a drowsy afternoon in another flat she is at odds with her domestic role. But she is ignored by her husband now and the Iles family settles down to eat.

'Anyone phone for me today?'

'Why?' Helen does not want him to know she has been out since noon. Her body will surrender no clues: her grey eyes are steady, there is no garlic on her breath, she has already floated in Badedas before her husband returned. Only her mind is divided.

Iles described his encounter in the restaurant.

Perhaps it was a good omen, she suggested, playing to his superstitions.

'You never know with those guys if they mean it.' He flashed some forgotten boastfulness. 'But when my agent sends him the new manuscript he can take me to lunch at L'Etoile.'

She reminded him with satisfaction that his agent had become a born-again Christian and emigrated to New Zealand. 'So you have decided to sell out.' Sometimes she does not understand why she needs to provoke.

But he kept his cool. 'Why are you such a puritan all of a sudden?' He smiled at his children who were eating their supper with peculiar concentration.

Ruth's question was inevitable. 'What's a puritan, Christopher?'

'Someone who . . .'

In her mind, Helen returned to the lazy afternoon: the cool light of a room half-curtained, the wine . . . He was saying something to her directly and she apologized.

'I'm obviously boring you. Hal said that most writers do it for money. No man but a blockhead and all that stuff.'

'Why do you have to quote Hal? You normally say he's a meatbrain.'

'He happens to understand my point of view.'

She began to collect the plates. 'I don't mind what you decide, so long as you're convinced it's the right thing for you.'

Was it a decision, a choice? 'Somehow,' he said, 'I don't think your choices are made, really made, from necessity so much as from some sort of secret knowledge of your own desires and powers.'

It was when he spoke like this that she knew why they were still living together.

He offered to wash up. Ruth, who is serious-minded and usually on her father's side, wanted to know what the book was about. She was old enough to remember the Time-Life project.

Iles loves to entertain his children. He painted an exaggerated picture of the stranger on the train. Rebecca wanted to know if this man was coming to stay; strangers were her idea of heaven, they usually brought presents. Iles looked at Helen. Then the telephone rang and she went to answer it.

He brooded. The writing would be a lot more work than Hal realized, but a strict régime would do the trick. Stop drinking. No parties, no late nights. Get down to it in the evenings and at weekends. Stop watching TV with the kids. He poured himself a whisky.

Helen came back. 'What have you done to Hal?'

'What do you mean?'

'That was Lizzy. She rang to say that he's been on to her. He's told her that you're very excited about a new book and she was calling to hear all about it.'

Lizzy was Helen's oldest and best friend, an extrovert Australian, a women's page feature writer with a habit of saying (and printing) what most people only think. She was immensely tall with clouds of bleach-blonde hair and the body of an Olympic swimmer. Iles knew this well: he enjoyed a brief fling with her when Helen was expecting the twins. Lizzy (a diminutive of Margaret for reasons that no one could remember) was fascinated by Iles and seduced him without difficulty, loudly protesting her loyalty to his wife. She was obsessed by what she called 'creative people' who in her guide to life were allowed extra quantities of licence. Iles exploited this for all it was worth and experienced hours of hectic, slightly sea-sick intercourse on the water-bed of her mansion-block apartment in Belsize Park.

'If Lizzy knows,' he said, 'then the whole world will know.'

'At this rate,' Helen added sharply, 'Hal and the gossips will have finished the manuscript before you've even had a chance to speak to this man again.'

Her attitude to Christopher's plan is so complicated. She will welcome anything which gets her husband out of his rut; on the other hand, it must be a project that works. If she finds it difficult to relate to Iles it is because there is a part of him unfinished; her anxiety about his latest scheme is to do with her fear that this will just be another botched attempt at self-definition that will add yet more confusion to their lives. At the same time she wants to encourage him; selfishly, she would like him nicely occupied for a bit.

Many of these complications have been eased recently; at last, there is something at the centre of their relationship which is finally maturing. I like to think that this, *The Fabulous Englishman*, has had something to do with that. I've grown very fond of both Helen and Christopher. They are so ... crazy. That's the only word for it. Screwballs, really, to use one of Christopher's own favourite expressions.

Just now their conversation was interrupted by the twins wanting to watch late television. It was only when they were going to bed that Helen resumed her line of thought. She was plucking her eyebrows, sitting at her table in a dressing-gown.

'This book,' she said. 'I suppose it would mean travel.'

He put his face in the mirror and kissed her warm skin. 'Only short trips.' He thinks he knows what she's thinking. 'He'd pay, of course.'

'If you have to go, you have to go.' She concentrated on the tweezers. 'Thank God for Sarah, that's all.'

'And if the thing is successful ... .' On another wavelength, the prospect of massive royalty cheques suffused his imagination.

'Yes?'

'We'd have money in the bank. We could travel together.'

'Yes, of course.'

But he missed the ambivalence in her voice. Now she could see him, fragmented by the mirror, dancing in a slow circle. She continued to comb her hair, watching the turning of his milky-white body. He seemed to be in a world of his own, waltzing around the room, humming off-key, *Every breath you take, and every move you make, Every bond you break* . . .

She smiled, though perhaps even she could not say why. Then she went into the bathroom and fitted her diaphragm again.

Four

[1]

At the beginning of April 1975, Václav Havel, the playwright, addressed a long open letter to Dr Gustáv Husák, General Secretary of the Communist Party of Czechoslovakia and President of the Czech Socialist Republic. The letter began:

> Dear Dr Husák,
>   In our offices and factories, work goes on, discipline prevails. The efforts of our citizens are yielding visible results in a slow rising standard of living: people build houses, buy cars, have children, amuse themselves, live their lives . . .
>   The basic question one must ask is this: *why* are people in fact behaving in the way they do? Why do they do all these things that, taken together, form the impressive image of a totally united society giving total support to its government? For any unprejudiced observer, the answer is, I think, self-evident: they are driven to it by fear.

Christopher will discover that fear in Czechoslovakia has a special meaning. For the moment, he simply added the document to his collection, but was sufficiently stirred, by Havel's concluding words, to make his first contact with *Index on Censorship*, offering his services for nothing.

> What I am afraid of [Havel had written] is something else. The whole of this letter is concerned, in fact, with what I really fear –

the pointlessly harsh and long-lasting consequences which the present violent abuses will have for our nation(s). I fear the price we are bound to pay for the drastic suppression of history, the cruel and needless banishment of life into the underground of society and the depths of the human soul, the new compulsory 'deferment' of every opportunity for society to live in anything like a natural way.

This letter was widely published in the West. Havel spent much of the late seventies in and out of prison for what the authorities called his 'subversive activities'.

With Prague very much in mind, and with his contact there renewed, Iles himself replied to Císař's March letter on 15 May that year.

Wandsworth

Dear Peter,

It *was* good to have your letter. I'm sending a couple of books in a separate packet, though there's something of a dearth of good writing at the moment. I hope you continue to make a good recovery: I do like your typewriter!

I've had a bit of luck recently and feel very excited by it. I've been recommended to the Time-Life people as an author for their book series, 'Great Islands of the World'. Apparently, they've persuaded themselves that I'm expert in the history of Sicily, and, subject to approval from World HQ, I'll be getting the job. It's an extremely lucrative assignment (lucre is something I badly need just now), and I hope to use it to re-establish myself in the freelance market. I've had it up to here (as we say) with advertising.

I do hope the books get through. Helen sends her love. I'm enclosing a photo of Ruth's second birthday party. The other man in the picture is one of Helen's Fleet Street friends who happened to be around at the time.

As ever,
Christopher

Rather surprisingly, he says, the Time-Life contract material-ized almost at once, and while he was away in Sicily another letter arrived from Prague. It was typewritten, like the last.

Praha
1st July 1975

Dear Christopher,

It is being very nice to hear your news again. The books do not arrive, but I am not expecting them at this time. It is very difficult for us just now.

It is being good summer here. The farmers complain all the time. I think that is how it is with farmers.

I have keeping of your letters in this box. Yesterday I am reading them all from the very first time. You are so good a writer of letters, Christopher, and it is so very interesting for me to see how you have changed in this time. I think you are very good man to always continue writing with me. We look forward to what you are sending us each month, and, even when nothing is coming through, we are being sure you have tried, so we do not give up hope. Now you must read the letters to you and tell me how much the better is my English now.

Forgive me, please, if I say like an old man, but I do not think you should write with Time-Life company. You are good writer. You do not need to do that.

Now I understand Sicily Island is beautiful place. I am reading this in history book by Professor M. I. Finley, published by Chatto & Windus, London, 1967. Same year as your book!

Sincerely your friend with blessings for dear Helen and the little Ruth,
Peter

Up in space, orbiting American and Russian astronauts successfully carried out the Apollo–Soyuz mission and were temporarily united 140 miles above the planet.

In August 1975, two Dutch journalists who tried to visit Dubček's apartment on Mouse Street found it guarded by three soldiers. Instead they waited for him outside his office. When Dubček saw them he said, 'You must go away. I am running a terrible risk. I have never seen you.' A couple of quick questions, please. Was he being persecuted? 'I'm not a free person, you know that. I live in a prison without walls.' Would he ever play a political role in Czechoslovakia again? 'Not any more in my lifetime.'

In late November, Dubček, who was fifty-four, collapsed to the floor of a crowded tram with what was said to be either a nervous crisis or a mild heart attack. (Friends who heard about it remembered his illness in the Kremlin during the negotiations with the Russians in 1968.) The secret policeman tailing him stood by as other passengers helped him to a doctor, and then tried to force his way into the surgery. Dubček pointed out that even in gaol prisoners are left alone with their doctors and the policeman withdrew. Who knows if he was ashamed? The former First Secretary continued to live in Mouse Street, guarded day and night, effectively under house arrest.

[2]

A few days after his return from Vienna, Iles went into work with two envelopes in his briefcase. The first, addressed to Peter

Císař, he posted by the tube at Green Park, Then, walking on past the Ritz and down into Pall Mall, he delivered the second at Kuhn's London address, his club.

Christopher is adamant that he soon lost the sense of bitterness he had felt towards Císař. Be reasonable, he told himself. There could be a thousand and one explanations for the missed rendez-vous. It would be enough to know that his old friend was safe and well. There would be other chances to meet for sure. Besides, he was grateful for the trip across Europe in a way that he could not have anticipated. Thus the drift of his short letter.

His note to Kuhn, a simple request for a meeting at the earliest opportunity, was pigeon-holed by the hall porter with a flourish. The name obviously meant something. Iles asked if the doctor was a regular visitor.

'Dr Kuhn, a very remarkable man,' replied the doorman with portentous gravity. 'Being as how he's such a very gifted physician, sir, it amazes me what else he is conversant with.' He considered Iles with interest. 'You're a friend of Dr Kuhn, are you, sir?'

This was clearly an advantageous condition as far as the porter was concerned and so Iles, who generally expects to be bounced in such places not greeted, admitted that this was so.

'Well done, sir.' He was a short, tyrannical-looking man with a greying toothbrush moustache; his military manner was clouded by a tone of ingratiating deference. 'Would that be a professional association sir, or a sporting partnership? Beg pardon for the inquiry, sir, but I was wondering' – he inspected the visitor's flak-jacket – 'if you had participated in one of Dr Kuhn's rallies.'

'Rallies?'

'Dr Kuhn is well-known for his speed across the Sahara, sir.'

Iles apologized for his deplorable ignorance. 'I'm just a friend, if you know what I mean.'

The porter consulted the guest ledger with a show of thoroughness. 'Not booked in, sir, but you know how it is with a busy man.

Here, there and everywhere. He'll be under this roof some-
time soon.' No, of course he would not forget to pass on the
letter.

Iles took the tube to the office. In the Piccadilly subway a
busker with a tarnished trumpet was playing 'Hey Jude'. He threw
his loose change into the empty hat; the melody stayed with him
all the way up the broken escalator into Holborn.

Strachan hurried over the moment he came in. He was in his
latest Italian cream suit and, although the light in the office was
entirely artificial, celebrating the brighter days with a pair of
kir-tinted aviator glasses. 'Was he there?'

Iles is no longer surprised that his boss knows all the details of
his private life and looks on it as a kind of flattery. 'I left him a
note.'

'Get in touch, that's my advice. Before he changes his mind.'

'I've suggested a meeting.'

'Terrific. I can't wait.' He came closer. His skin was soft and
powdered like a baby's. 'You're making notes, of course. You
should, you know. This is the big one, Chris.'

He became defensive. 'I don't want to rush. Anyway, I haven't
the time. It will take at least a year.' He found Strachan's readymix
enthusiasm faintly ludicrous: after all, he hardly knew the elusive
Kuhn. It was typical of his circle and their empty fantasies that
they should snatch so greedily at this latest scrap of gossip.

Strachan jerked his head in the direction of his office and Iles
followed, a giraffe striding awkwardly behind an exotic jungle
bird. As he anticipated, the moment Strachan closed the door he
became personal. 'Now, I know I shouldn't say this to you, Chris,
because we're always run off our feet, but honestly it's a privilege
to have you here.'

Iles was silenced by the breadth and audacity of his admiration.
He sat in the canvas chair while his boss improved his perch on
the low perspex table.

'These people,' Strachan continued, pointing contemptuously
at his staff beyond the glass wall. 'Utter wallies. No talent. No

imagination. All I can do is keep them up to the mark and hope for the best. But you,' he gestured a circle with a manicured finger, 'you need space to be the person you are.'

Imagine Christopher Iles as he sat there that morning. His long figure was hunched in the chair; Helen would say he needed a haircut. Today he was wearing his brown corduroy suit, in honour of Kuhn's club, but it was warm for April and a dribble of sweat ran down his side. He was not really at ease but he managed to thank Strachan for the encomium and, seizing his chance, hinted evasively at his overdraft.

Strachan shook his head. 'Beyond my control, Chris,' he said seriously. 'Nothing I can do.' He might have been a seismographer discussing the San Andreas fault. 'But I can give you all the freedom you need. I want you to know that. If you write the thing under my aegis – is that the word? – then I shall have my reward.' He pointed past the window; five storeys below, the London traffic snarled and hooted. 'I should be proud to think that this is where they have to put the plaque.'

Iles knew that he was about to embark on a favourite theme, the demise of the private patron. 'I'm not a Medici,' he had once remarked, 'but I do my tiny best.' In this, as in everything, Strachan undertook his responsibilities (as he saw them) with a special gravity, arriving at his decision about a new painting or sculpture with immense deliberation. His flat was filled with the evidence of his patronage and, as Iles says with that quizzical smile of his, it is not for this generation to pass judgement. Perhaps he is just protecting himself. In the world of letters, Iles himself was Strachan's one and only investment. 'If I get half a page in your biography,' he had admitted late one evening after too much Buck's Fizz, 'I shall be content. Hal Strachan, who made it all possible.'

The writer himself, managing self-mockery without self-pity, is only too quick to ridicule these pretensions. He often has long discussions about his boss with friends. Hal is the kind of man people like to argue about. How was it, they ask, that someone who boasted his tastes and preferences as he did should settle for a job that lacked any obvious glamour or status? The answer, in Christopher's view, was simple. Beneath it all, Strachan was afraid. He wanted security. He would pay for others to have the life he could not risk and get his kicks that way. Deep down, Iles says, Strachan probably hates himself.

Now, in the office, slick with sanctimony, he repeated his gratitude and said that he did not want to sell the company short.

'*Entre nous*, you can sell the company as short as you like. I won't mind. They do it to us.'

He said he would bear it in mind and, improvising, explained that when he had finished his first draft he would be glad to have a break from the distractions of the office.

Strachan permitted himself a thin, Levantine smile of self-congratulation. 'I knew you were already at it. You're a sly one, Chris. You keep your cards close to your chest, but you're still playing the game. A deep game, if I may say so. Keep it up!' He hopped off the desk and, picking up his red telephone, he asked Germaine to get his piano teacher on the line. The interview was over.

Iles went back to his typewriter. Among the notes on his desk was a message to call Lizzy. He threw it away. Phoning Lizzy was the last thing he wanted to do at the moment. He stared in front of him, lost in the friendly hubbub of the office.

He had applied for this job seven, eight, Jesus, *nine* years ago, after the Time-Life fiasco. His letter of application, in answer to a Creative and Media advertisement in the *Guardian*, seemed like the final defeat.

A desperate last throw turned out to be a stroke of luck. Strachan, dismissing the other candidates on the short list as 'Cortina men', had offered him the job on principle. 'I need people close to me whom I can respect,' he had said, looking up at Iles with frank fascination. They had already shared a lament for what Strachan called 'the paranoid seventies'. The diminutive advertiser wanted an ally. 'We must stick together,' he explained, somehow suggesting that he too had been on the Magical Mystery Tour. 'When can you start?'

Iles was privately grateful for an end to the depressing cycle of compromise forced on him by his family responsibilities. Regular, undemanding work anaesthetized the pain of having nothing to write. It was not exactly T. S. Eliot in the City, he would say, self-mocking again, but it gave him a strange, indeterminate pleasure to find that Strachan's corporate bosses, who were not generally aware of anything that did not relate to the macro-economic situation, were intrigued by their new recruit. At the end of his third year, he was mentioned in the company report, a detail he passed on to Peter Císař with ironic pride. His relations with a hostile credit system improved. His spending limit was doubled and he discovered that his bank manager was a morris-dancing Sagittarian called Eric who believed in horo-scopes.

Iles and Strachan, had they met at a party or a pub, or indeed in any other context, would have found nothing to say to each other. The PR department brought them together and made them friends in the peculiar way that happens in offices. The rela-tionship was sustained by its unlikeliness. They came to know as much about each other as two ill-assorted brothers. Strachan, with a rare show of affection, became an uncle to the Iles children, spoiling them with expensive birthday presents and occasionally taking them to a Walt Disney movie or the zoo.

Strachan was even allowed to hear – as few were allowed – the full story of Milena, and he knew, as perhaps only Helen knew, the emptiness that this pointless death had left in Christopher's life. Such are the unsuspected things that two colleagues will say to each other over a boozy lunch. To Helen's annoyance (faithful to her ideas of cool, she has never asked too many questions about Císař), Christopher has even shared one or two pink-stamped letters from Prague with his boss.

Now those times were over and there was a new shadow in the

wings, the stranger on the train. Hey Jude, he murmured, as he watched Germaine xeroxing artwork, don't be afraid.

She smiled at him. 'Tell me your dreams, writer man.'

'Nightmares, not dreams,' he said and switched on his typewriter.

It was the same at home. He sat upstairs at his desk staring beyond the lamp into the spring darkness at the back of the house, listening to his children practising their parts in the school play with Helen.

There are just two sentences in his notebook for this day:

I saw Milena's face on the tube this evening and followed it as far as White City. I almost said something, but I lost my nerve: of course I know I shall never see her again.

Rebecca came in. 'Christopher. Come and see our scene. I'm a witch and I put horrid things in a pot. Double, double, toil and trouble.'

His daughters were changing into their witches' costumes, fighting for earrings and make-up with thespian glee. He sat and watched them rehearse the famous lines, thinking that Ruth was not really cut out for a career in sorcery. When they finished, he clapped. 'Bravo.' He smiled at Helen.

She saw that he was elsewhere. 'You're not with us, darling.' She touched his cheek. 'What is it?'

'Oh.' He sighed. 'Nothing.'

They know each other so well. 'I've seen that face before,' she said. 'Old memories.'

He began to hum, off-key as usual. 'I was dreaming of the past, and my heart was beating fast.' The words and music swam in his head, and when Ruth and Emma and Rebecca came to kiss him goodnight he pressed his face deep into their rich brown hair to hide his emotion.

Helen's instincts were sure and cruel. 'Are you afraid?'

'That's right.' He hated to be drawn; why must she always

seem to use her understanding against him? 'This . . . thing. It scares me. It shouldn't, but it does. Does that make you feel better?'

She went to bed, not answering. He sat up late and watched the midnight movie. Alone in front of the TV, with the family asleep upstairs, for the first time since his return he felt at home.

Five

[1]

Wandsworth
17th November 1975

Dear Peter,

You were right. The Time-Life contract has been a nightmare. Five thousand pounds seemed a fortune when I signed the contract, and the solution to half my problems. Now it seems like blood-money. In future I shall resist the lure of cash.

The only good part was spending the summer in Sicily, though after all I had to go through back in London those weeks have become a faint, poignant memory.

While I was travelling I kept a detailed notebook and when I came home I began to write up my text. This turned out to be a lot less simple than it sounds. As everyone had warned me, a contract with the Time-Life people allows them to do anything they like to your deathless prose.

Never again. The first chapter, like each successive chapter, went through countless drafts, each the work of more and more editorial collaborators. You won't believe this, but no less than thirty-two people are credited on the copyright page.

When I bring myself to remind myself of the comments coming out of Head Office – 'Not enough of the author in it' (first draft) or 'sounds too self-centred' (second draft) – this now seems to me a rather modest team of assistants. The desk editor assigned to my efforts was very short-sighted, but too vain to wear glasses and apparently allergic to contact lenses: half her corrections were mistakes.

Finally, a curious patchwork of prose was deposited in

135

the memory bank of the Time-Life word-processor to the satisfaction of all parties and the team received a congratulatory telegram from the moguls in the States.

After a month I was more than ready to walk out, but, naturally, I had not been paid. Helen insisted I stay, and when the cheque finally came through I'd earned it in blood. The finished volume is a garbled compromise tricked out with alliteration and cliché. Here's a book I shall not be sending you!

How is your own work progressing? Is the bibliography nearly finished? Here's another photograph of Helen, Ruth and me, taken at a party last month. The beard was after Sicily. I vowed I would only shave when the book was done.

> As ever,
> Christopher

[2]

From time to time at weekends, Helen and Christopher give dinner parties.

'When is Granny coming?' Emma was not past the age of repetition. She and her twin raced up and down the aisles of Sainsbury's like puppies. It was the beginning of a hot Saturday in June, just after eight-thirty, and Iles, the shop-hater, was making his weekly effort to beat the rush.

'I've told you already. Granny's coming next week.'

'Will she bring me a present?'

'I expect so.'

'What do we need, Christopher?' Ruth, always practical, was playing Helen's role.

'We need everything.' He pulled out his list. 'Our guests believe they have exquisite taste.'

'What does exquisite mean, Christopher?'

'It means the best in the world,' he replied, rattling his empty trolley past a pyramid of Heinz baby food.

'You mean like the West Indies?'

How could he explain that good cricketers were not necessarily exquisite? Why was he irritated by Ruth's thirst for knowledge? He said he would explain later. 'We have lots to do just now.'

He trundled on a whirlwind tour across to the market garden stalls and weighed new potatoes, red peppers, garden peas, broccoli and French beans into polythene bags. He chose the meat, a marbled leg of New Zealand lamb. The joint tipped in his hand like a club and he made space for it in the trolley next to the soft fruits of the season: early English strawberries, cherries, grapes and also a Spanish honeydew. He negotiated with the smiling cheese man for stilton, gruyère, dolcelatte and a Normandy camembert in a good-looking state of ripeness.

Ruth, pleased with herself, said that he had forgotten something.

'What's that?'

'The wine you drink too much of.'

'Get stuffed,' he replied cheerfully, and loaded the dinner into the car. Rebecca asked to drive; he sat her carelessly on his knee.

They set off past the Common for home. The wide green space was alive. There were pensioners with dogs, a ring of fishermen round the pond, bicyclists and joggers passing in and out of the sunshine among the heavy-leafed trees, and a police car parked next to a pile of litter.

'One man went to mow,' he sang, 'went to mow a meadow. One man and his dog went to mow a meadow.' When they reached No. 7 they were all singing 'Ten men went to mow' at the tops of their voices.

Ruth looked at him curiously. 'Why are you so happy, Christopher?'

'Because –' There is no answer. He is not happy; he is sad. 'Because tonight we have visitors.'

'Can we come?'

'You can say hello to Hal, if you're good.'

So the day passes – Christopher and Helen referee their children's tireless enthusiasms – and on summer Saturday evenings they sit in wicker chairs in the small gnat-crazed garden, reading or drinking, while their daughters run in and out of the house in bare feet.

This evening he is fitting candles into white porcelain holders. Flags of black flame fly up and the hot wax drips on to his fingers. Helen is chopping vegetables on her knee.

'I wonder what Hal will bring with him tonight.' She is cynical about his girlfriends. 'Does he ever get it together, do you think?'

'They say he plays to them half the night on the pianola and then rings for a taxi.'

And so they gossiped. The smell of cooking filled the house. A fiery Egyptian sun went below the roofline and one or two lights came on. Helen went upstairs to have a bath and wash her hair. The water creaked in the pipes; sitting under the cherry tree Iles could hear Helen and her daughters in front of the mirror discussing what she should wear: happy, careless, united. He flexed his toes on the grass; the ground was hard and dry.

His thoughts went to that inevitable subject, their predicament. Look at us now, he might have said, Mr and Mrs Iles of Wandsworth (the good part), with our three children (at local state schools), our five-year-old Volvo (family size), our annual holidays (Cornwall or Donegal), our friends (A1/B1), our progressive, metropolitan tastes (subsidised theatre, supermarket wine, art movies), our three Sunday newspapers, and our walled-in emotions. This is what we have settled for. He is hating it.

In the past, introducing pain into their lives was always the way for them to say to each other, we are not what they think we are. But now he is growing older. This time he feels bitter towards the other man, imagining some thoughtless young prick from Fleet Street or the BBC. When you are young experiences are more important than feelings. This boy might be relishing an affair with a married woman. For Christopher, the hurt which used to authenticate a novelty has now become real emotion. He is discovering, finally, that he does care. For the first time in his life he thinks he would like to be able to beg Helen to stop.

He came inside and considered all their preparations, feeling oddly detached, as though he too was a guest. Why are we doing this, he asked himself? Is it only to reaffirm to the outside world that we live in conventional happiness? Does Helen, who suggested the evening and invited the guests, feel guilty, defensive? Do I, who acquiesced in her plan, hope to find a moment of reconciliation in these rituals?

At eight-thirty Strachan phoned to say that he was on the point of departure. Christopher said, 'Everyone always wants to be the last to arrive.'

Helen observed that Lizzy was always late for everything. She fired a hot draught from the hair-dryer at Rebecca on her lap. Warm suggestions of perfume wafted between mother and daughter. In summery white cotton and a few pieces of silver she was smart in the simple way she preferred. Her lover had a balcony; she was well bronzed in the heatwave. In the shadows there was a hint of gipsy in her looks.

Outside in the street there was the rattle of a London taxi, followed by a confusion of raised voices.

'Hal,' said Iles and went to the front door.

But it was Lizzy, in the full flood of an argument. 'We don't tip these blokes at home and I'm too old and too ugly to change my spots,' she said, kissing him cheerfully. As usual, she looked stunning: baggy Turkish trousers, a saffron tee-shirt, her blonde hair cropped close to her fine-boned features in the latest fashion. She had obviously spent the day in the sun.

The taxi driver revved off with obscure yelps of abuse. 'This is Ray,' she added, introducing her host to a tall Australian with a sandy moustache and a raw grin. 'Ray is over here from Down Under to watch the cricket.'

'Pleased to me you, Chris,' said Ray, shaking hands like an explorer.

As they turned to go in, Hal Strachan, in a smoke-blue

Porsche, cruised up and parked in front of them with a crunch of broken glass. He had come with a girl called Susannah who seemed almost illegally young.

More introductions; then Iles served drinks while Hal made a fuss of his daughters. They sat out in the gathering darkness and chatted. Later on, describing this evening, Christopher will say it was as though No. 7 had been invaded from outer space. He says he can remember listening to the sun-baked Australian in the Hawaiian shirt compliment Hal on his Porsche and Hal saying that it moved like shit off a shovel.

Lizzy was talking about old times. 'There's only one difference between then and now when you get down to it.'

'What's that?' asked Strachan, joining in.

'Herpes, darling.'

He watched her smoking a cigar, her face turned arrogantly to the last of the light, a thin brown hand clasped behind her head like a claw. The self-questioning returned: Is this my home? Are these my friends? Is this what we talk about? Completely estranged, he fixed an inattentive smile on his face and tuned out, coming to only when more drinks were needed.

Lizzy followed him into the kitchen. 'You're very quiet,' she said as she watched him dropping ice cubes into the glasses.

'I'm sorry.' He tried to say the right thing. 'Ray looks all right.'

'He's a bore. I'm doing my bit for the folks at home. He doesn't know a soul, poor love. I'm praying he won't expect to have it off with me into the bargain.'

Dinner followed, a meal punctuated by flurries of appreciation. *We are all such foodies now*, is Christopher's observation. Still on another planet, he listened to his guests discuss some of the issues of the day: capital punishment, a controversial film, female circumcision, the Test series, the state of the Left, and natural childbirth.

Hal, who was always uneasy with talk about babies, asked if it was true that some mothers ate their placentas. He is inclined to affect an ignorance that turns out to be genuine.

Helen, who finds it so easy to humiliate him, yawned ostentatiously. 'Sometimes Hal,' she remarked, 'I simply don't understand how it is possible to be so ill-informed.'

'They wouldn't have it any other way, darling,' said Lizzy across the table. 'Sautéed, of course.' Her smile was full of innuendo. 'You should see my postbag on the deep-fried placenta question.'

Only Christopher knows that she has had two abortions. He poured more wine. The evening was warm; their faces shone in the candlelight. Susannah who had only said 'Please' and 'Thank you', suddenly emerged from her shyness and observed, 'What I don't understand is, why doesn't the women's movement accept that lots of girls want to have babies?'

Christopher rescued her from a lethal silence. 'Sometimes,' he struggled diplomatically, 'sometimes, I think that's so right. There's nothing worse than self-denial. But when it comes to our emotions we often cheat on ourselves.'

Lizzy lit another cigar at the candle flame. 'Do you really think you can deceive your emotions?'

'I don't,' said Helen quickly, lying.

'I certainly don't,' said Ray, not understanding.

'Civilized people often have a taste for devious behaviour,' said Iles.

Helen was curious. 'Devious towards oneself?'

'Perhaps,' he answered. They had all drunk too much. 'You can live with it for a while. But in the end a price is paid.'

He fell back into silence; lost among these words were his real feelings. He felt suddenly vulnerable. Fortunately , Lizzy turned the conversation to books. Strachan, the self-improver, announced that he always had two or three on the go at once.

Helen, sarcastic, wondered what these might be.

'*Beowulf* and *The Last of the Mohicans*.'

Helen paused musingly and then said, 'I read somewhere that *Beowulf* has the same plot as *Jaws*.' She smiled. 'So I suppose we could say you're reading the book of the film.'

There was a small, awkward silence and then Susannah said, 'I thought *Jaws* was incredibly scary. Do you know what I mean?'

Even Ray seemed to understand that things were not going well. He made the self-conscious effort of the half-invited guest who has been thoroughly briefed. 'So how's your own plot going, Chris?'

'Oh fine, thank you, fine.' Now his own planet was being invaded. He felt almost offended. 'I expect you know the story,' he added, heroically civil. 'I'm just waiting for my collaborator at the moment.'

'Hasn't he taken rather a long time to show up?'

'I thought you were on my side, Lizzy.'

'Oh I am, darling. But what's happening? We've had nothing but Kuhn this and Kuhn that, yet no sign of the bugger. We'll begin to think he doesn't exist outside your head, darling.'

Now Strachan was joining in. 'You have to admit there's this credibility problem.'

'Do I?' He felt angry and betrayed, and glanced at Helen in a way that said, did you organize this?

He began to talk. Kuhn would come, they'd see. He was going to continue believing in the project. He had to. 'Hanging on in quiet desperation and all that . . . I remember when I got taken up. People were talking. There was this old agent hanging around the Pillars of Hercules. You see the scene was changing. Style was on the move. The old chap was panicking. He knew his clients were singing out of tune; he was afraid the public would stand up and walk out. The number of times he tried to get me on to his list.' He laughed to himself. 'He needn't have worried. I'm the one who's panicking now.'

Strachan said something indistinct about 'only adjusting'.

'You talk about adjusting. When you're nearly forty, time begins to move too fast. You're running just to keep up.'

No one spoke.

He stood up and went over to the record player. He ran his fingers along the spines of the sleeves like a child: Led Zeppelin,

The Who, Wishbone Ash, The Jam, Uriah Heep, Steppenwolf, Queen, The Cream, Police, The Bay City Rollers, the Beach Boys, Deep Purple, The Incredible String Band, Wings, The Stranglers, Earth Wind and Fire, The Monkees, Bette Midler, Dr Feelgood, The Doors, Black Sabbath, New Riders of the Purple Sage, Emerson, Lake and Palmer, Jefferson Starship, Roxy Music, Procul Harum, Fairport Convention, The Plastic People of the Universe . . .

The music began. He wanted to drown the evening in rhythm; he wanted to forget. *Hope I die before I get old.* He turned up the volume thinking, Stuff the kids. *Why don't you all fade away?*

Lizzy came over and offered him some cocaine. He didn't take enough; nothing much happened. Changing tracks, he wondered if he could get his guests to dance, but saw that Hal and Susannah were leaving.

'See you on Monday.' It was impossible to disguise how distant he felt.

'Have a nice weekend.'

'Bye.'

He watched Lizzy phone for a taxi. Ray was reading out the numbers from the book as if it was another way of saying will you go to bed with me?

It was twelve-thirty. Soon the house was silent and the only noise was the splashing of Iles washing up.

'What's the matter with you?' Helen was demanding an explanation.

'What do you think?'

They went to bed, leaving the evening unexplored.

It was another breathless night and even under a sheet he could not sleep. Several times he was on the point of going to his typewriter and putting it all down in a letter to Císař. He felt extraordinarily lonely. The light came, blue and fluffy, and the city birds began gossiping in the early morning trees. He fell asleep at last.

Most Sundays he wakes up with a hangover. That is simply the way things are. Today, a laser beam of hot sunshine is breaking through a crack in the curtain, hurting his eyes, making him sweat. The digital clock clicks softly, 09.37. He lies in bed and counts weekends. More than two months have passed since his return from Vienna.

Helen is dozing next to him, her face half driven into the pillow and her dark hair blown across the sheet. She has strong, witty eyes that make people flourish in her company, but in sleep her personality is missing. The gaily coloured duvet has slipped off her shoulders. He leans over and examines the faintest spine of hair running down the nape of her neck. There are no marks, just that familiar mole between her shoulder blades, almost her only blemish. She has always been considered photogenic; her friends used to say she should be in films.

Helen is asleep because she is exhausted. In the last two months the other relationship in her life has made a serious takeover bid. The pursuit of happiness has left her miserable, 'shattered' to use her word. She worries about neglecting her children; she is ashamed to leave so much to her sister; she is anxious about the fictions by which she has to live. Her life is an oscillograph; unbearably tense, then wildly happy. She sleeps badly.

To make it worse, Christopher says almost nothing about it. Occasionally, when she shows him her stuff in proof, he will make some pedantic criticism about usage and they will argue about that instead.

Iles covered her bare shoulders. With the movement, she stirred. 'What time is it?'

'Time I went and picked up the papers.' His head was thumping fiercely. He stood naked in the bathroom, dropped four Disprin into a tooth mug and, feeling his belly with his fingers, watched the fizzing pills turn to white scum.

Rebecca, in a nightdress printed with elephants, came in. 'Hello sexy Christopher,' she said.

'Hello, darling.' He took her in his arms and kissed her. 'Are you coming with me to the shop?'

Of course she was coming with him. In a few minutes Iles and the twins, who insisted that he smelt like an old ashtray, were walking in the sunshine to the corner.

He always buys the same newspapers: the *Sunday Times*, the *Observer*, and the *News of the World*. If his daughters are with him, he buys a carton of orange juice. They have come to associate the cold beads of condensation running over their fingers with the day of rest, a day that always follows the same pattern, unless he is playing Sunday cricket.

Today, with no match in view, they walk slowly back to the house, Iles absorbed in the front page, Emma and Rebecca chattering beside him. While they leaf through the colour magazines discussing the fashions, he makes coffee and toast, with his hangover pounding away in his head like a civil war. In due course, he goes to the foot of the stairs and tells Helen that breakfast is ready in a voice muted with neuralgia. By the time she appears, tousled and sleepy like her eldest daughter, he has become immersed in the book pages.

The language of newspaper reviews always struck him as curiously stilted, a mandarin vernacular hovering indecisively between the formal codes of literary criticism and the sloppier constructions of news journalism. Some writers of his acquaintance claimed not to care about or even to read their reviews, which he suspected was a lie. It was disconcerting how easily he could still remember his own cuttings, still stored upstairs in a brown envelope.

'Mr Iles has got what it takes,' the *Sunday Express* reported. 'A sharp young talent and a voice for our time,' noted the *Guardian*. The *Daily Telegraph* commented that he had written 'a mad, sick, twisted book – but I couldn't put it down'. The *Punch* review remained, in retrospect, the most painful: 'Christopher Iles has given us an unusual story in which fact and fiction are blended indistinguishably. It is a brilliant device for coping with the fantasy world in which so many young people today are living. I predict that Mr Iles has a future that will take him somewhere near the top.'

His self-image, besieged by hyperbole, did not stand up too well. Soon he was going at eight o'clock on Monday mornings to the Institute of Psychoanalysis just off Weymouth Street. He sat in a small bare room next to an electric fire and talked about himself to a balding, wooden-faced man with an eczema-raddled scalp. Iles did not enjoy these visits, although the anticipation exerted an unexpected fascination. He did not make any startling discoveries about himself but when, after nine months of weekly £7 cheques, he decided to stop, he was forced to admit to curious friends that his psyche's unsmiling navigator had mapped an archipelago of personality traits only half-glimpsed before.

What did he say about Milena? That was my immediate question, too. It was, he says, almost too painful to mention. He is sure he repressed a great deal. That was part of his problem. He could never forget, but somehow he could never articulate either. Only time could sweeten his bitterness. When he deserted Weymouth Street his letters to Prague became a regular habit.

Sunday was the allotted day. He would browse the newspapers, then go up to the box-room they called his study and hammer out two or three pages on his q-less Olivetti before lunch. For an hour or so, the small book-cluttered space saw a writer at work, intent features rehearsing variations of phrase and emotion.

These last few weeks the typewriter had been silent in front of him. Several times he typed the address and then stopped. Instead of a letter he was doodling.

Words Helen prefers: bliss, wonderful, empathy, schism, hybrid, magical, hopefully.

'Hopefully' was a word they had argued about in her latest piece.

Words the twins use: fart, terrific, Big Mac, fishy, disgusting, movie, fuck.

When their children copied their schoolfriends, he and Helen, good liberals, found themselves wondering what they should do about it.

Peter Císař's words are: nice, English, sincerely, please, help, book, galley proof.

Words I like: peace, symphony, majestic, rallentando, miracle, penguin, balm.

If anyone had looked over his shoulder, he would have defended himself: These are five finger exercises. A writer has to be ready for his material.

In the bookcase next to the desk was a pile of Císař's letters, stretching over the years to the beginning. Iles had the first one almost by heart, 'Dear Mr Iles, Excuse me, please for writing to you. But as I suppose, that if you be so very kind, you can help me very much with my problem . . .'

Today this reverie was interrupted by Ruth, in a stage whisper. 'Helen says why are you writing letters now? She says you know there's no point.' She looked up at him seriously. 'What does she mean?'

He stood up decisively, pulled the page off the roller and crumpled it in his hand. 'She means we should go for a walk, enjoy the sunshine and stop worrying about the past. Come on.' He took her by the hand, heartbreakingly slight and trusting. 'We'll go and see the funny keeper with the red nose.'

They would all associate that year with Kew Gardens. They went many times. Iles always made an adventure for his children out of the cherished Victorian park, finding mystery and romance in the Chinese pagoda, the Palm House, the rhododendrons and the monkey-puzzle tree. They watched the seasons change: from daffodils to bluebells to lilacs. Now there were roses in bloom and white bodies sunbathing on the parched grass. Christopher admits that he would lie there with the Sunday newspapers, or perhaps telling the inquisitive Ruth that he would rather die of heart failure than cancer or pneumonia, and look up at the grey metal bellies of the jets as they flew low overhead towards the airport and wonder whether, even as he watched, the globe-trotting doctor was perhaps on his way in for the rendezvous, a character possibly in search of an author.

[3]

'You can't get there from here.' I have to confess to an uneasiness about giving away the details of Christopher's private-life (even though I have his full approval). I'm trying, of course, to convey something about who he is, his tastes and style, the sense I have of a man caught in a time-warp. Somewhere between here and there something got lost. The young man who once said 'I feel in a hurry to find out what my thing's going to be' can now sit back and complain that 'our parents were different. They made their dreams come true.'

But that's the problem. I can't bridge the gap. No amount of careful research can really convey what he's like now or what he was like then, in the old days. And it won't help much if I write about Led Zeppelin rather than the Animals, or if – as Christopher himself has corrected – I refer to the Fresh Cream not the Cream. Even the act of teasing out the memories and of putting everything in order is a fake; lives are not ordered, memories are incomplete. I have to come clean: this is only an approximation.

But talking of records, among the albums on Christopher's shelves, his Plastic People of the Universe discs are the most unusual, most treasured. They are old now, more than ten years old, cracked and scratched; for millions of Czechs their music says it all.

The Plastic People were one of the most talented bands to be thrown up by the Prague Spring. Under Husák they were suppressed and harassed by the authorities, but refused to stop playing. Their impromptu concerts became underground events and their repertoire changed from the songs of Jimi Hendrix and Frank Zappa to the poems of the best Czech poets, Jiří Kolář and Egon Bondy.

In February 1976, Ivan Jirous, the artistic director of the Plastic People, got married in a small village just outside Prague. There were several hundred guests, many of them fans, all of whom arrived in secret to stop the police banning the event in advance. Here was the Czech underground at its most potent: more than a dozen groups performed protest songs all day. No police turned up, but a month later the reprisals began.

On 17 March, the members of the Plastic People (together with many other fans and rock musicians) were arrested, interrogated and had their homes searched, an operation carried out by the combined forces of the Secret and Public State Police. All private correspondence, manuscripts, typescripts, tapes, films, photos and all musical and electronic instruments were confiscated. In April, a media campaign, vilifying the imprisoned musicians as anti-social layabouts, long-haired drop-outs, alcoholics, drug addicts and psychiatric wrecks who engaged in orgies and created a public nuisance, highlighted official anxieties about the band.

On 21 September the trial of four of the arrested Plastic People opened in the District Court of Prague West. Security was extremely tight; neighbouring houses were searched and foreign journalists were excluded 'for lack of space'. Among those who did manage to attend was Václav Havel.

On the third day of the trial, after the Department of Art and Culture had pronounced that the Plastic People's songs extolled decadence, nihilism, anarchism and clericalism, Ivan Jirous was sentenced to one and a half years in prison, while his co-defendants received lighter sentences of twelve, eight and eight months apiece.

'Hundred Per Cent' is the song for which the Plastic People are remembered:

> *1. They are afraid of the old for their memory.*
> *2. They are afraid of the young for their innocence.*
> *3. They are afraid even of schoolchildren.*
> *4. They are afraid of the dead and their funerals.*

5. *They are afraid of graves and the flowers people put on them.*
6. *They are afraid of churches, priests and nuns.*
7. *They are afraid of workers.*
8. *They are afraid of Party members.*
9. *They are afraid of those who are not in the Party.*

What else are They afraid of? Here – as the song goes – are some of them: writers and poets, radio stations, telephones, letters, détente, tennis players, St Wenceslas, archives, philosophers, the future, jokes, Marx, Lenin . . .

96. *They are afraid of truth.*
97. *They are afraid of freedom.*
98. *They are afraid of democracy.*
99. *They are afraid of the Human Rights Charter.*
100. *They are afraid of socialism.*

So why the hell are WE afraid of THEM?

Six

At the beginning of 1977, on 6 January to be precise, something happened in Prague to suggest that not all the memories of Dubček's 'socialism with a human face' had been eradicated.

Just before noon that day, three Czechs – an actor, a novelist and a playwright – were arrested as they drove to the city's main post office. On the back seat of their battered white Saab were envelopes containing a document, now known as the Charter, intended for its two-hundred-and-forty-one signatories and a number of party officials, including Dr Gustáv Husák.

In this way Charter 77 – a manifesto of fewer than two thousand words protesting the loss of freedom, justice and privacy in Czechoslovakia – was born.

The actor was Pavel Landovský, the novelist Ludvík Vaculík, and the playwright, Václav Havel.

> *16. They are afraid of journalists.*
> *17. They are afraid of actors.*

In the course of the summer that year, Christopher Iles wrote to Prague on flimsy French notepaper.

Wandsworth
July 10th, 1977

Dear Peter,
    We have just come back from a very lazy two weeks in the Dordogne: Helen is expecting her second child in December. I

must confess that with the prospect of another baby, I'm afraid of getting really housebound. Do you know *Enemies of Promise* by Cyril Connolly? He writes in a spine-chilling way about the threats to a writer's life, among them what he calls 'the pram in the hall'.

I had a story (not a very good one) in a magazine called *Woman's Journal* last month, but that's been my total output this year. The office takes up a surprising amount of my energy and when I get home in the evening all I want to do is watch TV, play with my children, or go out with friends.

I'm ashamed of this country when I read the news from Prague. We have all gone crazy with Jubilee madness. This Queen has been on the throne of a stable but clapped-out country for twenty-five years (not a very remarkable achievement in an age of world peace and antibiotics), yet the nostalgia merchants in the press have managed to whip up a frenzy of royalism.

For weeks now, little Ruth has been making drawings of horses, castles and crowns. I do my best to preach sturdy republicanism, but kings and queens make better pictures than freedom fighters. Our street had a bonfire party on the evening of the Jubilee itself, organized by a couple of local Conservatives. Everyone had a good time and our neighbour's seventeen-year-old daughter was, apparently, seduced on the Common by a local lad, a sexy disco-hound with small buttocks.

This is no longer the country of your dreams, I'm afraid. Czechs who remember England from the war would be disillusioned. It's a corrupt, demoralized and confused sort of place with no future. There's a sense of failure, of everyone grabbing what they can while the going is good. That's what I think, anyway.

As ever,
Christopher

> *63. They are afraid of today's evening.*
> *64. They are afraid of tomorrow's morning.*

In October, Havel and three other Chartists were brought to trial, charged *inter alia*, with 'damaging the name of the State abroad'. In the words of Tom Stoppard, 'Franz Kafka, meet Lewis Carroll.'

Christopher Iles read about the case in *The Times* and the *New Statesman*, and took several clippings. Then he wrote this letter, in reply to one that is, presumably, lost.

Wandsworth
Nov. 77

Dear Peter,

For God's sake don't ask me about my work again. Not writing, not having or finding anything to say: it's become an obsession. When I sit down at the typewriter to answer you it's an escape from a nightmare. Suddenly, there are words to savour again, words that matter. If only you knew how much I look forward to my Sundays, and to the postman's visit. There – I've said it, and got it off my chest.

It's ghastly in the office. A friend and I have got this idea to make a fortune selling badges, I HATE OFFICE LIFE. I'm sure there's a market. I look at the faces on the bus and on the tube and I can see them full of loathing. My company is full of unscrupulous careerists in fashionable suits. There's a desperation about the way people live now that terrifies me. Everyone is horrifyingly selfish and dreadfully cynical. Even the kids in the office. God knows what they'll be like in twenty years' time.

Helen asked me to send you this recipe for Christmas pudding.

    With love from us both
    Christopher

65. They are afraid of each and every day.

At the same time, a leading Chartist spokesman wrote:

> The aim of the Charter is not to collect as many signatures as possible, it is to win over the greatest number of people to our idea that it is possible and desirable to behave towards the State as free and courageous citizens . . .

52. They are afraid of Santa Claus.

There is no way of knowing what Peter Císař, the bibliophile, thought of this movement. His letters remained studiously neutral and in December 1977 he sent the Iles family a special recipe for baked carp together with this typewritten note:

> It is being very beautiful and nice here now. There is snow everywhere. At time of Christmas we celebrate as we always do. A week ago it was Feast of St Nicholas. We have saint who brings nice things and nasty things for the children. Hana is liking this very much.
>
> With special good wishes to your family and to your new baby.

By the time this recipe arrived, the twins had been born, and Helen was back from the hospital. Slowly, Iles became accustomed to being the father of three daughters.

86. They are afraid of light and darkness.
87. They are afraid of joy and sadness.

[2]

Kuhn swam like a Regency buck at a seaside resort; his style was an absorbing compromise between keeping dignity and keeping afloat. When Iles, watching unseen from the side, announced his arrival, the stately breast-stroke did not falter. Only a slight turn of Kuhn's head betrayed his interest. He reached the end, pulled himself forward, executed a racing turn and, surfacing again, wallowed back up the pool, lost in the oblivion of the water.

At seven-thirty in the evening, the Roman-style baths in Kuhn's club were deserted. The light was soft and dim, diffused from opaque lamps shaped like pomegranates. A fashion team on location, session over, was folding away cameras and tripods in the pillared atrium. The echo of many footsteps going up the staircase to street level and the bright summer evening joined the slop of trapped water and the banging and whistling of the attendant cleaning up after the day. The empty space with its religious light and disembodied sounds made an affluent sanctuary.

Out of the water, Kuhn stood tall and powerful, his strange whiteness tinted with thick reddish hair. He was in excellent condition. 'Yes,' he said, spotting his guest's admiration, 'You see a healthnik. Two miles a day. That's my régime.' It was only then, as he bent down to dry his calves, that he referred to his sudden invitation.

'So you had my message?'

'Fortunately you spoke to my sister-in-law. She knows all about you . . .'

'Ay-yay-yay!' He was both affable and cruel. 'My dear Christopher, I hope you have not been telling stories out of school.'

Iles stammered with anxiety. He had forgotten Kuhn's dislike of publicity. 'It's okay. Sarah's learned to keep a secret –'

'Please – it is too early for apologies.' He cloaked the towel round his shoulders. 'But you are alone?'

Iles looked away, playing the pause like an actor, testing Kuhn's apprehensions. The pool was still, reflecting the pattern on the ceiling, and now so silent that he could hear the water dripping in the empty shower rooms. 'Yes,' he said, releasing the tension between them. 'No one knows where I am. My wife, Helen, believes that I am at a party for a well-known brewery.'

Kuhn approved. 'He is a wise man who keeps things from his

wife.' He would dress, he said, and they would have a quiet dinner upstairs. 'You will accept, of course. My time is short, but let's *shmooz* while we can.'

The writer was delighted. At last they could get down to business. He sat and waited, full of happy expectation. When a wet-haired girl in a white blouse came out of the ladies changing room and passed him with a shy, self-conscious glance, he smiled.

Kuhn was a quick dresser. In his linen suit and spotted bow tie he looked like a journalist of the old school. 'It was good of you, my friend,' he said as they climbed the stairs to the club dining room, 'to come at such short notice.'

'A pleasure.' Iles was only too relieved that the elusive figure everyone took to be his patron, partner and collaborator had finally materialized. After all the scepticism, it was going to give him great satisfaction to spring this surprise on Helen.

'How I have been travelling these days!' said Kuhn as the first drinks – a bourbon and a campari-and-soda – arrived. 'Once you start running you never stop. Since I saw you last I have been twice round the world –' he consulted his pocket diary '– at least half in my own plane. Your Lear, there is no equal. Cheers.' He looked boastfully into his guest's face. He was, Iles said later, so childishly eager to impress.

'I think I know you well enough,' he replied, with a hint of familiarity, 'to let you tell me how your affairs are going.'

'No problem. You I trust. So, I am with gold again. The whole *schmeer*. I am discovering one thing: the mentality it is always the same. You have to flatter like blazes; lay it on with a trowel you know.'

'And how are you making out?'

'How am I making out?' He composed his reply. 'I met this Texan lawyer. What a chap! A playboy, a pilot. We make a partnership. Nuggets. Bars. Bullion. It's the real thing. You can't beat it.' He looked at Iles with that queer smile. 'You remember that recent gold rush on the exchanges?' He dropped his voice.

'All my work. Scout's honour. One day I will explain. A dirty story which shows you should never trust a bank, especially a Swiss one.'

'You lost your shirt?'

'Excuse me? Oh no – I was not liable personally. What do you think I am, some kind of numbskull?' He considered the writer shrewdly. 'There are only three rules of business. Never ask a question to which you don't already know the answer. Never trust a man who uses three names. Always negotiate in a language you understand.'

Iles was curious to know how many languages that might be.

'In French, German and English I can discuss anything you like, from the floating exchange rate to antique silver. In Russian I can conduct most business necessaries. Italian and Spanish I understand with the heart of course.' He winked. 'I can ask for a boy in Arabic, a donkey in Greek and I once wrote love sonnets in Magyar.'

'Bravo.' Iles applauded the performance, glad to have reconstructed their rapport. 'Are you going to tell me any more about your career in gold?'

Kuhn always took himself very seriously. He leaned forward. 'My sphere of operation is confidential, but I have real money behind me and I am in touch with what they call good London delivery. Sitting in a vault, wrapped in cotton, stored in boxes. I am – how do you say? – pig in the middle.'

'A go-between.'

'Very necessary, this go-between.' He raised a teacher's finger. 'Look, there is only so much gold in the world, perhaps a block the size of a house. You need negotiations.' He paused to look over his shoulder. 'But – *ach, tsores*, I have had such *tsores*. I'm getting pushed, as you say. Bullion, it's a *glitch*. To be perfectly frank with you, I have to be in Zurich tomorrow morning.'

Iles said he was in no hurry. This, as he saw it, was only a preliminary meeting. He was glad he had come, though. 'To be perfectly frank myself,' he added riskily, 'if you hadn't answered

157

my note by the end of the month, I'd made up my mind to do as my wife has suggested and abandon the idea.'

Helen would have smiled to hear this conversation; it would have soothed the tensions in her mind to hear her husband speak of her in this way. She is sitting alone in the bath, listening to a concert on Radio Three. Outside, while Christopher is eating Parma ham and melon with Kuhn, the light is fading, the trees have gone purple in the summer night, and the earth, after thundery rain, has filled even the trashy metropolis with a breath of wet grass. A small quiet jet, winking like a UFO, passes the window; a voice in the bedroom asks her what the music is and she says Janáček she thinks.

Soon, her face remade, she would be driving back down the hill and across the river, to be home when Christopher returns. They have become so used to exchanging small and not-so-small domestic fictions that occasionally she was uncertain about the value of the currency. Was Chris at a party, really? Was he not, after all, out with some girl? She was grateful that the long-suffering Sarah, who knows everything, was there to babysit.

Did their daughters believe their lies? Did they suspect Christopher when he said that Helen was visiting someone in hospital? (Strange, these infrequent bouts of philanthropy.) Did they understand when he said she was seeing a friend? Perhaps one day, with lovers and husbands of their own, Emma and Rebecca would look back on their childhood memories and realize what it had all been about.

She turned on the tap with her toes, noticing for the third or fourth time that it was time to paint her nails. The fresh current of hot water sent a browning fern leaf drifting between her breasts. She looked upwards through the steam to the hanging basket, reflected in the clouded mirror. It was a bachelor bathroom, tidy, deep-carpeted, pampering phials and jars arranged in order, a place for grooming. The man who lies next door smoking a Camel is like all the others, she says; it's not serious, an affair of the heart, not the mind.

She heard her name, felt the touch of familiar lips, an inaudible sigh answering an unspoken question, and she swirled half-defensively in the water, putting up her long brown arms to be kissed and kissed.

Kuhn has no time for wives. 'Do not become too married, my friend. Women are such *kvetchers*. Also tough. You must not let yourself be bullied. I see from your look, she has you here.' He made a crude gesture and ordered another bottle of wine.

He seemed in a mood to talk, so Iles asked the question that had been tantalising him ever since their first meeting. 'Is that how you got your doctorate – in gold?'

'Good question, good question.' For a moment the impassive white face was almost disconcerted. 'To be perfectly honest, it's a *nom de guerre*, so to say, the doctorate. My friends in many of the world's business centres,' he went on with shy candour, 'will tell you that it is for music, or medicine or even classical archaeology.' He clapped his hands, a magician vanishing a watch. 'All wrong.'

'You made it up to get out of a tight corner?' he suggested.

'How did you guess?' Kuhn, who prided himself on his intuitions, suspected the facility in others. 'But of course, you are a writer. You know the secrets of a man's heart. That is why I did not try to deceive you.'

Iles recognized the lie but, accepting flattery, swallowed it whole, like an oyster. He indicated that he would like to know more.

'Yes, yes,' Kuhn warmed to the idea. 'Of course I will tell you. Now when was it?' He searched for the memory, tapping his nose absently with a finger. 'Nineteen seventy something. How time flies when we have fun. I was in London, staying at my club. In those days I had this great *amour* with vintage motor cars.' He began to recite with pride. 'Rolls Royce. Bentley. Jaguar. I was the real Toad of the Toad Hall. You know that stuff? Poop-poop. Out of my way.'

Iles nodded encouragingly. When he is not actually inventing stories for his children, he is a regular reader aloud, often from the favourites of his own childhood.

'And then I have sports cars. Porsche, MG, Ferrari. Such vehicles are a provocation to your London coppers. So, here I am, bombing along in my dear old Ferrari, after dinner with my intimate ladyfriend in Barnes.' When Kuhn became excited his syntax broke down. 'I am, how shall I say it, pissed like a newt.'

The writer resisted the temptation to make an editorial correction.

'Suddenly, nah-nah, nah-nah. Police! Disaster!' He put up his arms theatrically. 'Augustus Kuhn under arrest. If I blow into the little bag I am finished. So I start to argue. Buying the time, you understand. What else can I do?'

'It must have been a bad moment.'

'It was.' He smiled beatifically. 'And then, Christopher, I tell you, God in heaven heard my prayers. I forgot to say it is raining dogs and cats. The road is like slalom. Right in front of us this Mini has a prang. Brake. Skid. Crash-wallop-bang. Straight into a wall. What a mess. Blood everywhere. I seize my chance. Excuse me, officer, I am a doctor. Allow me. Big con-trick of course, but first aid is no problem. I know it from – from Budapest days,' he emphasized with happy inspiration. 'So there I am sitting next to this poor boy in the ambulance, pissed like a newt, pretending I am Doctor Kuhn.'

He was fascinated by his own narrative; his watchful, cat-like eyes were expressing an emotion Iles had not seen before.

'To cut a long story into a short one, the coppers catch up with me in the hospital, drinking black coffee like there is no tomorrow. One good turn deserves another, they say. If I collect my Ferrari before the next shift, never another word. So now I am Doctor Kuhn – thanks to your London bobby.' He indicated the chintzy luxury of the club with amusement. 'Why even here I have attended a dying man. It's true.'

Iles, not wishing to mar the evening with scepticism, looked about the half-empty dining room and complimented Kuhn on his choice of club.

'You would like to join? Sure, I can put you up.'

He shook his head with a smile. He was grateful, but no. 'These places remind me too much of school.'

'How is that?'

'It's hard to explain. But it's to do with elderly men in blazers, and with pigeon-holes and porters, and – and the smell of changing rooms, and generally the atmosphere of well-scrubbed conformity.'

'I see you were not happy at school.'

'I was neither happy nor unhappy. At that age you accept it as the way things are. Afterwards you say to yourself, did I really go through all that? But then it's too late. So much of growing up here seems a foreign country to me now.'

Kuhn was attentive. 'To me, this foreigner, your English school is an odd fish.'

'Yet – yet this is your London address. Do you feel at home here?'

'Listen, my friend. England is a good place for homeless Europeans.' He wiped his heavy lips on his napkin. 'In your country I am always a foreigner, but I am safe and free – well, usually.' He seemed unable to resist sustaining a note of mystery in his conversation.

Away in the warm city streets there was the sound of a siren in the dark. Among the pink tables and soft-footed waiters of the club, the threats and violence of ordinary life seemed to belong to another society.

'But here I am,' Kuhn continued, introducing a typical note of false modesty, 'only thinking of my troubles again. Tell me, Christopher, how's the book?'

So Kuhn had not forgotten after all: he masked his relief. 'I've made a few notes.' He smoothed an invisible crease in the tablecloth. In the course of a dinner he will hardly taste, he will work through a repertoire of tactful gestures, tracing the warp of the linen, sipping his claret, buttering a crusty roll, etc., etc. 'I've been waiting,' he added.

'Waiting?'

'As I said in my letter, once we've come to an arrangement, we must make a start. There must be interviews. You'll have to give me some of your time.'

Kuhn seemed puzzled. 'Perhaps we have a little misunderstanding. You know it is impossible for me to speak to you on the record. There are things to repeat that would be dangerous for both of us.'

At first, the writer is merely surprised. 'What do you mean, dangerous?'

'What I say.' His host looked almost excited. 'I've known contracts involving the Vatican, the Shah, God bless him, the US government . . . When you are dealing with those people things can get pretty hairy. In gold, you see, there's this total dedication thing.' Once again he had become absorbed in his adventures. 'There was this Mr David. Oh boy, he was very strange. Some of these guys play very . . .' – he was speaking as if their table was bugged – 'permanently.' The memory of Mr David brought a note of astonishment into his voice. 'You know what he did?' He made a tiny but extraordinarily menacing gesture with his fingers.

Iles played a five-second pause.

'So I had to caution him.' Kuhn shrugged. 'I suppose he didn't realize he was talking to someone . . . real. You know what he did next?'

His guest shook his head and executed another silence.

'He just cleared out, closed his office and quit.' Kuhn leaned across his plate significantly. 'That was a very stupid thing to do. In fact it caused him some rather massive problems. I'd told him, goldwise, that he had to recoup what he had released – at any cost – and he didn't do it. Was this guy a nutcase! Exactly what I told him would happen happened . . . Well, that's his problem.'

'He was . . . Is he still . . . in business?'

'I can't comment on that.' His expression was a Chinese riddle. 'All I know is his office stays closed. You see what I mean about this total dedication?' He bared his teeth arrogantly in an approximation to a smile. 'That's how dangerous my business can be.'

Now Iles was despondent. He made a lame, optimistic reference to their evening together on the Vienna express.

'You know already. I am afraid of the written word. It is too permanent. You are talking about an autobiography, no?'

Hope stirred faintly; he nodded with enthusiasm.

'You flatter me, of course, but it's impossible. On the train, I assumed we had too much to drink. I say to myself, No it's not serious.'

Iles became uncharacteristically pressing. It was serious. The good doctor's big chance. He could have the words on his side for a change.

'You will take dictation like some nebbishy hack? You told me you will betray anyone for your story. That is a writer I respect, but that is not my biographer.'

Christopher says he tried to disguise his disappointment, conscious of Kuhn enjoying his discomfiture. He became unavoidably petulant. 'I simply don't understand. I thought I was coming here to make an agreement. Instead you back out. You don't realize – no one need know it's you.'

'What's with you tonight, Christopher?' Kuhn smiled his dead white smile with a kind of malice. 'You know as well as my grandmother that everything has to come out in the end.'

These are Sarah's opinions too. She has just washed her hair and has her head in a towel. She is an older, plainer version of her sister, a disappointed woman. Standing in the kitchen of No. 7, she is having a row with Helen about the way she and Christopher are carrying on. She is, in her own words, fed up with the deceit. 'How can you live like this?'

'Is it any of your business?'

'If I'm looking after your children, I think it is my business.' She knows she has missed out; she hates to sound jealous.

Helen ignores her; she wants to know where her husband has got to.

'He said he was going to a launch party.'

'I happen to know that's a lie.'

'Well, I promised I wouldn't tell.'

'Don't be ridiculous.'

'Do you want me to give away your secrets too?'

'He wouldn't ask.'

'Want to bet?'

'You're playing games, Sarah. Where is he for Christ's sake?'

'You're the one who's playing games. And it's getting on my nerves.'

'I'm sorry. You know I can't help myself. If you want something, you try to have it.' She sighs. 'Think of your own life.'

'You can't always get what you want, that's what they say, isn't it?' Sarah lights another Winston. 'Whatshisname. The man he met on the train. He's in London. They're having a meeting. It's to be a surprise.' She is pleased. 'You didn't think of that, did you?'

But it will not be quite the surprise Christopher intended. Nothing he can say will dissuade the doctor from his decision. 'You ask: what is the secret of Augustus Kuhn? I will tell you. No soft feelings. I like you, Christopher, but if I will talk to you on the record, it is wrong. This world of ours, it is full of *kibitzers*. I must be careful. Sorry. No deal.' He lit a Beedie and offered his guest a cigar, which was refused.

'You can't stop me using what I know already. Have you thought of that?'

He had not found an Achilles heel; Kuhn expressed great satisfaction. 'I should be delighted. I have always said that fiction inoculates the public to the truth.'

'Perhaps you will dislike what I write.'

Kuhn was unmoved. 'If I have to sue, I will.' He put up

his hand. 'Please. Let us not fight. This is supposed to be a pleasant dinner between friends. There has been a little misunderstanding. Now we will draw a line, clean the balance sheet and start again. Okay?'

At ten-thirty, after too much brandy and some awkward silences, they walked through the club together to the hallway. Torches flamed over the portico. 'Stay in touch,' said Kuhn. 'Next time you must bring your wife.'

They shook hands. The door began to spin. Iles stepped through, and when he looked back Dr Augustus Kuhn was no longer there.

Seven

[1]

Kuhn's unexpected departure at this point in the narrative is a problem that Christopher and I have discussed to the point of distraction. He, the great improviser, with real experience behind him, is inclined to glissade past the bumpy bits with a well-turned prolepsis, 'Look folks, no hands!'

For my part, I must confess: a character who breezed so auspiciously into Christopher's life has just backed out at the moment of maximum inconvenience, from everyone's point of view, i.e. just when (1) the writer thought he was about to begin the collaboration of a lifetime (2) you, the faithful reader, were perhaps getting interested in him again and (3) I, the master-of-ceremonies, might have made him the centrepiece of a compelling finale.

Both of us have, of course, been only too conscious of the impending difficulty ever since our first reference to the errant Doctor on page 6. I can now reveal that we have wasted much time and effort speculating (a) how to be truthful to events and (b) how to satisfy the reader's expectations.

There is, naturally, no necessary contradiction between (a) and (b), it's just that so many readers today have been brought up on a diet of surrealist-inspired foreign language films and the teasing games of fictioneers like Nabokov that they are inclined – conditioned might be a stronger word – to make clever-clever assumptions and interpretations where none are intended. I am aware, *par exemple*, that much contemporary writing is devoted to what the critics call 'subverting traditional prosodic modes' but this, it seems to me, is to gain academic credibility at the expense of the common reader. I – should I say we? – am for Everyman. I am not going to pass off Kuhn's annoying reticence as the most fashionable thing since Robbe-Grillet.

Knowing Christopher as I do, I place great faith in the narrative charm of his experiences and will continue to unfold his story regardless of any little local difficulty. It is, in fact, almost a matter of professional pride that I should do so. What is the use of an editor without prosopographical consistency?

Besides, paradoxical as it may seem, I have to admit that Kuhn's exit, abrupt and dislocating though it was at the time, provoked responses in Christopher that have led in a strangely logical sequence to our present collaboration.

Very briefly, Iles decided to conceal the dashing of his dreams from his friends, announcing, instead, to general astonishment, that he had met Kuhn in private and that they would soon rendezvous again to start work on his story. In retrospect, he says he had no idea in his head, just an instinct to buy himself some time. Shortly after this he began to make an arrangement, ostensibly part of the Kuhn project, to visit Prague.

This, the journey from which he had flinched so often in the past, was, I must confess, essentially my own idea, for it was at this stage that he and I met for the first time.

It happened by accident. I have already described the encounter with his publisher (my boss). Several weeks later – during the Wimbledon fortnight, I remember – I had the following memo from Upstairs:

I expect you know who I mean by Christopher Iles. We published his book years ago in the sixties and did very well with it. He turned out to be a nine-day wonder like so many of those characters and, although we kept in touch for a while, he has never produced anything since. I ran into him the other day at lunch and he mentioned something about a new manuscript. Would you mind getting in touch with him to see if there is anything in the pipeline (? for the Spring). I'd be surprised if it was any use, but it might be worth a phone call. Over to you.

This typically enthusiastic instruction lay among the papers on my desk – I am not a tidy person – for several days. Then, one evening, when my wife Jane was away visiting her mother, and I had nothing better to do (we were, I recall, sweltering in a midsummer heatwave), I looked up Iles in the telephone book and rang the number. One of his precocious twins answered but he soon came on the line and I explained who I was and whom I worked for. In due course, I asked if there was a manuscript in the works, received a lot of evasive burble and suggested, my curiosity aroused by his charm and diffidence on the phone, that we should get together for a drink one evening after work. (It was only then that I ordered up our library copy of his book, together with his author's file, from the archives in Harlow.)

I was not prepared, on first meeting, for his wonderfully sympathetic manner. He seemed only interested in me and my work and talked, with a mixture of bitterness and nostalgia, about the company in the old days, keeping me in stitches with one or two wildly funny stories about our present Chairman. He seemed pathologically anxious not to discuss his own writing.

Gradually the Boswell in me got down to business and he began reluctantly to explain his predicament. After we had both drunk a great deal (I like to think there was an element of trust at work as well), he confided in me about the Kuhn fiasco, begging me to keep it to myself. I have often observed that there are no secrets in publishing. Gossip travels like a bush fire. In me, however, he was lucky. I prefer to save the tittle-tattle for myself, the Boswell streak again.

I don't remember how the subject of Prague first came up. Apropos Kuhn, I think, I asked him why he'd been on the train to Vienna in the first place. He explained. All innocence, I asked when he expected to be going across the border to find out what had happened. He looked a bit surprised, as though he'd never thought of such a thing. He said he hadn't made any plans. I pushed a bit, hoping to find out more, but he resisted. There, apparently, the conversation ended, and shortly afterwards I staggered home on the late tube.

A few days later I received a postcard, thanking me for the drink. There was a scribbled postscript. 'You are right. I should go to Prague. I'm trying to fix a w/e there. Let's meet again when I get back.'

I took the bus to work as usual. Oddly enough *The Times* that morning had a 'Letter from Prague' on the back page, just above the anticyclones on the weather map. In a way that I now see was a touch predictable, their correspondent had a report about Charter 77:

> In a cavernous wine bar near Kafka's birthplace, I drank with a dissident who has recently been released from prison . . . Once a senior journalist, he is about to begin work as a night porter. What was it like in jail? 'Inside?' he said. 'Inside is just like outside.'

Unlike Christopher, I am not superstitious; nonetheless the piece seemed something of an augury.

[2]

When you make the right choice in your life, Christopher says, it's wonderful how you find the unrelated parts of your experience coming together and making a pattern, a whole. It was like that with his ticket to Prague: the decision to go gave him an almost-forgotten sense of purpose and excitement. All at once his moonlighting for dissident journals, his émigré acquaintances and his repressed fascination with Czech politics moved sharply into focus. Coming alive, he asked himself: why did I wait so long? Why the cowardice?

Everyone had something to say to him, advice to give, a favour to ask. He felt amazingly wanted: someone hoped he would take a letter, another asked him to take bananas and coffee to an old friend, a third insisted that he visit so-and-so. It was, he told Helen, a bit like joining a family.

Two days before his departure, he went to the offices of *Index on Censorship* in his lunch hour and collected two copies of the latest issue. It was only a small-scale act of political defiance to take the magazines in his hand luggage, but it made his trip seem less selfish, less personal. It was, besides, the way to pay a debt of gratitude to people who had given him help and encouragement in some of his darkest moments.

The next morning, on his way to work, he went to the Czech consulate for his papers. There was a small queue ahead of him, one or two elderly tourists, a journalist in a seersucker jacket and a few businessmen in flash blue suits. He waited patiently for his number to be called.

The visa clerk was a Czech dumpling in a shapeless printed dress. Her potato-coloured skin was blotched with a birthmark. 'You are writer?' she asked, waving his passport.

'Yes.'

'What do you write?'

'I work in public relations. I write slogans.'

She looked disapproving. 'You do not write poetry?'

'No.'

'Then you are journalist.'

Iles did not challenge this conclusion.

'Why are you going to Prague, please?'

He leaned forward and suggested a conspiracy between them. 'I am running away from my wife,' he whispered.

As I, Mr Know-all, can vouch, this is not remotely true. They are probably closer now than they have been for months. Helen has supported Christopher's decision to go to Prague with something approaching total generosity, and instead of exploiting the opportunity to see her lover, has actually refused the offer of a weekend in Wales, preferring instead to have the time to herself.

Today, in a sudden mood of self-indulgence, she is having her hair done in Covent Garden. Zero, her regular, always treats her like a celebrity. Zero was pale and twenty and his plumage was a permanent advertisement for the salon's more outré styles.

'Is this for special?' he asked, playing with the dark strands like a lover.

She smiled at herself in the mirror. 'It is.'

'How's Christopher?'

'He's fine. Busy. He's going to Prague tomorrow.'

'That's nice.'

Soon she was surrendering her scalp to Zero's soapy caress, savouring the scent of coconut oil and dreamily anticipating the pleasures of a quiet weekend at home with her daughters, probably with the phone off the hook.

Iles was looking forward as well, collecting badly printed tourist brochures from the Čedok offices in Old Bond Street.

Someone was trying to catch his attention, a young student, a girl, in jeans, football jersey and tennis shoes. He apologized.

'Please, excuse me. You are going to Budapest?' She was speaking very fast about a family left behind. Already there was an envelope in her hand; her voice was faltering.

'I'm sorry,' he said. 'It's not possible. I'm not going. Just planning,' he lied, making a half-hearted gesture with the leaflets. He pointed to a fellow browser, a donnish figure in a long mackintosh. 'Ask him perhaps.'

As he went back into the street, he felt ashamed. He could have posted the letter in Prague. But there was something about the girl's request that restored the wrong memories of his own letters: inspired by a new sense of freedom, he wanted innovation not familiarity.

Outside in Piccadilly the air was heavy and the morning sky was puffed up with bruised clouds. He had set out in a lightweight beige suit, now he stepped on to the escalator at Green Park wondering whether he shouldn't buy a cheap umbrella.

At the other end, the rain had started. Ranks of timid

commuters stood in the shelter of the station looking up at the water sheeting down. He barged his way into the street, put his newspaper on his head and began to run. Thunder rolled in the distance. The rain came down even harder. He was soaked already; slowing down, breathing hard, he threw the sodden newspaper into the swirling gutter. Mad with a strange happiness and apprehension, he walked the last hundred yards to the office, his face turned up to the sky and the water running down his neck.

Strachan was late too, waiting for the lift, laboriously unbuttoning a yellow oilskin and shaking out a large red-and-white golfing umbrella. It was typical that he should be well-prepared. Underneath, he was dressed in boots, jodhpurs and a blue silk shirt: on Thursday mornings he always went riding in Hyde Park.

'It's raining outside,' he said. 'Did you notice?'

Iles ignored him and went off to the Gents to dry himself on the broken hand towel. Actually, Strachan was lending him the money for this adventure, but doing it with a kind of maddening sympathy, as if humouring an obsessional lunatic, that he found exasperating.

These favours had, naturally, been discussed over lunch. A light dew of vinaigrette formed on Strachan's moustache as he disembowelled his avocado and, offering a patron's encouragement, granted his colleague's requests for another loan and more time off.

Iles thanked him in a don't-care manner that said he would have bunked off anyway. A depression had settled over the table. They started to talk about cricket, but no one listening to the conversation would have detected that this was a shared enthusiasm.

Today, they had a tense, farewell drink in the pub at lunchtime and conducted the rest of the day's work in an atmosphere of strained finality, as if Iles was never coming back. When six o'clock came round, Strachan strolled over to Iles, still firing off last minute memoranda, and wished him *bon boyage*, shaking hands with comic solemnity, like an Italian commander sending a trusted volunteer on a suicide mission. 'And if you decide not to come back here, I know we'll stay in touch. It's been a privilege. Hail and farewell, old boy.'

'Pip, pip.'

The miniature publicist collected Errol and Samantha from his office and left his protégé clearing up his desk.

Iles took the number 77 home, hoping to be more or less packed up before Helen appeared. He did not want another row about the cost of his trip. He crossed London in a daydream of anticipation. The storms had cleared, as they often do, and it was now a summer's evening at its finest and brightest. The red buses on London Bridge were like new toys; the Thames was on fire; the green on the trees by the water was full and freshened by the rain. In the parks there were girls in light dresses, folds of cotton snatched and played with by the warm flirtatious wind; next to him the coy smiles of girls watching a baby on the bus; girls everywhere, laughing, free. He sat back and stared out at the passing shops, and the people going home, the London parade.

Helen was looking out for him when he returned. She had packed his suitcase ready for his early morning departure and felt almost romantically happy to see his loping figure come through the gate in the evening sunshine. And he, too, was pleased. He admired her hair, came close and sniffed it with approval. 'Suits you,' he said.

She smiled, pushing her head absurdly into his shoulder. They stood very still and heard each other's breathing, hearts bumping unevenly. Iles stared over her dark head into the kitchen, feeling truant but strangely wanted. Out in the garden, his daughters were splashing about in the plastic paddling pool.

They moved apart; their eyes met but could not quite communicate. Perhaps they were both about to speak, falteringly to hint at their lost emotions. But then Rebecca with no clothes on, dripping wet and shivering, came running in through the french windows. 'Christopher, help! The hose has come off the tap. The water's going everywhere. It was all Emma's fault.'

'You'll catch your death, darling.' Helen was suddenly solicitous. 'It's getting late. Time to get dry and go to bed. Where's your towel?'

'I don't want to go to bed. I want to watch *Top of the Pops*.'

He said he would fix the hose. The nozzle was lying in a pool of mud and gravel with the cold London water splashing out of the tap. Too hasty, he tried to push it back on again and got soaked.

Emma was gleeful. 'Christopher's all wet,' she shouted, running over the grass, pretending to be a Harrier like the boys at school. 'Christopher's all wet.'

Iles turned off the tap and after a damp struggle rammed the hose on again. He watched Ruth dancing under the rainbow spray.

The phone rang twice and then stopped. There was no sign of Helen, but after a moment she appeared, calm and maternal, wrapping a towel round Rebecca.

He couldn't help himself. 'Who was that?'

'It was for Sarah.' She smiled her you-know-how-I-love-you smile.

Rebecca, suddenly quarrelling with Ruth, distracted their attention. Helen lost her temper and both girls began to cry.

He will do anything for a quiet life. 'Don't you want me to tell you a story?'

'No I don't,' said Rebecca, swollen with tears. 'Your stories are boring.'

But later, the mood forgotten, he sat watching the twins doze towards sleep as he unfolded a simple tale about a glow-worm on the razzle.

There are so many stories in his head, anecdotes and memories from the past. Tonight, with the flight to Prague a strangely unpremeditated reality, images of Milena came racing back. She was hardly more than a girl when she died; twenty passing easily for seventeen. Ruth would be a teenager soon.

The phone rang again. 'It's your mother.' Sarah was calling up the stairs. 'She wants to wish you safe journey.'

'I'll call her right back.' His mother was always a half-hour gossip. 'And that,' he concluded, 'is the sad story of Willie the worm, who came up for air.'

The twins were asleep, breathing steadily. He pulled the curtain to and moved quietly onto the landing, shaking with love and fear. 'Goodnight, ladies,' he murmured as he closed the door.

Downstairs, he said 'Hi' to Sarah at the ironing board.

'Your mother's had to go out to a meeting. She'd like you to call after ten.'

The phone rang once more. 'I'll get it.' He clattered over their fashionable polished floorboards, a hunter in full cry. Helen looked up casually, hyper-conscious of his suspicions.

'Who was it?'

There was colour in his cheeks. His tie was loose. 'They rang off when I picked it up.'

In the past this might have been an accusation; the emptiness between them used to call dangerous fantasies to mind. They have both told me that the poignance in the gap between them has been at times almost unbearable, the inaccessibility of their hearts as remote and tantalizing, in Christopher's phrase, 'as a telephone ringing unanswered in an empty house across the street.'

Now he was looking at her and all at once regretting his surge of mistrust. He came over and kissed her.

'Would you like a bath?'

She reknotted her kimono. 'I'll just say good-night to Ruth.' She paused, playing with the sash. 'Sarah will be going out in half an hour.'

He said, 'Fine.' He could wait. She kissed him again and he touched her. The unexpected intimacy scared him. Suddenly he wanted to be alone; perhaps he would pop out for a breath of air while she dealt with the kids, he said.

'Don't be long,' she replied, teasingly.

At the corner of their street, under a leaf-hung Spanish chestnut, there was a young man in a public call-box. Iles watched his silent lips with fascination, unseen. On the far side of the

Common a police car with a hot blue light flashed through the shadowy trees. He walked on in the Mediterranean twilight, half mesmerised by the crunch of his feet on the gravel, breathing deeply to calm his excitement. 'Zlatá Praha,' he said to the evening star rising in the west.

Just Across the Border

V naší zemi je i nemožné možným.

In our country even the impossible
is possible.

Bohumil Hrabal

One

Prague is just across the border. As that primordial air traveller, the crow flies, it is nearer to London than Florence, Barcelona or Stockholm, and by a quirk of geography almost the same distance as Nice. Even closer to home, its people, according to one theory, are proto-Celts, ancestors of the native Britons. Yet for many English-speaking readers Czechoslovakia is remembered in Neville Chamberlain's phrase as 'a faraway country' inhabited by 'people of whom we know nothing'. Would he, you ask yourself, have said the same of Greece?

For all that it was a short flight on a British Airways Trident full of diplomats and their families returning to embassies in Prague and Budapest, the journey, for Iles, was nothing but tension. He hates flying. He sat in the smoking carriage of the Piccadilly Line tube and lit a Rothman's with a shaking hand. There was power failure on the track. The train went stop-go through the parched, blameless suburbs, Stamford Bridge, Northfields, Osterley, Hounslow. But he was so preoccupied with his anxieties about the trip that until he saw the clock at Heathrow, he had no idea he was in danger of missing the plane.

We know about his travelling superstitions: no delays, a clean getaway. Despite his fears, he still races up the escalator and through the concourse to the check-in desk. He has one squashy bag; he's wearing sky-blue denim: it's the look of the gipsy, at home on the move. He's always, he says, had this permanent sense of impermanence.

Now, as he queued in the press of impatient business travellers with their close shaves and baggy eyes, here was a metallic voice announcing that flight BA 827 was delayed by an hour, due to a technical fault.

'Owing to,' murmured the man in front, looking up from his newspaper.

Someone suggested that the pilot was stuck in the traffic. Iles was not reassured. He has always boarded aircraft in the belief that he is forfeiting an already feeble control of his destiny, and now a second set of apprehensions came into view, more Space Invaders on his *Angst*-screen. He began to harbour disaster-movie fantasies about metal fatigue, blazing engines, electric storms, jinxed hydraulics and mid-air collisions. He found himself looking about hopefully for a bar that served something stronger than croissants and coffee.

Then the flight was called, the safety belts fastened, the latest cigarettes extinguished, and the seats placed in the upright position. The jets began to make a noise like the spin-dryer at home – yes, he loved his wife, loved his mother, and loved his children, yes, he wanted to see them again soon – the fuselage creaked, the horizon tilted, the undercarriage banged, whoosh went the air pressure, his ears popped and then ping! he could smoke again.

It was a brilliant day. Europe was laid out beneath them with all its scars and wrinkles. Plumes of steam rose in the Rhineland: shiny ant-like cars moved up and down the criss-crossed *Autobahnen*; the sun, slanting past their wingtips, glinted on obscure bits of water far below. The Club class passengers were hardly into their second whisky when the pilot announced that they were passing over Frankfurt and Iles, remembering the Vienna express, decided that flying was transport, not travel. Craning in his seat he saw that the plane was full; there was a distinctive mid-morning smell of farts and aftershave.

When he looked down again, the land was agricultural. He wondered if the dust track cutting between the trees and stretching away towards the unfocused horizon was the famous frontier. Were those tiny dots the goon-towers and machine-gun nests that separate East and West? His next-door neighbour, a silent German absorbed in *Stern*, did not seem likely to be able to answer this speculation.

Sudden turbulence distracted his attention from the tranquil, almost dreamlike, scene below, and then he felt the nose dip as the aircraft began its descent into Ruzyně. Iles pressed his face to the window, hoping to catch a first glimpse of the city but saw instead only grey tower-blocks, rubbish tips, building sites and the rolling, sandy-brown Czech countryside. 'Nearly there,' he murmured, and the perspex fogged slightly.

The plane bumped onto the runway, the engines were thrown into reverse and shortly afterwards they were filing out onto the tarmac under the eyes of a young soldier with a sub-machine-gun. It was a desolate place. Dirt-smeared jets were parked on distant airstrips; the wind was gusty and, despite the glorious sunshine, the emptiness of the huge field was almost haunting. He followed the other passengers away from the screaming turbines towards the terminal building; on the observation platform, next to the huge letters PRAHA, a pair of binoculars flashed in the sun.

Inside, the first impression of provincial shabbiness was emphasized by the vacant concourse and the unattended duty-free stands thinly stocked with Bohemian dolls and local brandy. Bored but forbidding officials checked his papers with doltish thoroughness. He changed his money into crowns, remembering to keep extra currency for the black market, and went over to the carousel to wait for his bag.

He says he tried not to think about the two copies of *Index on Censorship* neatly folded into his shirts. There have been moments in his life when, out of boredom, curiosity or fear, he has done things for the sake of the unexpected consequences. He was now beginning to wonder if an impulsive gesture towards an old friend was not about to jeopardize the whole visit.

The customs officer was a plum-faced bureaucrat with the shortest haircut Iles had ever seen, an intolerant demeanour that mobilized all his worst fears. He handed over his documents and weighed in the bag like a time bomb.

How long was he staying?

Attempting a note of casual normality, he explained, dry-mouthed, that this was a holiday.

'My country is beautiful land.' His varicose inquisitor was thumping the passport with a cherry-red stamp. 'Like United Kingdom.' He yawned and pushed the papers across the desk.

That was it. He was through. He could be smuggling enough Solzhenitsyn to keep a small university high for a term. Pushing through the frosted glass door of the *douane*, he found himself in another half-empty hallway.

Now, all tension gone, he stood by the exit, avoiding excited family groups, and feeling free for the first time that day.

'American?' A young man in a donkey jacket was offering a taxi into the city. He took it.

The traffic was light, just a few heavy trucks grinding along in clouds of black exhaust. Soon they were coasting through the suburbs, high-rise apartment blocks on both sides of the empty dual carriageway.

The road ran down the hill, over potholes and cobblestones, round a wooded corner and then all at once the old city, much smaller than he expected, came into view, spires, Habsburg façades and jumbled roofs. Fine trees in fat green leaf crowded towards a brown river spanned by many bridges.

'Zlatá Praha,' said the driver.

The first time Iles had heard that phrase all those years ago, Milena had whispered it to him like a charm. When he thought about it she had tears in her eyes. It was the New Year, after an all-night party somewhere in Lambeth. He remembered a lot of wine, pot, speed, and one or two people dancing without clothes. *Will you still need me, will you still feed me, when I'm sixty four?* There were so many faces; Maoists and flower people; partygoers in uniforms from *I was Lord Kitchener's Valet*; the smoky corridors were jammed with a media mob holding paper cups; a boy and a girl made love on a pile of coats in the bedroom. Milena stood out, austere and beautiful, distinctly foreign: in their spaced-out way everyone wanted to talk to her. He too was sought after; definitely known; marked by a tiny but significant mention in 'Books of the Year'. Someone asked 'Do you fuck?' 'It's all happening,' he replied, 'but not here.' This was the country of Now, where everyone was beautiful and nobody grew old.

He and Milena left long after four and walked back home through the rain. There were no taxis, the streets were deserted – yes, she had said it was like Prague, without the snow. The awesome stillness of a big city at the dead of night, its emptiness and silence, made them excited, as if it was all theirs. He remembered standing on Westminster Bridge shouting, 'All you need is love' across the water, and hearing the echo coming back from the Houses of Parliament, love, love, love. Of course he was stoned, but that did not take away from the emotion. Her arm was round him. She said she wished she was in Prague for the New Year. And then she described it. The bright, midwinter noon. The snow. The skating. Frosty stars. The gold gleaming on the churches in the dark. 'Zlatá Praha,' she concluded. He kissed her and her face was cold and wet with tears. Perhaps that was the first time he realized she would have to go home. *I don't know why you say goodbye, I say hello.*

The taxi driver was wanting to know where he was staying. He pulled out his Čedok vouchers. Single room, Hotel Palace.

The car jarred over some loose cobbles. There were many pedestrians with shopping bags in the street. To a Westerner, it was strangely quiet, almost deserted; a few taxis, one or two cars, and in the distance a clanging tram. Hungry for a first impression, he took in every detail – red flags and slogans (PROLETÁŘI VŠECH ZEMÍ SPOJTE SE! AŤ ŽIJE MÍR, DEMOKRACIE A SOCIALISMUS), dusty street fronts propped with rickety wooden scaffolds, and long patient queues, mainly of women.

The red-and-cream trolleybus was crowded with passengers. They stopped to let it skate by and then turned into a side street. The driver, jiggling the steering wheel between his legs, turned round. 'You have dollars, pounds, please?'

They exchanged £20 at double the official rate.

'Very good,' said the driver stashing the note in his wallet. He swung the car into another street. 'Hotel Palace,' he announced.

Iles looked at the meter. Eighty-three. Crowns, presumably. 'How much?'

'*Hundertzwanzig.* One hundred twenty.'

He pointed at the meter.

The driver shook his head. 'We have new price now. You know, gasoline – big up! *Handkoffer,*' he indicated the incriminating bag. 'Is extra.'

Iles paid, halving his black-market profit.

On the pavement the porter was already taking charge of his modest luggage. As he escorted the Western visitor through the heavy glass doors, he said, 'You want change?'

He shook his head.

The receptionist took his passport, and gave him a key and some dining-room coupons. The hotel manager was on hand to take him upstairs. The room was simple and clean in a style oddly reminiscent of the Festival of Britain.

The tail-coated patron had his own sheepish smile. 'You want crowns? You like change?'

Iles retaliated with an expression of great charm and sincerity. 'Why don't you go and stuff yourself?' he suggested, opening the door with gallant but persuasive alacrity.

Two

[1]

On 1 July 1980, Karel Soukup, a former member of the Plastic People of the Universe, was arrested in Prague charged with disturbing the peace. He had been singing some of the group's songs at a friend's wedding. He was later sentenced to ten months' imprisonment. Some pop groups now adopted songs without words as a way of avoiding the censor.

> *19. They are afraid of musicians and singers.*

The spirit of the Prague Spring lived on despite the repressions. A translation of *Night Frost in Prague*, the memoirs of Zdeněk Mlynář, one of Dubček's closest associates, appeared in the West, reviving the historical record.

> *22. They are afraid of the free flow of information.*
> *23. They are afraid of foreign literature and papers.*

Christopher Iles received an undated letter from his old friend by hand via a Dutch reporter.

Dear Christopher,
 I am sending this letter safe with a friend. You are very nice to me, dear Christopher, to tell me all the things you do in London. Of course we are never able to be meeting, but I am thinking I know about you like we are 'old mates' as you say. I am reading this is Alan Sillitoe's novel, *The Storyteller*, which I have just now from Artia agency.
 I must tell you about a student, Jiří, who is going into

Jugoslavia soon. Then he will get out of Jugoslavia into Italy. There is ways. He is very much liking to go into England. I am telling him where you are living. I hope this is all right on you and I am thanking you very much for your nice help.

How is family? On television we have the games. Your runners Steve Ovett and Sebastian Ceo (sic) are being wonderful. Your country is very proud I think.

Can you send copy of P. G. Wodehouse story, *Love Among the Chickens* (Herbert Jenkins, 1937)? Mr Wodehouse is nice funny writer. I have friend who likes him to translate.

Write again soon please.

Your friend,
Peter

For the record, Czech athletes in Moscow won two gold, three silver, and nine bronze medals at the controversial XXIInd Olympiad. But unlike the heady days of March 1969, the ice-hockey team was defeated by its Soviet opponents.

47. They are afraid of gymnast girls.

Throughout August that year the crisis in Poland grew as the strikers took over the Lenin shipyard in Gdansk. There were threats of Soviet intervention. It was impossible not to remember Prague; but that was history now. The TV cameras were focusing on the grave, moustachioed figure of Lech Wałesa and on the Polish workers celebrating Mass. The present was elsewhere.

Speaking on British television, Vladimir Bukovsky remarked, 'The lack of bitter experience of people in the West makes them incapable of imagining tragedy'.

Iles found this quote on a scrap of paper in his cuttings file. He posted it over with a note to say that in any really efficient system I would have been locked away years ago.

What did he mean? Naturally I questioned him and prompted a flood of self-assessment. His feelings towards me are so ambiguous. Part of him chafes at my intrusion into his life, my reorganization of his affairs; on the other hand, part of him is rather grateful that I've Boswelled him into print. He says it will give him the confidence for his next project. But I'm running ahead . . .

On my side, the admiration I've always had for him has only grown stronger. I'm so used to the lies and evasions of the written word in my day-to-day routine (from self-serving celebrities and out-of-office politicians) that Christopher's freshness and candour is almost miraculous. Courageous too. He has kept back nothing. And in the process he has begun to be healed. That's his verdict, not mine.

> *55. They are afraid of historians.*
> *56. They are afraid of economists.*

[2]

The room was very small, cramped by a clutter of books and newspapers piled on the shelves and table. The cheapness and overcrowding of the apartment was emphasized by the flat white glare from the humming overhead striplight. The two women were on upright chairs, ill at ease, like refugees about to go on a long journey. They stared uncertainly at Iles, at once welcoming and defensive, while he, keyed up with the drama of his visit, adjusted to the fact that this was indeed the address familiar from so many letters. The freshly smuggled copy of *Index on Censorship* lay on the table between them.

Císař's household was apparently not used to visitors and was hard for the stranger to find in the first place. The taxi, having taken the long road to Kosmonautů, had identified the address only after many inquiries. When he rang the bell, the woman he assumed to be Peter's wife had obviously wanted to close the door on him. Her severe round face, framed by straight black hair tied

in a heavy pigtail, crumpled with hostility. 'Mr Císař is not here.'
She spoke with deliberation as if from an old-fashioned grammar.

Iles spelt his name on the back of his ticket wallet, in large
capitals.

She looked at him with astonishment, and spoke peremptorily
over her shoulder. He thinks he caught his name in the gabble of
words. Then she ushered him into the crowded living-room with
the awkward courtesy of someone for whom it is a tradition, not
a habit.

Now he was considering her daughter. This must be Hana.
She was perhaps twenty, with fair, dull hair, also parted in the
middle, drawn in an arch over her forehead. He judged from her
appearance that she was a student or perhaps an assistant in the
bookshop, wherever that was. Like many of the girls he had seen
in the streets, she was wearing too much eye shadow. There was
something familiar about her that he could not place. She caught
his eye just then, a spasm of emotion passed across her baby-doll
features and she began to cry with a suddenness he found
inexplicable and embarrassing.

There is a note, made after his return home, which (in
retrospect) is an observation prompted by this scene. In Prague,
he wrote, ambiguity is a way of life. In an unfree society it is the
approximation of freedom. You feel there is always another
narrative, a different set of subtitles. People say and do things
whose explanation, especially to outsiders, will remain only half-
understood.

Mrs Císař spoke briskly to her daughter, mingling reproof with
endearment, it seemed. Then she turned back to their visitor.
'You like some tea?'

He thanked her and, speaking slowly, apologized once more for
his intrusion.

The girl got up and, awkwardly hiding her face, went into the
little kitchen next door.

Making conversation, he said he happened to be passing
through Prague on business. He thought he would take the

opportunity to visit his old correspondent. (He says he did not want to make the trip seem threatening.) Of course she knew about the letters?

She looked alarmed and uncertain, but, yes, she knew very well about the letters. 'You are nice writer,' she said. 'Very nice.'

The girl came back into the room, fully composed, carrying the tea. She said: 'My name is Hana.' She put the tea things down and extended her hand with great seriousness.

'Christopher.'

The older woman stood up. 'Olga.' Her handshake came with a slight bow.

They sipped the tea. The frankness of Hana's interest was disconcerting. He smiled at them both appreciatively. Císař had never discussed his household in detail, and Iles had never pressed blunt questions on him. Now he said, 'Is your husband away?'

Hana looked at her mother. The effort of translation showed in the older woman's eyes. She thought for a moment and then replied quietly. 'Excuse me please. Peter is not here.'

There was a short silence.

'You can certainly tell he's a bookseller,' he said. There were books everywhere. Now, for the first time since he sat down, he says he saw that even the pictures, mainly engravings and photographs, hanging on every wall, were also of writers – Shakespeare, Virginia Woolf, Johnson, Wilde, Keats and Edgar Allen Poe. He spotted one of his own gifts, a caricature of Bernard Shaw.

She explained that they had lived in this apartment for many, many years – ever since the building was put up. Housing was always short; it was the best they could get. She was so pleased to have a visitor from England, she said, and almost smiled. 'How is your Queen?'

He said he believed she was very well.

The conversation stalled again. If Císař was away somewhere, he would have to sit it out at the Hotel Palace and await his return. He tried to break the ice by saying how strange it was to be here after so many years of correspondence. It was as though he had been here already, he said, thinking, as he spoke, that nothing could be further from the truth.

Hana joined the conversation, darting nervous looks at Olga. She was very shy and spoke her English precisely, as if a mispronunciation would leap out of her mouth like a frog. 'We like your letters very much. We keep.'

He nodded encouragingly, miming enthusiasm. 'Oh. Good. I thought so.'

'We have your book.' She became almost animated and her pale cheeks were touched with colour. 'I am liking English writers so much. American writers also. F. Scott Fitzgerald, Ernest Hemingway, Truman Capote, Christopher Isherwood, Herr Issyvoo.' She laughed. 'Look,' she stood up and went to the bookcase. 'This is my father's ... library,' she pronounced carefully. 'His work.'

All the books were in English. There were hardbacks, in cheap English bindings, fine American editions with headbands and gold blocking, Penguins, pocket editions, spiral-bound books, even proof copies and xeroxes. Iles recognized the names of many publishers in London and New York: Faber & Faber, Alfred A. Knopf, Hamish Hamilton, Random House, Farrar, Straus & Giroux, Jonathan Cape, the Viking Press, Doubleday, and many others he had never heard of.

Hana pulled out a volume at random. Inside was a note, in flowing biro. 'For Peter Císař. Paul Theroux.'

He asked if her father obtained all his books in this way.

'Of course. We write away for anything we want. Half the time we are lucky, sometimes more.'

'You write to the publishers as well?'

'No – always the writer.' She began to recite again. 'John Updike, J. D. Salinger, Saul Bellow, Isaac Singer.' She pointed at a poster portrait of Norman Mailer. 'Look.' He stood up and went over to study the signature. 'For Hana, with best from Norman.' She laughed again. 'Yes, I am writing a lot to Mr Mailer.'

'You prefer Americans?'

She shook her head. 'No difference. I write them in England too.' She hesitated. 'Do you go to the British Museum?'

'Occasionally.'

'Some English writers say to my father they write in British Museum.' She looked at Olga as if for approval. 'The British Museum is in Bloomsbury. And Bloomsbury is near to the Covent Garden. And the Covent Garden is next to Strand Street, which goes to Fleet Street. This is where English writers are. One day I will go to England and see. I am looking forward.'

This, he judged, was the moment to introduce the magazine. 'It's for you,' he said, handing Olga his awkward credential. 'The latest edition. I brought it here for you – and Peter, of course.' He was not going to say what it had cost his nerves at the customs.

'Thank you.' She put on a pair of reading glasses and studied the freshly printed cover. 'What is it please?'

'Oh – you are not familiar?' He explained like a good liberal: a record of political injustice, a forum for the banned, a lifeline to the literary underground throughout the world. 'It's the only way for *samizdat* work to appear in the West.'

She took off her glasses with an expression of Scottish disapproval. 'No thank you, sir. I do not want.'

Hana, blushing, tactfully took down a large black volume from the shelves. 'Here,' she said, smiling. 'This is our *samizdat*.'

The book was hand-bound. He could make no sense of the characters on the spine. He began to turn the pages. Onion copypaper, faint mauve type. It was the bibliography.

He picked out the familiar names: Kingsley Amis, Hilaire Belloc, Noël Coward, J. P. Donleavy, T. S. Eliot . . . His own name was there, a tiny entry on page 83. Christopher Iles, the title, the publisher, the date, 1967. He pointed to the line and shook his head sadly. 'It seems a long time ago,' he said.

'You were a very young man in those days.' Hana was almost teasing. All at once he placed the familiarity of that expression:

she had her half-sister's ironic smile, the same playfulness.

'And you were a very young woman,' he replied, looking straight into her eyes with mildly flirtatious amusement. She could not hold his gaze. 'Yes, I was very young and very rebellious,' he added, closing his eyes in self-deprecation. 'Now I'm just a boring old has-been.'

'Excuse me. I do not understand.'

He noticed her mother watching her inquiring features with pride. 'Out of fashion. Out of date.'

'All my father's friends know your book,' she said.

He said he was grateful for her kind words. There was something so impressionable about her: he could not express his immediate mood of bitter resignation without seeming impolite. 'All these other books. What does the censor say?'

Olga intervened. 'Understand please. There is no censor. We do not ask for books we cannot have.'

Hana said, 'I take the metro train, two stops from Kosmonautů. There I go to Chodov, to special post office. It's easy. They know me. The books come.'

Mrs Císař asked him where he was staying.

'Hotel Palace.'

'Excuse me, what is your business here?'

He found her severe, interrogative stare rather disconcerting and made up an answer, mumbling evasively about an assignment for a magazine.

'You have left your wife at home?'

He simulated regret. 'We could not both afford to come. She has her work.'

'Of course, you have children.' To his surprise, she repeated their names. 'Rebecca,' she said. 'A lovely name. It is name of famous English book I think.'

He agreed. The teacups clinked in the silence. Tomorrow, he suggested, rising to his feet, tomorrow perhaps it would be possible to meet his friend, her husband.

'How long do you stay here?'

'A few days.'

She looked down quickly. 'I will see what is to be done,' she replied with an enigmatic pursing of her lips.

Hana said, 'It is good of you to come this way and see us.'

Hesitating, he mentioned Císař's visit to Vienna. 'Please tell your father. I was there. At the station. I did wait. Something happened, I suppose.'

She reacted as if to an indecent suggestion, first flushing, then frowning, and put her cup down, unable to say anything.

'I did write explaining. Perhaps he did not have my letter.'

Olga intervened, strangely regal and conclusive. 'We thank you very much, Mr Iles. You are very good to us. You are very nice writer.'

He looked from one to the other, but found no clue to their reaction. The habits of this household were so reserved. The subject was closed.

'Oh,' he said, touching the coffee in his pocket. 'I nearly forgot. I brought you a little something which I thought you might like.' He pulled out the neat packet. 'A taste of England.'

They were both delighted. The atmosphere lightened. With his departure, Olga became more relaxed, less the school-mistress. 'On Sunday,' she said, 'we have friends here. Peter's friends. You come then please. They will like to meet.'

'Won't Peter be there?'

'I hope it will be possible.' She seemed threatened by his question. 'He is away just now.'

They shook hands again. Hana showed him to the door. As he turned to descend the gritty stone staircase, he felt her touch on his arm in an almost childlike plea for attention.

'I must speak with you please. Tomorrow at twelve o'clock, I will come to Hotel Palace.' She spoke low and hurriedly, and broke off quickly, indicating her mother inside.

He was bewildered but encouraging. 'Fine,' he said.

Already she was gone. The door slammed and he could hear her feet on the bare boards as she ran back into the crowded living-room with its strange literary jumble. He expected to hear voices raised in conversation, but, as he began to go down, there was only silence.

Three

[1]

Iles advertised for a clean, second-hand copy of *Love Among the Chickens* in the 'Books Wanted' column of the *Spectator* and was soon in correspondence with a retired schoolmaster in Bournemouth, a lifelong collector. Negotiations successfuly completed, he posted the distinctive Herbert Jenkins edition to Prague without his usual message. Then, full of good intentions at the beginning of the new year, and reproaching himself for letting his contact with the old bookseller fall into abeyance, he wrote one of those letters which are somehow only possible to someone you have never met.

Wandsworth
6 January 1981

Dear Peter,

I feel very bad about my silence these last few months. To tell you the truth, I've been very preoccupied. Towards the end of the summer I met a recently divorced woman of about thirty at one of those parties we all go to from time to time, one of those 'And-what-do-you-do?' kind of parties. I suspect it was pure flattery, but she seemed to know all about me. At the end of the evening a crowd of us went out to dinner and we found ourselves sitting next to each other (I say *found*, it was what we both wanted), and spent the rest of the evening talking. She was amusing, cynical and flirtatious. I saw her the next day for lunch, two evenings later we had a drink after work in Covent

Garden, and shortly afterwards went back to her flat in Maida Vale.

At first, this was the most glorious secret, two people taking the most wonderful delight in each other. At the time it felt like love. Looking back, I can see I had become bored. However . . . what began as a light-hearted fling, soon became serious. She said she hated the deceptions; hated being treated like a mistress. She understood the delicacy of my position, she said, but I was lying to myself if I thought I could avoid a decision. Sooner or later I had to choose.

Of course I procrastinated. At times I thought: this is it. I'm leaving. But the more I thought about it, I realized I was really only in love with the idea of her. 'Conscience makes cowards of us all.' I stayed.

Sometimes I look back and think what a fool I was; I was happy with her in ways I've not known for years. But I don't believe in lasting happiness. Do you?

I had to tell you about this. I feel you will understand.

Your last move was a clever one. It's taken me some time to work out a reply. Here it is: P – K7.

As ever,
Christopher

44. *They are afraid of chess-players.*

I've mentioned already that Christopher likes to make fun of my 'March of Time' passages. My revenge, so to say, comes with this snippet from the 1981 *Index on Censorship* which Christopher (for reasons best known to himself) insists on putting in here, together with his comment that 'the Husák of the new decade was much like the Husák of the old one.'

Jiří Lederer, a leading journalist of the Dubček period who had refused to leave the country following his release from prison early last year, sought political asylum in West Germany at the beginning of September after the authorities had ordered his Polish wife, Elizabeta, to leave the country by the end of August. Lederer said that they had refused to extend her visa after fourteen years of residence in Czechoslovakia because of her contacts with Polish dissidents . . .

> *31. They are afraid to let people out.*
> *32. They are afraid to let people in.*

[2]

Hana was late. Iles waited at noon in the half-lit hallway of the Hotel Palace, browsing tourist brochures in Czech and German, languages he does not understand. The porter, an ungovernable black-marketeer who had already that morning offered the lonely English visitor a fistful of crowns, a nice girl, and two tickets for the Smetana Theatre, hovered by the switchboard, waiting to make another strike. Iles, avoiding eye contact, slumped deep in the broken-springed club chair and studied postage-stamp reproductions of a castle in Slovakia, a glassworks at Karlovy Vary, and the famous brewery at Pilsen. From time to time, when the porter's attention was distracted, he mounted covert watch on the street beyond the door and the weekend shoppers enjoying the city sunshine.

When she came swinging in off the street, an intoxicating flurry of talk and movement, he hardly recognized her. Her hair was loose and silky and she was dressed as if for a picnic in the country, a girl in a Russian play. Out of breath with lateness, she seemed to fill the dingy brown lobby with the spirit of summertime. For a moment he thought she was going to greet him with a kiss.

But she was not alone. 'This is Jaroslav – I mean, Dr Novák,' she said, introducing them with bubbling laughter. 'He is my father's best friend.'

Admiring Hana's white gym shoes and her colourful arrangement of ribbons and printed cotton, Iles wondered if her chaperone was not also her lover. He found himself shaking hands with a small, dapper, Jewish-looking gentleman, sharply bearded and with the strong, egotistical features of minor devils in medieval allegory. Novák's fussy, twinkling, slightly self-important manner was emphasized by professorial gold spectacles. The battered music case clasped in his right hand was bulging with the cautious tourist's plastic mac.

Hana said they would like to show him Prague.

'I have motor car,' said Dr Novák, speaking with enthusiastic deference. 'It will be great honour. Virgil and Dante I think!' From Hana's expression, he obviously delighted to parade his classical allusions.

Iles guessed what this offer would cost in petrol. Tactfully, he asked if they could start with Wenceslas Square. There were so many things he wanted to know.

'Sure,' said Dr Novák. 'Off we go.' He had this habit, Iles noticed in the course of the day, of apparently speaking to a class of ten-year-olds.

Later, Hana suggested, they could drive across the river to the Malá Strana.

'The castle is very nice,' Dr Novák interrupted. 'We will have a good view of our city.'

At the end of Jindřísská they stepped out of the shadow of the buildings into the open sunshine of the famous square. Crowds flowed up and down, uniforms strolling among camera-slung tourists. They began to walk up the slope. Iles commented that on such a day it was hard to imagine tanks and demonstrations here.

'Ah, but you must understand,' Dr Novák raised a pedantic finger. 'This is not the same Václavské náměstí.' He stopped the little party in its tracks and pointed like a corps commander. 'Here – there were tramways. Here – no flowers, no bench. Here – no metro. Oh – it was all different then.'

'And black and white, of course.'

Dr Novák sparkled appreciatively. 'That's it!' They moved forward again. 'In those days history was not yet in technicolour. Well, here we are.' He was rather small next to the statue. Iles pulled out his Olympus Trip.

'Smile, please,' said Dr Novák, showing off his English and pulling Hana into the picture.

Iles took his photograph and inquired about the building at the top of the hill.

Hana explained that it was the National Museum, adding that it contained no works of art, no sculptures, nothing in fact but natural history exhibits.

'Would you mind,' said Iles, 'just for a few minutes? Perhaps there's a view.'

They climbed the massive steps and, pausing at the top to draw breath, surveyed the panorama. Dr Novák pulled out a well-thumbed pocket dictionary and, alluding to the earlier conversation, described how, during the invasion, the tanks had massed at the foot of the museum.

'It's a commanding position.' Iles looked beyond the long green boulevards stretching to a perspective point at the end of the square and into the distance; dark woods snagged with radio masts crowded the northern flank of the city.

Novák insisted on buying the tickets. 'It is great pleasure to try my words on you, sir. I must make up the most of it,' he said, risking an idiom.

'Make the most of it.'

'Thank you, please. You must . . .' He consulted his vocabulary again. 'You must be the schoolteacher, please.'

Inside, there were a few children with their parents; otherwise the museum was deserted. A cold shaft of light fell on the marble staircase. Hana looked about in nostalgic wonder. 'I haven't been here since many years.' Her voice filled the stale silence as they went up to the first floor. 'You like animals? I know where to find them. When I was so high' – she stooped – 'they were favourite with me.'

Dr Novák, who had been fingering through his lexicon, touched Iles on the sleeve and took him to the casement. 'Next door is our Parliament House. Next to that is Smetana Theatre. We have joke. "Where is Czech Parliament House?" '

He said he had no idea.

'It is half-way between a museum – and a theatre.'

He showed his appreciation and Dr Novák chuckled self-indulgently. Iles is fond of jokes, however feeble. 'How do you form a Soviet string quartet?'

'How is that?'

'You send a Russian symphony orchestra on a tour of the West.'

Hana laughed. 'It is nice here.' She bowed to a stuffed bison, patting its hairy flank. 'How do you do, sir?'

Iles, relaxing in her company, invited the beast to dinner. Dr Novák, watching with envious amusement, started to hum a little tune. 'You see,' said their guest, as they strolled into the next gallery, 'this is not so boring.'

Nothing had escaped the taxidermal frenzy of the Victorian zoologist. The museum had captured, stuffed and labelled a Noah's Ark of fur, fin, fang and feather. The only sound as they moved past this unnerving menagerie – dogs, cows, birds, sheep, wolves, fish, eagles – was the faint squeaking of the polished floor.

Turning a corner they came upon twisted skeletons in foetal poses displayed in dirt trays on the floor. Chipped plaster-of-Paris models of Bohemia, Moravia and Slovakia in various prehistoric ages – Ice, Iron and Bronze – gathered dust in cases by the wall. In other rooms they admired encyclopaedic displays of coin, fossil and stone, azure, opal and amethyst.

It has, as Iles will tell you, a certain cornucopian charm.

As they walked among these strange treasures, Dr Novák talked more confidently, pausing now and then to find the *mot* not so *juste* in his tiny *aide-mémoire*.

He praised the correspondence between Iles and his friend the bookseller, making no secret of the fact that any letter from abroad, but especially from his good self, had been widely read by a circle of like-minded bibliophiles. Yes, they were exceptionally grateful for the books and the press clippings. It was wonderful to know they were not forgotten. Of course, not everything would get through, they knew that. But then their little group was not at all – how should he say? – controversial. As they passed through a shadowy doorway, he peered up at Iles. 'You understand?'

He nodded. He had already made a mental note to throw away both copies of *Index on Censorship*. 'Your English is very good.'

'It is teached from the letters. You bet.'

Iles enjoyed the anxious search for approval that followed each idiomatic experiment.

Hana added her agreement. It was all true, she said. 'Like I told you yesterday.'

'You were very nervous, weren't you?' They were looking at Wenceslas Square again, higher still, from an open window.

She was also nervous now, for some reason, and parried his gentle probing. 'It was a surprise. We never thought . . .'

'Me too.' How he had repressed his feelings! 'But I was afraid.'

'What could you fear?'

Her directness made him candid. 'I was afraid to lose my sorrow. Without Milena in my heart I was afraid I would be nothing.' He faced her. 'I could not look myself in the eye. When you are young you think: this will pass. Life is full of distractions. I can handle these conflicts. Now when the party is coming to an end, I realize I should have come ten years ago.' He sighed. 'Well, I have paid for that arrogance.' Something about the angle of her face filled his memory with desire. 'You know, you have her looks.'

She blushed and stepped away, shaking her head, divided between pride and embarrassment.

Dr Novák came back into the conversation again like a guardian, looking up with a carefully researched question. 'Now tell me man to man, Mr Iles, did you like the letters of my friend Mr Císař?'

'Very much, of course.' He reflected on all those years. 'Peter's English has improved enormously. With the typewriter I think he made big progress. He's really quite colloquial these days. Do you share the writing perhaps?'

Dr Novák seemed discomposed.

'No, please – I don't mind. Of course I should have realized the letters were sort of public property.' Feeling awkward himself, he added how glad he'd been to provide help from time to time, a useful contact abroad. It was not much, but he hoped it had been something. Very tentatively, he mentioned Vienna. He was really sorry Mr Císař had been unable to get there.

His two companions looked at each other. They stood in silence. Eventually Hana, who seemed suddenly to lose patience with Dr Novák, said, 'Christopher, it was not my father who was coming to Vienna. It was a different man.'

Iles was only half understanding. 'Oh – I see. What happened? Couldn't he go?'

'No,' she said shortly. 'It was not possible. There was a difficulty.' Her voice was low. 'You know it is very bad here.'

The things unsaid left him chilled. 'Where –?' be began, 'where is your father?'

'He –' She stopped, and then seemed to make a decision. 'He died some years ago,' she said.

Their steady, echoing progress across the floor did not falter. They were passing from minerals to butterflies. Iles moved apart and stared at the rows and rows of faded wings, neatly labelled, neatly pinned. Of all the lifeless things in this lifeless place, these seemed the most completely dead, the most far-removed from the glory and movement of the open fields.

Peter Císař . . . So they would never meet. Perhaps . . . perhaps he had only been a fiction, the making of Dr Novák and his friends for certain obscure purposes. Turning round, he asked her in a voice he hardly knew why he had not been told. Why the silence?

Hana said nothing. Dr Novák licked his finger and stuck it in the turquoise dictionary, searching out the bits and pieces of

English with which to build an explanation. 'I am sorry,' he said at length. 'But we are afraid you stop the letters if we tell you.'

Iles pulled out his wallet and found the photograph. 'You sent this?'

'Yes. It is Peter.'

He felt the stirrings of anger. 'How can I believe you, for Christ's sake?'

Hana turned away.

'Please,' said Dr Novák. 'It is he.'

'Is it a good likeness?'

His question stayed unanswered. Hana was in tears, the awkward girl in the apartment again. They stood still for a moment. A door slammed in the distance with an ominous booming. Iles held the tiny print stupidly in the palm of his hand, unable to move or speak.

Once in an interview with an American journalist, exasperated by banal and aggressive questioning, Iles had resorted to metaphor to explain what he called his method. Now, by one of those quirks of memory, the moment and the image came back to him.

He had wheeled his cigarette in the air. 'I imagine a circle.'

'A circle,' she repeated, entering the diagram in her notebook.

'Corresponding to the space in my head.'

'Space in your head.'

'As I write I fill the space. I fill it in, like a child. And when it's completely filled in . . .' He drew on his cigarette. 'Then I know I've finished.'

'Know you've finished.' She looked up from her shorthand with puzzled admiration. 'Fantastic.'

Thinking of Císař, he realizes that while he was faithfully writing to him there was still a part of a circle to fill. Now that space was blacked in, done with. Imagination, forced to work only on what was past, would become merely nostalgia.

He stared dully at the meaningless labels under the glass.

Parnassius Imperator, Papilio Aegeus, Uraniidae . . .

The curator's penmanship was generous, italic, precise. But was this, any more than Peter's crabbed biro, a guide to the man himself? That ultimate curiosity – what are they like? – could have no satisfaction. Like one bereaved, he found his thoughts going into flash-back. He says he had this overwhelming urge to be alone in his study with a bottle of scotch and Peter's letters, a pile of rustling onion skins.

He looked up. 'The butterflies, they're very dead, aren't they?'

The indecisive little group began to move through the museum again. His companions seemed deprived of speech. Dr Novák's polished shoes tapped on the floor. Hana, who had collected herself, stared at the ground in shame. He forced himself to be bright. 'I suppose there's not much I haven't told you about myself already. It's true: I've written things to Peter I could say to no one else.'

Hana said, 'We have arguments on this.'

Dr Novák nodded. Falteringly, he explained how, after Císař's death, his little circle had doubted to take advantage of their correspondent. They had wanted to keep in touch and how grateful they were, he repeated, for the books and the cuttings. Also they had wanted to preserve an illusion. They thought he would never come to find out. His minor devil's jauntiness was quite lost in the stumbling apology.

'So there you are. I should have come sooner. Found out the truth. Put you out of your . . . dilemma.' In a way, says Christopher, the idea of this dogged little circle was rather touching, even funny. He couldn't deny it appealed to his exhibitionist side. 'Who is the chess player?' he inquired, signalling forgiveness.

Dr Novák's defeated expression brightened. 'I am the one now. Pawn to queen four.' He twinkled cautiously. 'We have tough end-game.'

'You can say that again.' They shook hands spontaneously. Once he had despised the game; now it was strangely good to know an opponent. 'Perhaps we can finish it off while I'm here.'

'I would not like.' Novák looked down, humble again. 'I would like to happen in letters.'

Christopher was uncertain of his reply. In his heart he knew the letters were over. He had written to one man, someone who had in his time made a unique gesture of sympathy; and in gratitude for this he had spoken freely and with passion on all subjects, as to a priest or a lover. But – a committee. It was impossible.

Hana seemed to understand his doubts. 'You are disappointed?'

How could he reply? How could he speak what he felt, that his mind, as he put it in his notebook, had been burgled?

Dr Novák had an idea. 'You would like to see his grave?'

He shook his head.

'His . . . funeral, you know, it was so beautiful.'

He expressed a silent appreciation of this news. There are times when such gestures speak the sense of sadness and pride more eloquently than words. He might have spoken freely of his feelings to Hana. Novák was different, someone who would repeat a good story, suitably improved, in the first cellar bar down the street.

They were back in the chilly entrance hall again. The tour was over. It had taken nearly an hour. They stood, a small uncertain party, each waiting for the other to make a suggestion. Novák was humming with nervousness, fiddling with a handful of small change.

'And now,' he said, 'a change of scene. How about we go to the castle?'

Hana, a sad figure trapped in her summer cotton gaiety, looked doubtfully at Iles, who hesitated.

'If you don't mind –'

'We understand of course.' Novák had an answer for everything. 'Please. You be alone just now.' He rubbed his hands briskly together. 'Perhaps this evening I come, and we go –'

Hana broke in quickly, speaking in Czech.

'Yes, yes.' Dr Novák was absurdly proud of his English. 'Yes, I understand.' Self-importantly, he began to interpret. 'She says she has to go to her mother. She says you and I will meet again tomorrow.'

'Yes, tomorrow,' he repeated, turning to Hana with a bleak expression. 'I've arranged to come to your apartment.' He turned back to Novák. 'I look forward to meeting all his friends.' He gestured up at the museum. 'Thank you so much for the guided tour. Very instructive.'

'It was a pleasure.'

They shook hands and he watched them going down the grey stone steps into the sunshine. They might have been father and daughter. He followed their progress through the crowds until they were lost among the colour and movement of all the people in the square.

Four

[1]

26. They are afraid of typewriters.

Of Christopher's visit to Prague, there is still much to narrate, but I will anticipate, as they say. Dr Novák's admissions in the museum demand it. Naturally, when Iles returned home his first move was to pull out all those letters and look at them in a new light. He wanted to understand how he could have been fooled. The answer: cleverly. The onion skin was the same. The typewriter – well, how could he have guessed? He held the originals against the fakes. The cramped signature was almost perfect. The style, well-matched. It was hardly surprising. A circle that had been used to helping the old bookseller with his English would have had no difficulty counterfeiting his responses. Look, for instance, at their reply to that last confessional letter. First of all, it was not an immediate reply. They posted a bland New Year message which made no mention of Christopher's affair, exactly as Císař would have done. Then, about a month later, they wrote as follows:

Praha
20 February 1981

Dear Christopher,

Winter is heavy now, with snow and ice and it is very cold. I think this is good time for reading books. I am happy here with a copy of *A Time of Gifts* by Patrick Leigh Fermor (John Murray Ltd, 1977). Do you know it? It is very nice to read how a young

Englishman see Europe in those days, the Nineteen Thirties. That is how I am remembering it from my days of a boy, what you say is 'a golden age'. Now, I say nothing about.

I hope you and Helen and family are well. Last year you write me about yourself. Please forgive me in my letter of Christmas I am not knowing what to say. You are very honest with me I think. I will be honest with you. I think marriages should stay. Of course I know how it is. You look at the other lady and she is very nice for you. You say, This is what I want. But, please, I will say you do not know. You must be thinking of your wife. I look at your letters which I have here and I know it is she you love.

Please write to me soon and tell me about English Spring. This I like to know. I have read Geoffrey Chaucer in Penguin Books translation by Nevill Coghill and it is so nice.

When in April the sweet showers fall
And pierce the drought of March to the root, and all
The veins are bathed in liquor of such power
As brings about the engendering of the flower . . .

I do not understand all this, but I think it is so beautiful a poem. I am sure you know.

    With love to Helen and children,
    Your friend,
    Peter

I should add, by way of a personal footnote, that when, after an understandable hesitation, he showed me this part of the correspondence I, too, was astonished at the verisimilitude Dr Novák and his friends achieved. Perhaps, I suggested, even Císař's own letters were the work of many hands.

Christopher was adamant that this was not so. Císař, he said, had first written off his own bat, for his own reasons. The little group had only come into existence as time passed; only then could they have played a part in the letters. All this he learned from his meeting that Sunday.

[2]

Afterwards, Iles would say – when trying to explain what had happened in Prague – that the meeting with Císař's friends was by far the most difficult moment. Many are the times he has sat back after dinner and tried to recapture the scene. And when he has finished he will often protest that his words are not adequate for the subject. There is, he will say, something about the place and its inhabitants for which *weird*, untranslatable Anglo-Saxon, is the only word. 'But you have to go there to know what I'm talking about.'

Prague, *par excellence*, is a city of secrets, and all the more so for being, at first blush, like any other central European capital. You walk through it, he says, and you might be in Austria or Germany, though it is perhaps grimier than most of the cities of the West. Here, in the heartland of old Europe, there is everything to persuade the tourist they are on familiar ground. Unbombed by the Nazis or the Allies, it has the miniature charm of Florence or Edinburgh: all the sights and treasures are within easy walking distance. You turn a corner and there is the Tyl Theatre where they gave the first performance of *Don Giovanni*. Some parts of the city are so unspoilt it requires no effort of imagination to picture a bewigged Mozart hurrying over the cobbles to a rehearsal with the score under his arm. On a deserted Sunday afternoon, you can walk in the sun and hear a Brahms clarinet quintet through an open window, or, on a Saturday night, the beat of disco music in the three-star hotels. Crowds of tourists with Russian cameras pass to and fro across the Charles Bridge. Up in the castle there are taxis on the rank, a restaurant in a renovated stables serving *Wiener Schnitzel*, and off-duty soldiers photographing their girlfriends against the misty background of the golden city.

Appearances are so misleading. The famous architecture is propped up by wooden scaffolding. There are at least eighty-thousand Soviet troops stationed on Czech soil. The restaurants serve the same tasteless menu six days a week. The taxi drivers are running a currency racket, like everyone else. The man who punches your ticket in the picture gallery may be a disgraced writer or teacher. Watch the Czechs and you will see the lethargy of people living in an occupied country. The only escape is jokes.

When they laugh – there was plenty of laughter that Sunday – Iles will tell you that the Czechs look English. It is not just that they seem to have bought their clothes from an Oxfam shop, or that they have the same love of irony and understatement, it is that they have an actual physical resemblance to the English. (Perhaps Dr Novák is right: we are both of Celtic stock.) They have the same lumpish, sallow, raw, potato-eating faces. It was the faces, full of curiosity and apprehension, that struck him as he came into Olga's apartment that Sunday morning.

The room itself was so clean and bare it was hardly recognizable. All the books and papers had been tidied away, the table pushed against the wall and loaded with plates and bottles. In the space that remained, nine or ten people, sitting or standing, the men in tidy jackets and ties, the women in summer skirts, were crowded together in serious talk. As Iles was led in by Olga, they all stopped, staring at him with wide-open faces, making the kind of envious circle that he knows only too well from the regional Arts Council groups he has visited in the past.

Dr Novák stepped forward. He greeted Iles warmly like a spokesman and began a round of introductions. Their hand-shakes were keen and genuine; their penetrating looks full of admiration. He rose to the occasion like a celebrity. How pleased he was to be here, how delighted, how grateful, how do you do . . .? Miroslav, Stefan, Dana, Karel, Vladimír, Ivan, Oldřich, Anna; the names whirled past like figures in a Slavonic dance.

He looked for Hana. She was playing the dutiful daughter again. Her hair was caught in a tight pony-tail; this time there was no sign of make-up. But when she intercepted his sly wink, her submissive demeanour faltered into a smile.

'So here we all are,' said Dr Novák, breaking the ice. 'Living and partly living.' He looked knowingly at Iles, who flagged his appreciation.

Hana began to serve drinks. One of the men, a pipe-smoker, explained how their Czech beer was the best in the world. The others listened to him practising his English with secret mocking smiles. Little skirmishes of conversation began to break out again.

Iles found himself talking to a woman who had relatives in Minnesota. She had once visited the States for a holiday.

'Did you not think of staying there?'

'This is my country,' she replied with severity. 'This is my home.' She indicated solidarity with the other guests. 'We are Czechs. We love our homeland.'

He suggested that some Czechs had no choice.

'Not everyone can run away.'

He replied, naming one or two famous exiles.

'Great artists, but . . .' She seemed to regret expressing her opinion and fell silent.

A tall, emaciated, scholarly-looking man with parchment skin and hawk-like features, who had been standing on the edge of the conversation, spoke up. 'In the end, silence.' He seemed content with this enigmatic pronouncement, folded his arms and looked at Iles expectantly.

Dr Novák was on hand with an introduction. 'This is Franta. Franta is our printer.'

'Roneo, you understand.' He looked as though he had spent most of his working life in a half-lit basement bent over badly stencilled typescripts. 'Now, Mr Iles, you are fine writer. We have your book. We like your letters very much. Where is next book? What is happening up here, please?' He tapped his temple with a ridiculous gesture.

'Words, words, words.'

Dr Novák nodded approvingly, but Franta was baffled and, seeing his confusion, Iles apologized. 'Excuse me,' he said, speaking slowly, 'at the moment I am toying with an idea.' A significant glance at the little circle that had formed round him. 'That is partly why I am here.'

'Tell us, please, a little of what you are doing. What is your story?'

'It is about a man who discovers that autobiography is fiction – and, of course, that the reverse is also true.'

'You are writing memoirs?'

For all that he is everyone's friend, the joker at parties, the fool on the bus, Iles has the killer instinct. More than once on his visit to Prague, he found that the effort of English as a foreign language became simply boring. Now, for instance, he struck. He spoke only to hear himself think aloud.

'I am considering the questions of innocence and experience. Take an Englishman who has led a quiet life – on the Isle of Wight perhaps. One day he chances to meet a man who knows all about crime and politics, the Moriarty of international capitalism. He falls under his spell and, masquerading as a publisher's copywriter, undertakes a literary collaboration, playing Sancho Panza to his Quixote, little realizing that the man is wanted by police in three continents. Will he escape? Will the blonde flight attendant with the lacy underwear save him from his fate? Will the villain strip his assets, plagiarise his ideas, and merge his quotations? Find out in next week's instalment.' He smiled gleefully and saw in the faces of his hosts the suspicion that the famous English visitor was drunk. 'As you see, I'm still at the planning stage.'

'Are your characters from life?'

'Every word is researched. My motto: for every anecdote a footnote.'

'How is he ending, this story?'

'I have no idea. All I know is that it will have incestuous rape, violent death and bad cheques.' Changing the subject, he turned to Franta, the roneo expert. 'Isn't it you who've printed Peter Císař's bibliography?'

'That's it.'

'Tell me about your friend.'

Franta searched for words, hesitated, and was then distracted by Olga giving orders from the kitchen. Lunch was being made ready. They were pulling the table into the middle of the room, spreading out the knives and forks. Soon everyone was edging round, perching on stools and chairs. Dr Novák leaned across to Iles. 'A tight squeeze,' he said. Glasses were filled again and soup passed from hand to hand. Someone knocked the table and the dishes slopped. There were shrieks of alarm. 'Too many cooks spoil the broth,' said Dr Novák, showing off again.

Iles saw his game. 'Well, make hay while the sun shines,' he replied and had the satisfaction of watching the autodidact plunge back into his dictionary for assistance.

The others seemed indifferent to English proverbs. They were concentrating on their soup, a clear chicken broth with bits of carrot floating like goldfish in its shallow brown waters.

'It's strange,' Iles began, wanting to sustain the conversation, 'you know all about me, yet this is the first time we have met.'

A disconcerting silence followed this remark. He took a mouthful of goldfish soup and nervously filled in with more talk about his special affection for their late friend. The mention of Císař's decease struck the indifference of people who have come to terms with loss. Only Hana, smiling with sadness and embarrassment, seemed to be responding to his words. (This was the most difficult moment, he says, the realization that they could not really share his sorrow.) The man next to Dr Novák – was it Oldřich? – spoke quickly in his own language, and Iles afterwards wondered whether he had not caught a mention of Milena.

'It is a shame,' he remarked, speaking to the Sunday circle generally, but almost thinking aloud, 'that we did not meet sooner.'

Hana knew what he meant; she was watching her mother.

Throughout the lunch, Olga's look never lost its fear that the conversation would take an awkward turn. Iles knew instinctively that he should never refer to yesterday's meeting in her presence, even though she had surely approved it.

'But,' said Dr Novák happily, 'better late than never. Yes?'

Iles, commending his latest proverb, helped himself to beer and passed the bottle round. The atmosphere was beginning to relax.

Led by Novák, under Olga's watchful scrutiny, they began to talk about the late bookseller. His death was a tragedy, but of course he had never been fit. After so much pain, perhaps it was merciful. His great work, the bibliography, could never be finished. But then perhaps it should never be finished.

'He has read everything,' said Dr Novák.

'He has a great memory.'

'He is a fine chess player.'

'He loves quotations and limericks.'

Their voices round the table were chiming like bells. Iles was moved to hear them all talking, as of a friend who has just popped out to buy a packet of cigarettes. The soup was taken away; chicken and potato salad followed. More beer was poured. The pale bookish faces began to take on a more convivial colour.

Olga described how, every Friday, her husband would take the tram to the Cultural Section of the British Embassy, an unbelievably dingy first-floor office in the Jungmannova, to read the reviews in the English newspapers. Everyone always liked him. He was so simple and unselfish. The staff there came to know him well, respecting his strange dedication. Some of them would bring back books for him from England. Yes, English writers were his passion. His letters to Iles were the source of his greatest happiness. After the great tragedy in his life when the Russians came – she did not say more – his books and his letters were everything to him, a way of life. He was not political. No, he'd not bothered with the Charter. Occasionally, he tried to help people who wanted to go to England. There'd been some trouble with the police a long time ago, but that was all.

'In Prague,' said Dr Novák, 'everyone has their own fabulations.' He looked at Olga for approval. 'But you knew you could always trust him.'

Iles says that only after a week in the city would you realize what praise this was. For the moment he only felt the satisfying fullness that follows a good meal. There was a flash. Franta was taking snaps.

'A group,' said Novák, 'we must make a group.'

They all crowded together in front of the table, Iles in the middle. Someone pressed a book into his hands. 'Now smile, please.' They all laughed.

'In England we say cheese.'

'Say cheese,' repeated Dr Novák.

'Cheese.' The happy faces achieved a broken unison.

Franta waved the camera at Iles. 'Now. You. Please.' The others stood aside to watch.

Once there was a time when he was often in front of the lens – the publicity department still has several Do Not Bend envelopes – in various sod-you expressions. Now he feels diffident about the attention.

'Please. Hold up book.' Coming out of a nostalgic daydream he realized that it was his own and simulated horror. Flash. Laughter. He turned the pages.

Here was that speech, his hero's climax, the forgotten rhetoric of his times.

What, you ask, is our programme, our scene, our freak-out? Let's say we have more fun, more sex, more money and more talent than our parents did. Let's say we're making it happen – Now.

What is the happening, the now that we're into? Let's say our aims are a magic sevenfold.

ONE: the spread of an ego-dissolving delirium for a tribal

telepathic understanding among all the people of the earth.

TWO: To re-ignite the spark of wonderment at the Universe.

THREE: To expand the range of human consciousness.

FOUR: To institute the international tribe of People.

FIVE: To outflank the police, the educationists and the moralists who still maintain the death machine.

SIX: To release the forces of our movement into the prevailing culture and to dislocate the reality of the old.

SEVEN: To bring a sense of festivity into public life whereby people could fuck freely and guiltlessly, dance wildly and wear fancy dress all the time.

Erotic politicians, that's what we are. We're interested in everything about revolt, disorder, chaos and all activity that appears to have no meaning.

Ongoing vibrations will be highly relevant. We are into the exploration of Inner Space, the deconditioning of the human robot, the significance of psycho-chemicals and the transformation of Western European Man.

What are our source materials? Nothing could be simpler. We are into Artaud, and Zimmer, and Gurdjieff, and W. Reich, and K. Marx, and S. Freud, Gnostic, Sufi and Tantric texts, and Pop Art and Comic Books . . .

The words seemed very old and distant, faint signals from another galaxy. The edition was heavily annotated. Flash. Now Olga was asking him to sign and date it. He did so graciously, thanking her for the lunch.

A clamour from Dr Novák. He, too, had his own copy, an American edition. He would be so proud to have a signature. Iles flipped the pages: the garrulous self-improver had underlined many words and phrases.

Iles is fairly illegible at the best of times. Now, at his most indecipherable, he wrote: 'For Dr Novák. In fond memory of your tiny genitals. Love Christopher', and handed it back with a smile.

Dr Novák stared keenly at the scrawl. 'So,' he said, apparently enlightened, 'another proverb.'

Iles gave him a just-between-the-two-of-us wink and turned to answer questions about Helen, his children, his job, his future, English politics, American fiction, etc., etc. A contented postprandial calm fell over the party, punctuated by gassy burps.

The lunch table was cleared. With much ceremony, Olga brought out a set of hand-painted Austrian cups and served coffee, indicating that they had their English visitor to thank for the luxury. They showered him with more gratitude; they were still so apprehensive about their deception, he says. He adds that he did what he could to put them at their ease. Surrounded by these shy, inquisitive, scholarly faces, he says he wondered about his own family's Sunday lunch. Was Helen making coffee too, while the girls played in the garden, and Sarah relaxed with the colour magazines? There's now an important part of him that would like to be at home: he feels the new closeness to Helen is too precious to be squandered. Coming to Prague has brought so much of his floundering life into focus, he is impatient to see what coming back will add as well.

The afternoon draws on. In London, the Sunday film distracts the Iles children. Helen works in the garden; Sarah has a migraine coming on. At the same time (allowing for the time difference), Iles begins to think about going back to his hotel. Promises are made and addresses exchanged. They must all come and visit him in England. Franta, the printer, offers him a ride back to the city centre.

When he stood up to go, Dr Novák stepped forward, beaming with self-congratulation. He was holding a neat black box file. 'Please,' he began. 'We should like to make present to you.' He looked about for support; Olga and the other guests nodded approvingly. 'Here,' he said. 'Your letters.'

'Oh – no, surely –' Iles says he felt the magnet's dilemma: an almost physical revulsion but also a quite overwhelming attraction, a kind of mega-curiosity. He saw they wanted a release from their absurd conspiracy. Dithering, he found himself holding the box of letters and making a banal little speech of thanks.

Then Peter Císař's friends applauded awkwardly, and Iles says he felt nothing so much as the sense of their extraordinary relief.

They came out of the grey concrete apartment block like a crowd of sightseers, Sunday best at odds with the drab workers' housing. It was a windy, unfinished landscape. Dust devils whirled among the parked cars; a litter of cassette ribbon and newsprint danced and tumbled among piles of dirt. Clouds were sweeping across from the west, low and rain-heavy. Hana was standing next to him. He drew her aside briefly.

'Thanks for coming yesterday.'

His words made her flinch; instinctively, she checked that her mother was out of range.

'I have more things to ask. Tomorrow? Do you have time?'

She seemed to be expecting his request. 'Tomorrow I must work. There is one hour at lunch. I can see you then.'

'Shall I come to the bookshop?'

She shook her head. 'It is difficult to find.' She paused for thought. 'Please. Near Old Town Square is a monument to Franz Kafka. Next to church. You cannot miss.'

He felt elated, adolescent. 'One o'clock?'

Dr Novák interrupted. 'What's this? More secrets?'

'No, no,' said Iles quickly. 'Just tourism.'

'Ah ha.'

They made another round of farewell handshakes and then Iles climbed into the tiny car. They laughed to see him crammed against the dashboard. Hana slammed the door, a flat, dry sound. She patted the bodywork. 'See,' she said. 'Cardboard.'

'East German,' said Dr Novák, informative to the last.

Franta pressed the accelerator; the engine sounded like a motor mower. With a wave and some feeble tooting they swung into the road and set off for the city at twenty-five miles per hour.

It was only when the now familiar outline of the castle and the Old Town appeared before them that Iles pinpointed his sense of something unsaid, something held back by Císař's loyal circle. It was of course that none of them had even referred to Milena.

'Goodbye, Franta,' he said when they reached the hotel. He got out of the car and could not resist tapping the wing. 'Is it really?' he asked with childlike curiosity.

'It's true,' said Franta. 'Is painted to look different.' More handshakes. 'Goodbye, Mr Iles.'

Christopher stood and watched the little cardboard vehicle trundle absurdly to the corner. Then Franta was gone and he was alone in the evening. An elderly stroller shuffled past. 'Change,' he murmured hoarsely. Iles shook his head and went indoors.

Five

[1]

In his room in the Hotel Palace Iles took the letters out of the file.
Here was one dated 12 May 1981, written from an address in
Cornwall:

Dear Peter,

I'm on holiday with the family by the sea, just what I needed
after the traumas of the last few months. We've taken a cottage
near St Ives (I'm enclosing a couple of postcards). You will find
it on the map. Perhaps you know the famous English nursery
rhyme that starts, *As I was going to St Ives, I met a man with seven
wives* . . .

It's our first visit to this part of the world and we're enjoying it
thoroughly. It's been a wonderful week and we're hoping that
the weather will hold for another one. The children are
perfectly happy playing on the beach. They seem impervious to
the icy water and yesterday even managed to tempt me and
Helen into the waves. Emma and Rebecca are learning to
swim and are both quite fearless, which makes me strangely
proud.

Today is a day of high sunshine and flying clouds. There are
yachts frisking on the sparkling sea. The cliffs overlooking the
ocean are covered in tiny pink flowers – sea pinks, they're
known as – and the air is full of seabirds enjoying the sunshine.
Sometimes I look up at those white wings swooping in the blue
and I wonder if they can experience happiness, the glories of a
fine day by the sea, as we do.

Is there no way you could arrange for a visa? I can promise you that the moment you land in London you will have nothing to worry about. We will take care of all your needs. After all these years, it seems a shame that we should not finally meet. I would like to come to Prague, but I could not afford to bring Helen as well and I know she would feel aggrieved if I came on my own.

If your last move was K to K2, then mine is R to King's Knight 7.

Come to London.

Yours,
Christopher

He turned the pages. He had written twice on that holiday, and, he recalls, was reconciled with Helen. It was odd: even 1981 seemed a long time ago.

25. *They are afraid of printing presses, duplicators and xeroxes.*

That was the year of the big bust at Stará Boleslav. At the beginning of May, two French citizens, Gilles Thonon, a lawyer, and Françoise Anis, a student, were arrested on the Austro-Czech frontier at Stará Boleslav. The Peugeot van they were driving was loaded with a duplicating machine and a large number of banned books and magazines. They were finally released and expelled from the country accused of smuggling 'anti-state matter'. In the van itself, the police claimed to have discovered a list of Czech dissident contacts, probably planted.

Whatever the truth of the matter, immediately afterwards the police made a series of dawn raids in Prague, Brno and Bratislava and arrested twenty-six human rights workers and members of the Charter 77 movement. Of the eight finally charged with subversion 'in co-operation with a foreign power' (maximum sentence: ten years) Karel Kyncl, Jiří Ruml and Milan Šimečka were all well-known from the Dubček years. They were kept in custody for eleven months, awaiting a trial that never took place.

61. They are afraid of political prisoners.

In the interim, the police stepped up their brutality towards human rights activists in Czechoslovakia. The case of Mrs Zina Freund is typical. She was alone in her flat when, at about two o'clock in the morning, the police arrived and entered. Then they blindfolded, beat and kicked her. Banging her head against the wall, one of them said: 'We'll kill you next time. If you want to live remember that. No one will investigate this. The post mortem will show suicide by strangulation.'

In November 1981, Alexander Dubček retired from the Regional Forestry Administration into total obscurity.

74. They are afraid of their former friends and comrades.
75. They are afraid of their present friends and comrades.

[2]

Kafka's memory is preserved – 'honoured' is too strong a word for a society which has banned the publication of his work since 1969 – in three places in Prague. There is his grave in the new Jewish cemetery; there is the little house where he lived on the 'Golden Alley'; and there is the haggard bronze on the corner of the house in which he was born.

Actually, the house itself was pulled down several years ago and its place taken by a nondescript modern structure which, masquerading on the hallowed site, gets much more attention than it deserves. Perhaps this is why, Iles observed, most of the inhabitants of the city, passing by, seemed indifferent to its literary significance, despite the snap and clatter of tourist Kodaks.

He squinted at the monkey face through the lens of his own

camera, listening to a guide telling a group of Americans that a view of a bell tower seen through an upper-storey window was described by the famous existential author in one of his writings. Sure, there it is, the very same church, on the right there, neighbouring on what we call Old Town Square . . .

Iles, who is not particularly well-read, was baffled by the reference. There was a tap on his shoulder. It was Hana, all smiles. She was neatly dressed for work in the bookshop and, on her own, seemed relaxed and spontaneous once more.

'Let me take a photograph,' he said. 'Here.' He marshalled her in front of the building. She had been walking hard and was warm under her gaberdine. He crouched down, angling the lens like a *paparazzo*. There was enough of Milena about her to be memorable; it made him happy to have her with him again.

She stepped back and looked up at the bronze mask. Sometimes, she said, she was afraid that such writers would become completely forgotten.

'Sometimes,' he replied, 'I don't know what's worse, being remembered or being forgotten.'

They began to walk, looking for a quiet bar. Hana hurried beside his long strides, talking over yesterday's lunch and her father's friends. She seemed to know people. Three or four times on their route she was greeted with a wave or a shout. He told her how Milena had turned their street into a village. 'They loved her,' he said. 'I think you have the same gift.'

She shrugged off his compliment, saying how provincial Prague was. This, he admits, is true: the place is strikingly free from big-city paranoia.

'Would you like to see the bookshop?'

He would love to see the bookshop.

She laughed. 'Well, here it is.'

They had stopped just in front of it. Iles took another photo and followed her inside. It had the atmosphere of a small public library, quiet, clean and very subdued. The shelves were tightly stocked with well-bound textbooks on chemistry and economics.

Sometimes, Hana explained, a new novel was published. The customers always knew when. They would queue down the street. 'Overnight –' she snapped her fingers '– all gone.'

They went back into the crowds of lunchtime shoppers and were about to go into a popular cellar bar when she was stopped and greeted by a workman in a donkey jacket. Eager conversation, apparently of the how-are-you-and-how-are-you variety, followed. He was introduced. The man, who had sly intelligent eyes and a heavy grey beard, looked at him inquisitively. After a few minutes they parted. As they went downstairs, Hana explained that this had been one of her father's dearest friends, a former lecturer in history who was now working for the city as a street cleaner.

'You see,' she said sadly, 'he was on the wrong side. That is how it is here.'

Iles ordered drinks with the confidence of a three days' stay. The room, heavily raftered and gloomy even in summer, was crowded and noisy.

They took their drinks to a corner table. As they sat down she said, 'Do you know, yesterday was the first time since my father died when everyone was together.' Part of Hana's attraction was her candour. She was, he reported later, a person to whom you could speak freely, with trust, though that is also to do with her hold over his imagination as Milena's half-sister. 'It was like the old times,' she murmured.

'Your mother,' he replied, after a moment, 'she's really in control, isn't she?'

Hana sighed. 'She likes to think nothing has changed. It was her idea, to go on with the letters. She told to Jaroslav, Dr Novák, to do it. He said, no, we stop now. But she said, for my husband's memory, you do it. Quite soon he and the others like it. They like your letters and the books. That's how it happened,' she concluded.

He was intrigued. He has spent many hours awake in the Hotel Palace wondering about that bizarre compact, poring over his replies, delving back into his lost years. 'Tell me something else. Why did they say nothing about Milena? Is that also your mother?'

'Oh yes.' Now she was instructing him in first principles. 'She thinks Milena is what killed my father. How do you say, a loss of heart? Also,' she frowned, 'my father never talks of Milena after . . . well, after she died. That is not his way.' Iles was moved to see Císař's vivid presence in her mind. A look of regret passed across her face. 'You see how closed we are.'

'Perhaps you have to be.' He says that a repressed society makes its own repressions.

'My father's friends knowed everything about you and Milena,' she added, making a rare mistake. 'But they do not like to say.'

He poured more beer. 'They probably felt inhibited. It's not surprising really.' He looked at her, challenging, appealing. 'But you understand. Please tell me what they did not say. That is why I have come.'

'Oh yes; I can.' She was eager to inform. She did not seem to realize that he wanted to be with her and to hear her talk as much for her own sake as for his curiosity's.

'When you came to where we are living,' she began, 'you do not know what it is like for me. For us, you are –' she hesitated '– a sort of legend.'

Iles mocked the idea with an instinctive irony; Hana insisted on an explanation. He concentrated on her serious young features, that ghostly version of Milena, the quirk of the mouth, the broad forehead, and then, teasing again, remarked, 'But you – you were, what shall we say, hardly five when she died?'

'Yes, but I am told.' There was Milena's trick of closing her eyes to emphasize her words. 'My mother – Olga. She is telling me this story. What happened, you know.'

When Milena came back to her country in the midsummer of that distant year she was not, apparently, the girl they all remembered. She was serious, unhappy and spoke of politics like a crusade. She had left behind in London a young writer who, it was said in the way gossip says these things, had changed her life. At the same time she had come back to Prague to know for herself what was happening. In those times, Hana reported, people were like that.

She had forgotten to whom she was talking. He was strangely touched. 'Yes,' his eyebrows went up in a melancholy smile of agreement. 'They were.'

After her death, her father had found the English boy's address among her belongings. 'You,' said Hana, verifying.

'At home. I still have it. His first letter.'

Her father had always had an interest in England, she explained, but now it became an obsession, as if in some belated way it would bring him closer to his beloved daughter. So he had read all her books on the shelf; he had wanted to know all her thoughts. He was a bookseller; the bibliography came naturally. It was a way of keeping faith. Christopher's own book, well, that was always very special with them. 'We don't understand it,' she admitted, 'but it has her name in your writing. That is enough.'

Dr Novák had said: in Prague, everyone has their own fabulations. Iles will say now that when you're there it is like watching a play or a film knowing that the real drama is backstage or off-camera. He put his glass down. 'It's odd you remember Milena for her seriousness. When I think of her, I think of laughter – like you.'

She blushed. Now it was her turn, she replied quickly. He should tell her about those times.

'When she was in England, she was always at play. She was sometimes a true clown. A free spirit. Do you remember the way she laughed?'

Hana shook her head.

'Of course. You were too young. It's a long time ago, in another country, and besides the wench is dead.'

She was not following and he apologized.

'Tell me about her laughter.' She was not just making conversation.

'It was a transformation. It was – it was as though she was filled up with a kind of hilarious gas . . .' His eyes filled with tears. 'You cannot know how I loved her,' he confessed.

She put out her hand and touched him. For a moment or two they said nothing.

No one in this story ever saw Christopher and Milena together. The people who knew them well have passed out of his life a long time ago. Some went to Canada, Europe, the States, even Australia, mostly on lucrative contracts; others have settled down in four-bedroom Victorian houses in London suburbs like Barnes and Canonbury, where they conduct mild, useful lives as civil servants, bankers, publishers, accountants, publicists, TV producers; some have moved away to the country and run antique businesses, small farms and second-hand bookshops; a few are dead. If it was possible to solicit their memories they would tell you that the relationship between Christopher Iles and his Czech girlfriend was a love match; those that knew the end of the story would say it was the tragedy in his life. But none of them knew much about Milena's abrupt departure.

He had come home to their flat one day to find her sitting with the *Guardian*, snow-haired and tiny, on the edge of his cane chair. 'I have to go back,' she repeated. 'I have to be there.'

He said he would come too.

But she said, no, he would only be a tourist. She would go alone at first; perhaps he could come later. Or – *eventually*, as she put it, mistranslating – she would soon return to London.

They had gone the next day with the group to a gig at Windsor, got stoned, played to a summer audience and bathed at midnight in the dark, warm Thames. *Picture yourself in a boat on a river with tangerine trees and marmalade skies*. In the morning the girl with kaleidoscope eyes had got up like a commuter and simply taken the Dover train.

When he reached this part of his memory, he could not sustain his neutral murmur. He put his head in his hands feeling old and tired. 'You know, Hana, the moment she left something inside me . . . I've had to pretend, but it was never the same. Your father knew about that.'

A group of workers stood up and made their way to the door. The cellar bar was emptying. He sensed that her time was running out and asked about her father. 'Milena never talked about him much. I realize now that she used her mother's name. I never discovered why. It was not something I ever mentioned to your father.'

Hana knew what he was saying. Her father was an unusual man. He was extremely complex, half-puritan, half-liberal. He and Milena had fought much of her life, just as, she admitted, she now fought with her mother. To understand her father, she said, you had to know about his family.

He came of strict Protestant parents. He had been intended for the Church and was on the point of going to theological college when his life was interrupted by the Nazi invasion. The war broke out and Císař's father was called up, sent off to the Eastern front and never seen again. The young man, barely twenty-one, suddenly found himself the head of the family. Apparently he found the responsibility a burden, especially as his father's absence gave him the longed-for freedom. All ideas of the Church were abandoned. Like many young people then, he became a communist, with the intention of becoming a school teacher.

So, after the war was over, he went off to teach at a small town in Slovakia. There, with all these confusions in his head, he fell in love with one of the other teachers, a considerably older woman, a certain Ludmila Hamplová. To the amazement and scandal of their colleagues, she became pregnant. She was getting on and wanted a child. The baby was born in the year of the communist takeover, actually in the same month as Masaryk . . . Hana stopped, sensing that she was straying too far. To go back to the story, by one of those tragic coincidences that religious people pass off as the punishing hand of God, Ludmila Hamplová died when Milena was only four, leaving Peter Císař a widower at the age of thirty-two. By the time Milena grew up to be a student – at odds with her autocratic, she meant to say too-loving, father – it was her mother, romantically deceased, who inspired her imagination. That was why she took her name.

Iles wanted to know when Císař had remarried.

Hana explained that after his wife's death, her father had given up teaching, come to Prague, and joined the bookshop. The Church, school, books – it was a progression. Olga was one of the other assistants. They had married in nineteen-sixty-three, and she was born soon after. Her mother, she said, was almost more fanatical about the bookshop than her husband.

Hana looked at her watch. The lunch hour was over. Iles imagined Olga crossly checking her back to work. He hesitated. 'Thank you for telling me these things.'

'I saw when you first came that you know nothing.' She frowned. 'My mother is like father. Very strict. She says it is better you do not know too much.'

'You said before. Why is that?'

'She says it was this that killed my father. She says you are young, you should forget such things.'

'But I've told you, I've spent too long trying to forget. I can't help it.' He paused and considered her concern. 'Especially now I'm here.' There was only one more thing he needed. 'Do you – can you tell me how it happened?'

'At the end?' She seemed to be expecting his question. 'No, I do not know really. I've been told, but I do not know.' She added that she could remember bits of the funeral, singing the Hussite hymn, foreign television cameras, watching the crowds of mourners come to the graveside, white flowers piled on the wet grass. That was the aftermath. 'You do not know in England what that year is for us. It is a wound, always a wound,' she repeated, mispronouncing fiercely.

'Wound.'

'It will never heal. Some lives have been wrecked for ever.' She looked thoughtful, hesitant. 'There is a man.' Now she was deciding what to do. 'I will talk to him. Tomorrow – in the morning – stay in Hotel Palace. He will come. If not, I come.'

He was strangely pleased. 'Either way I'm lucky.' He considered her frankly. 'On – on Wednesday I must go home. I would like to thank you. Will you – would you like to have dinner with me tomorrow night?'

She accepted, delighted. 'I think you like to dance,' she said, and ran up the stairs to the street. He felt sad, lonely and middle-aged. She had the kind of presence whose departure one regrets the moment she was gone.

The hotel was half-asleep in the quiet of the afternoon when he returned. Three waiters were horsing about the empty dining room, flicking each other with napkins.

The receptionist, who was beginning to recognize him, coolly returned his smile. She had pale, watery skin. Her blood-red lipstick was like the first brush stroke on a new canvas. Everything about her said that she considered herself too good for the job. Iles, who was getting used to the idea that people in Prague often had absurdly contradictory identities – historians who were street cleaners, philosophers who were nightwatchmen – wondered if this girl too had another life, one that accounted for her wardrobe.

He walked across the foyer and into the bar, a smoky cubbyhole decorated with 'Fly OK Fly ČSA' posters that seemed never to close. Some soldiers in uniform were sitting at a table by the window staring blankly into space; the middle-aged American couple who had arrived the evening before with a mountain of matching baggage sat with their camparis and soda locked in the silence of a second honeymoon. At the bar, a solitary woman with a cigarette holder was ignoring her neighbour, a hopeful-looking character in a mac, and nodding abstractedly to the musak, a tune that Iles identified as Eurovision Song Contest nineteen-seventy-something. He took a bar stool next to the man in the raincoat, who rather surprisingly had *The Times* crossword in front of him, and ordered a beer in his atrocious Czech.

His neighbour abandoned the woman with the cigarette holder and switched conversations with the effortless skill of the traveller, introducing himself with a firm handshake. 'Harris. Reuters. Vienna desk.' He delivered the information like a telex and then, as if waiting for an answering signal, pulled out a pipe and began to play the flame of a throwaway lighter over the charred bowl. Harris had black, cropped hair starting back from a domed forehead, and a round, sickly, rather Germanic expression. He spoke like a middle-aged man, but would have been younger than Iles.

They talked politics. Iles asked about the future.

'What can I tell you? In theory the First Secretary controls the Party, the Party controls the state, and the state controls the poor bloody workers.' He singed his briar. 'In practice, of course, everything is fucked up by the system, everyone's on the fiddle and the top dogs take their orders from Moscow.'

'Which are?'

'Propping up the bloc. Listen. Last week there was a strike in a frozen chicken factory. Why? Because the proles objected to sending their birds to Poland in bags labelled "packaged in the USSR." So what happens?'

'I've no idea.'

'They draft in Vietnamese students as blackleg labour while they sort out the strikers. Crazy.'

Iles expressed his appreciation of this local colour. 'Another one?'

'Don't mind if I do.'

He reordered; the woman with the cigarette holder eyed him provocatively, got up and walked out.

'Cheers, m'dear.' Harris lifted his glass. 'And what brings you to this neck of the woods, if you don't mind my asking?'

'Do you really want to know?'

'I wouldn't have asked, would I?'

'It's a long story.'

'Tell me about it.'

'And so,' said Christopher, many months later, as we sifted through his papers together one winter evening, 'I did.'

231

[3]

Iles says it is curiously soothing to share your troubles with a crashing bore. He will add with a grin that, yes, he probably outbored him, sparing nothing of himself or his anxieties. Why else should Harris have let him lift his newspaper?

He had pointed to *The Times* folded on the bar.

'May I?'

'Sure. I know how you feel. Brits abroad always want to keep up with the old country. Go ahead; take it.'

'I'll drop it back to your room.'

'No problem.'

Iles said he would see him later. Upstairs, he threw his prize onto the bed, saving it up, and turned once more to Císař's file of correspondence.

Prague, 26 July

Dear Christopher,

Your last letter is much amusement for us. We like to hear about Rolling Stones. And thank you for the very nice photographs. I am thinking you like poems and stories, and I am sending you this one by very famous poet Miroslav Holub, translated by Mr Theiner. Perhaps you are knowing him: he is in London now.

The game of chess is now very interesting and difficult I think. My move is K to K2. We have news here of Karpov-Korchnoi world championship and he is very interesting to follow I think.

Write to me soon.

Your Friend,

Peter

Just Across the Border

The poem, *Fairy Tale*, is clipped to the letter:

Fairy Tale

He built himself a house,
     his foundations,
     his stones,
     his walls,
     his roof overhead,
     his chimney and smoke,
     his view from the window.

He made himself a garden,
     his fence,
     his thyme,
     his earthworm,
     his evening dew.

He cut out his bit of sky above.

And he wrapped the garden in the sky
and the house in the garden
and he packed the lot in a handkerchief
and went off
lone as an arctic fox
through the cold
unending
rain
into the world.

Christopher held the letter in his hand. The Rolling Stones! He'd persuaded a magazine to cover his expenses to the Madison Square Garden concert, hinting at an interview with Jagger. Of course he never got near the Stones. Well, if the editor believed him, that was his problem.

Here was his reply. 27 August. From Wandsworth again.

Dear Peter,

The poem is very beautiful. I read it aloud to my daughters. Ruth said, 'That's a sad story.' I suppose it is: but I rather like the idea of pulling up and off like that. If only one could . . . I heard an item on the radio the other day about the thousands, the tens of thousands apparently, of Americans who vanish each year. Not murdered. They just up sticks and start again in another state. Take a new name, a new wife or lover perhaps, a new job and start a new life. It has its attractions. That's the beauty and the curse of the States, anything seems possible.

Yes, I am restless again. Perhaps I should travel. It needn't cost much. Helen's freelance work would take care of the mortage for a month or two. That's all I need. A bit of time to have some new experiences. I'm fed up with the routine here, the children whining and fighting, Helen and her anxieties, the monotony of what they call domestic bliss, everyone's obsession with property, cars, holidays, jobs, money, and children, children, children. Oh yes, I would like to pack it all up into a handkerchief and go off alone into the unending world. Maybe I would find something that would give me renewal. Maybe not.

It's late: I must stop.

As ever,
Christopher

As ever, Christopher; your friend, Peter; Yours, Christopher; Dear Peter; Dear Christopher; Your Friend, Peter . . . He has never quite come to terms with the fact that Peter was no longer a friend but a letter factory, a forgery, a fake, a manipulation, a fiction.

There was a knock at the door. The maid wanted to turn down the bed. When she had finished, she stood in front of him and unfastened the top button of her blouse. He shook his head and picked up *The Times* with an awkward gesture of distraction. The maid looked at him for a moment, perhaps expecting second-thoughts, then turned and walked away without fuss.

Christopher rustled casually through the familiar pages, noting as he always did how introspective and local his country seemed from abroad. A photograph on page five caught his attention. Someone he surely recognised, or half-recognized, but could not place? Someone . . . But of course. It was Kuhn, without his beard.

'The virtuoso blank-cheque artist', ran the caption, 'Siegmund Dukatenzeiler – charm, skill, panache, and five aliases.'

Next to his photograph, an estate agent's view of a mock-Tudor ~ansion in Esher. 'Antiques, dozens of expensive suits, a Mer· cedes, a Rolls-Royce and a Jaguar. Gold décor throughout down to the taps. Guests were rare, neighbours said.'

Another photo. A familiar portico. 'Dukatenzeiler's club: he did his deals here, but the police waited in vain to trap him.'

The article, which filled the whole page, was headlined *How the man called Dukat lived high off the world's banks.*

At Interpol in Paris the last trace of Siegmund Dukaten-zeiler, or Dukat as he was known, came in Switzerland 10 years ago. The file says 'identity uncertain.'

On the Antwerp diamond *bourse*, dealers thought he was dead, killed in a mysterious car crash in 1974. And police in Rome wanted to talk to him about a billion lire fraud in 1976.

In London, Scotland Yard set a trap, but Dukatenzeiler never showed up. Now the authorities fear he has slipped the country, possibly to Latin America. Instead, they arrested his one-time partner, 'Gordo' Johnson, a Texan lawyer with a record in drug-trafficking.

Yesterday at the Central Criminal Court, Johnson, also known to the underworld as George Johns, was sent to prison for five years for his part in . . .

Iles read through the story feeling curiously satisfied. It was all half familiar; it was *his* story, Kuhn's story. Here was the Viennese childhood, the gold, the women and the fast cars. But there were also new, contradictory details. The name, for instance. No mention of Augustus Kuhn. The Italian bank fraud. And the death in the car accident. That was new. Iles looked again at the photo. Surely it was the elusive doctor? But without his beard it was strangely difficult to be certain. But yes, he was proud. There was a story there, a drama. And he had found it. Perhaps . . . he tore out the page and folded it into his wallet.

Six

[1]

His name, he said, was Míša. He would like to show Mr Iles a few of the sights. Apparently there was a renovated gallery, just open. 'Do you like?'

'Please.'

Míša was an actor, short of work; a bit player relying on voice-overs to keep busy. He was a chain-smoker: he had a wife and two children to support, he said. There was sick on his jeans and he wore grubby plimsolls. Looking at his exhausted pallor and wild, thinning hair, Iles would have cast him as a chess pro or a lab assistant.

Hana had asked him to come, he said. The affection with which he mentioned her name was a sufficient explanation for his appearance, but he was obviously in two minds about the rendez-vous: curious about Milena's friend, yet reluctant to open old wounds and talk about the lost, unmentionable past. His English was poor and he was rather bitter. When he discovered that Iles knew no German, he formulated his more complicated thoughts in French. On the way to the gallery, through the empty byways of the city, he abused the West in an idiosyncratic franglais.

What had Mr Iles to do here? Why had he come? This was a prison camp, not a zoo. With all that money and freedom the Yankees should do something real about the oppression. When he was in London all those years ago there was this stupid argument with the censor about buggers and shits. It was absurd, truly absurd. Here, there were writers who . . . Well, why didn't he tell him a story?

A friend of his, a poet, writes this poem in which he describes a housewife buying liver sausage. When the poem is submitted as part of a collection to the state publishing house, the editor takes exception to 'liver sausage'. Why? says his friend. Is liver sausage too prosaic? Liver sausage, replies the editor, a pig-faced toady, is the cheapest meat in the butcher's. The poem gives the impression that the average Czech often eats liver sausage. So what? Well, it will be understood by our enemies, the counter-revolutionaries in the West, to say that there is a meat shortage in the Socialist Republic. But, says his friend, everyone knows that there has been a meat surfeit during the Polish crisis. No matter, the line must be changed. '*Leberwurst,*' said Míša, angrily dropping into German.

Iles interrupted. (He will say it is part of Prague's spell that all free conversation in its open spaces becomes political.) Surely, the Soviet empire was falling apart, he suggested.

Míša was bitter about that idea too. That was what the smart people, *les mondains* liked to say. It didn't feel like that. With sixty, eighty thousand Soviet troops on Czech soil! And even if the Rusáci went away, there was still the state. Plenty of people had a big stake in the status quo. The tanks were one thing; the apparatchiks were something else. 'It is Hapsburgs again,' he said in English.

'Surely change is inevitable.' Iles tried to appease his rancour. 'The ice has to melt in the end.'

'Why?' They were passing the statue to Jan Hus, stony, looming, impressive. Míša added that his people were good historians, better fatalists. Apart from the First Republic, there had never been much freedom.

'Not even with Dubček?' The moment he spoke, he was ashamed of his eagerness to strike a vein of nostalgia. Here, unlike the West, the past was as loaded, as incriminating, as the present. For Míša, who resented so much, this allusion was inexcusable. He turned sharply off the main street and walked in a furious silence towards a small, white courtyard framed by the bough of an apple tree. At the door he argued briefly about who should pay, and came into the exhibition choked with irritation.

The gallery was once a convent. Within its cool, white shadows, among the paintings, Míša grew calmer. He began to speak again, breaking out of his mood to identify a favourite canvas. When they reached the third or fourth room, he suddenly turned to Iles and apologized. He was going through a difficult patch just now, and he hated to be reminded of the good times.

Iles said that he too was sorry; he had every sympathy; such memories were cruel. Telling this part of the story, he will say that here, unbelievably, was someone for whom the Great Dealer had stacked an even worse deck. Unlike his youthful good self, Míša had not aged well; he was losing most of his hair, he had the grey, pink-eyed stare of the sleepless father, the desperation of the under-employed for whom the future offers no sign of hope.

They should be good friends, Míša added. *Ils ont beaucoup de points communs.* He was a solitary man who seemed disturbed by the idea of trust.

Iles encouraged him warmly. They had a shared experience; that was something special. 'What happened with you here,' he said, 'affected all of us.'

Míša seemed slightly flattered; his self-confidence returned. He stopped in front of a brown Victorian landscape. He wanted his friend Mr Iles to know that the so-called Prague Spring was both a liberation and a *désastre*. He could see, he said, that the Englishman was, how could he put it, a bit romantic about what had happened. Understand, he repeated, a liberation, but also a disaster. It was a big surprise, the end of Novotný and all that. Yes, exciting, if you liked that sort of thing. Did he remember the student demonstrations here, when was it, in the autumn of sixty-seven?

Iles remembered. That was shortly after he had first met Milena, towards end of a year which had seen the Six Day War, *Blow-Up*, thigh-length boots, Red Guards, the Dialectics of Liberation at the Round House, the deaths of Che Guevara and

Joe Orton, Francis Chichester sailing alone around the world, *Bonnie and Clyde, The Naked Ape* and the fiftieth anniversary of the Russian Revolution. *I read the news today oh boy.* People were on the street again, but now they were singing and dancing, *It was twenty years ago today, that Sergeant Pepper taught the band to play, They've been going in and out of style, But they're guaranteed to raise a smile* . . . When Milena smiled fifty-four muscles in her face did a royal command performance. *I'd love to turn you on.* No, what did she say? What did he say? I want you now. I want you *now.* When you remember, says Iles, you're the man of a thousand voices talking perfectly loud. Míša was still speaking.

At first, he was saying, the man with the squashy face from Bratislava looked like just another grey figure at the top. But then the people realized something, and he won their hearts. They realized that this man wanted to give the party a human face. He was a good communist, but he was also a good patriot.

So – he raised his hands – along came the spring. Everyone coming alive. Plays, art, cartoons, satire, TV, newspapers. Himself, he wasn't too interested in *la politique*, it was the freedom of the people that was exciting. But then, of course – drawing a long face – as everyone knows, it was all a *désastre*. How did they say it in English, something about a little baby and the water in the bath?

Something in the way he struggled with a long-forgotten phrase aroused Christopher's curiosity. He said, 'Your English is very natural.'

Míša looked at him defensively. 'You know who learns it to me?'

In the fragmentary diary Iles kept at this time he noted how appropriate it was that Milena should slip into the conversation, as though she had just joined them from another part of the gallery. He didn't reply at once; they passed some more pictures with booming feet. He'd guessed already she was Míša's girl too, but so what? He felt calm and happy. Finally he said, 'I expect she was a good teacher.'

Míša reckoned she was very patient. Yes, she had tried to give him lessons from a book. He had wanted to go to England.

'On tour?'

'I like to see English theatre.'

Iles asked about his work in Prague. Míša described his last production, a modern-dress *Hamlet*. 'We was sensational,' he said seriously.

Old memories wake slowly. 'She was – Milena was – acting with you perhaps?'

'Of course.' He looked at the Englishman carefully. 'She talk about you all the time, you know.'

He laughed it off; he does not need his feelings spared. 'And when she was in England, she talked about all of you. She used to listen to the BBC World Service, the Czech station. She knew she was missing something.'

'It was . . . *sa grande honte, vous savez.*'

She had to go home sooner or later. There was no real work for her, an exile without proper papers. Her life in England revolved entirely around their relationship. He remembered her, with the radio on in the background, sitting by the telephone on the floor of their room, chasing jobs. When there was scent in the bedroom, he knew she was going for an interview. If it was a show, they would read through the script together first. He would throw himself into the other roles to encourage her, but his efforts only emphasized the awkwardness of her speech.

He tried to teach her: My name is Milena Hamplová. I'm from Czechoslovakia. I have worked in the theatre in Prague. Now I would like to start work in the English theatre. Or perhaps you need an A.S.M. . .?

It was hopeless. As the weeks passed and the spring turned to summer, the news from home underlined her isolation. Her pride ebbed away and she became depressed.

They were coming to the end of the gallery. Looking down into the courtyard Iles could see a school crocodile queueing for tickets. Míša dismissed a room full of *fin de siècle* canvases with a contemptuous gesture and led him downstairs to the exit.

Iles stopped at the souvenir stand and chose several postcards for his daughters; Míša suggested coffee in the gallery's gloomy cafeteria. As they sat down, he asked him to speak cautiously. 'You understand,' he said, looking over his shoulder. The tea-lady was an old acquaintance, the mother of a disgraced pop star from the good times, though, as Míša said, *on ne sait jamais.*

Iles recognized the ordinary fear of the ordinary citizen, someone whose anonymity is perhaps tainted by more than one entry on the police register. In a free country, he says, fear is the mugger's knife or the dangerous driver, a mundane, intermittent, physical business; in Prague everything is fear, a low-temperature drizzle of apprehension which, quite quickly, becomes indistinguishable from the atmosphere of ordinary life itself.

He began to reminisce about Milena. 'I only realized what I had lost when she was gone,' he confessed. 'When you are young you imagine you will forget. By the time I understood I had to follow, it was too late. Everything happened very quickly that year.'

Míša agreed that there were some years in which you had no time to think. 'Now,' he winced, 'we are tortured by time, *le temps nous écrase.*'

'Since those days, the more I regret, the more I remember. But it's difficult to talk about it at home. There is something about England that throttles your emotions. Instead, I used to write those letters.'

Míša said nothing, but he knew. He was listening. His doggy eyes, bright with emotion, had come alive, and perhaps he too was lost in the past as Iles went on speaking. It was easy to find sympathy in Míša; he understood the luckless and seemed, like a good comrade, to share in their misfortune.

'At my worst moments her father made my life bearable.' He paused thoughtfully. 'And now he too is gone.' He smiled with sadness. 'In this town, a part of my life has gone missing.'

Christopher says that it was Milena who had made the rendez-vous so tense at the beginning; now it was through Milena that they found each other and became friends. When he mentioned her death, he discovered that he had released the story that Hana had been unable to tell. Pressing one hand to his temple like a migraine sufferer and staring fixedly at the table, Míša began to talk about the invasion of Prague.

[2]

Not everyone knows, said Míša, that Shirley Temple was among the foreigners caught in the city by the Rusáci. At the end of a day 'eavesdropping on history' as she put it, and during which she flushed her souvenir photograph of Dubček down the lavatory in the Hotel Alcron, the former child star was evacuated to West Germany in a convoy organized by the US Embassy. Later, on her arrival in San Francisco, she announced at a televised press conference that 'The Soviets are machine-gunning all over Czechoslovakia. They're doing it without provocation in many cases.'

For those who could not take the train from Smíchov, Míša remarked, the arrival of the Rusáci had a different meaning.

It all began in the early hours of Wednesday night, he continued, speaking in his strange, private babel, English, French and Czech hammered into a language currency of his own minting. That was when the first troops arrived.

All over Prague people heard the transport planes throbbing in the summer darkness and, though many refused to believe the news when they heard it, they knew that something unusual was going on. He himself had been feeling very much under the weather and was sitting alone in his flat drinking whisky to kill his head. He smiled self-consciously; yes, he'd slept through the first hours of the invasion *comme un soûlard*.

The next thing he remembered was the phone ringing; a friend with the news. 'We have been occupied by Russian and East German troops.' It was early; about five-thirty. He switched on Radio Prague. Solemn music, the National Anthem and appeals to the people to stay calm. *Don't try to fight. Stay calm.* It made no sense.

At about seven o'clock there was a furious banging on his door. It was Milena. She had been up all night. As soon as the suspicious plane movements began, she and a group of friends had gone to the Central Committee building where Dubček and the others were thought to be in session. The leaders among the students had demanded to speak to the First Secretary.

As they had waited, there was a rumour that Soviet troops were already crossing the river. There were only a few lights; it was warm and dark. Apart from the noise of the planes, the city was quiet.

A grinding of trucks and then all at once here was the first wave of invaders, racing out of the shadows. Foot soldiers in black combat suits jumped out and took up positions. Others hurried obediently into the Central Committee building. Milena reported that at first it was businesslike but not really frightening. They had watched like sightseers.

One of the students went over to the cordon and began to argue with the troops in Russian. The commander appeared, very spruce in his combat gear, and shouted at his men not to speak to anyone. That was the first time anyone lost their cool. The officers treated their troops as though they were educationally subnormal. Many, it turned out, were peasants from Georgia, Tashkent and beyond. They had been told to expect a fraternal welcome from the beleaguered people of Czechoslovakia, and were stunned by the hostility. Most of the violence that week came from fear.

Then they caught the squeaky rumble of tank treads on tarmac, an oddly vulnerable, antiquated sound, like an engine in pain. How familiar these noises would become during the next few days! The crowd surged now, there was whistling and cat calls, and then the first shots were fired. A boy was killed and the crowd began to chant, 'Kill us, Kill us, Kill us.' Once the tanks arrived, Míša said, everything changed.

Milena had come straight to his apartment from these first demonstrations. Now she switched on the TV. Chaos there too: newscasters in open shirts, harassed and unshaven. More appeals for calm, a picture of Svoboda, then an announcement: *Harold Wilson has returned from his holidays.* They both had a good laugh at this, he said; shortly afterwards the TV went off the air. Now they could hear real shooting. So it was true.

He was feeling hung over, and thick and groggy with his cold but Milena made tea for them both, and after that they went out. It was universal, the urge they all felt to go out on to the streets to find out what was going on.

Outside, there was early morning mist, a hint of autumn, and a lot of people hurrying towards the Nové město. A few trams were running, packed with passengers. So much seemed so normal. Queues were forming outside the bread shops. The elderly were anxious that the occupation should not disrupt their lives. The war had taught them that when the enemy comes you are likely to starve.

Soon he and Milena and several others had reached Old Town Square. No, *il se fiche de la politique*, but he had to admit that the atmosphere was exciting. Milena was especially exhilarated, almost in a trance – that was the only word for it.

Talk, milling crowds, black smoke from burning vehicles, and chanting: Dubček, Dubček, Dubček. Some boys had draped a flag over the statue of Jan Hus. It was like before a big match. All the streets were sealed off by tanks. People were crowding round, talking to the crews. Why did you come, Ivan? Go home, we don't want you. There were some clenched fists among the demonstrators. As the city woke up, the tension began to grow. Fighting broke out as the Rusáci tried to take over the radio station on Vinohradská. Shortly after he and Milena arrived at Old Town Square there was more shooting, this time from the direction of Hradčany.

He'd already said how nervous some of the troops were. It was not surprising. When you got close to them you could see they were only *bleus*, with cub moustaches, acne, and round cheeks, trying to act big. Yes, they were probably shit-scared. Most of the people who died were innocent victims. A burst of flame from a trolley wire and the Rusáci opened fire in a panic. Five dead in a street car. Just like that. Is that what they call Fate? You see, for most people the invasion was not dangerous.

After Old Town Square, they made their way with some difficulty through the side streets to Václavské náměstí. No, there was no special reason to go there. It was just something a lot of people were doing, an instinct if you like. The king's horse was draped in flags and banners. Thousands of students were gathering under the gun barrels of the tanks, distributing leaflets already, and discussing the situation. As far as he could remember, they began a vigil that day which they kept up for two weeks, despite the curfew and the shooting. Two-by-two, they stood guard with the red-white-and-blue Czech flag and a black banner of national mourning. Big events, big gestures; it wasn't his style, but you had to admire it, he commented with regret.

Everyone seemed to know that Dubček and the others had been seized. At midday there was a two-minute standstill in protest. After the ebb and flow of the crowds, the chanting, the gunfire and the noise of sirens, the silence was extraordinarily peaceful, like a prayer. His cold was getting worse and his ears were blocked: everything seemed doubly remote.

He couldn't recall exactly what happened after that, except that later in the afternoon when he told her he was going home, Milena was furious. He tried to explain that he was not feeling well; after all, it was only politics. For her it was the moment of a lifetime and she had to do something. You are here in Prague when they trample on our freedom, she was saying, and you take your cold off to bed like a bourgeois! Well, he was sorry, but that was how he was made. Even now he seemed embarrassed to have been so short of anger and passion.

He moved his hand absently over the table top, making patterns in the grease with his bony, undernourished forefinger.

Milena certainly wasn't going to rest. She was already making plans to print leaflets and posters. It frightened him, he said, to see how she had fallen in love with the event. But that was true of so many. For a week or two, everyone played truant from their ordinary lives.

When he thought about it now, it was obvious she was getting into a mood where she'd do something stupid. He should have restrained her. He found it hard to forgive himself. But then, at the time, everything was so unreal; quite a lot of the violence seemed to be for the benefit of Russian TV cameras. No one thought they were going to die. In truth, most of the bullets ended up in the wall.

What was Prague like? Well, he could recall certain images. Broken glass everywhere for one thing. On the pavements, on the road, crunching under every footstep. He didn't know that windows could make so much glass. It was like after a big car smash, *un carambolage*, he said.

Well, night came. It was wet and quite warm. Odd the thoughts you have at such times: he imagined the rain might dampen the situation. As it happened, there was only sporadic gunfire that night, from all parts of the city. The Rusáci sent up flares, lighting up the action. War can be very beautiful, he was afraid to say. But yes, some people died, and many others were hurt. He sat alone in his apartment, feeling terrible, drinking whisky, and listening to the radio which, *par miracle*, was managing to keep up an independent broadcast. The Radio Prague story, he'd have to tell him about that one day.

He must have got a bit pissed on his own because he woke up in his clothes on the floor. Milena was outside, shouting to be let in. She came through the door, slightly out of breath, almost joyful with her adventures. She had been up all night again, plotting and drinking. She was now desperately tired, and a bit wild. After another argument about his cop-out, he persuaded her to rest for a while, and for a few hours she slept.

Occupation isn't all drama. Sometimes it was waiting, waiting,

waiting. To pass the time, he went out and stood in a bread queue. There was a rumour the shops were running low; people said that transport was a problem. The women in the bread line were discussing what they had seen. One had witnessed a fifteen-year-old boy shot down in Václavské náměstí. They couldn't believe what was happening. As he took his loaf back to the apartment, a truckload of Asiatic-looking soldiers trundled past.

Et maintenant? Some things stand right out in your memory. The thing that came back to him now was Milena, flushed and crumpled with sleep, standing in the doorway of his bedroom wearing only a pair of black knickers. She wanted to take a shower. Where would she find a towel? Now Míša looked awkwardly across the table. She had a perfect body, he said.

'Yes,' said Christopher Iles. He felt his eyes brighten with emotion; looking away, he let Míša continue.

After her shower, she borrowed one of his shirts, tucking it into the belt of her jeans. One of his shirts. After all these years there was still a hint of sexual pride in his expression. He made coffee and they broke into the new bread. At midday horns and sirens sounded again, and for an hour the streets were empty. At one, the protest stopped. They joined the crowds outside again. For the rest of that day, he said, all he could remember was walking, walking, walking through Prague.

The streets had become an extraordinary sight. There were tanks or armoured cars at all the junctions. The walls of every building had become scarred with posters and graffiti. MOS-COW – 1,500 KM. LENIN AWAKE! BREZHNEV HAS GONE MAD! DUBČEK! DUBČEK! EVEN HITLER CAME BY DAYLIGHT. IVAN GO HOME! If there was a hammer and sickle it was painted like a swastika. Remember, he explained to Iles, we were shocked. This was the army that had liberated us from the Nazis.

Street lamps, rammed by tanks, tilted at crazy angles. In some parts of the city the trams were still running, but slowed by debris. In other places, the cables were down. The worst damage was by the radio station, which had seen real fighting. The tanks racing through the streets had bulldozed dozens of cars into shop fronts. Food, paper and bric-à-brac were scattered across the streets. There must have been looting, but he didn't see any, only the endless queues. The Rusáci seemed suspicious of the passage-ways that run between streets and houses in Prague: these had been crudely blocked with wrecked cars, Skodas, Volgas, VWs and Minis, some with foreign plates. He remembered thinking that even the West was getting its share.

Here and there, piles of flowers, wreaths and posies marked where someone had been shot down.

As they walked, Milena talked politics, abusing the Rusáci. They were still holding Dubček and the rest of the government. No one knew what had happened to them. The people should demand the release of their leaders. Now was the time to stand up and be counted. Why didn't he do something about it? It was only afterwards that he realized how wrong his cynicism had been. She was right. He had failed.

He looked at Christopher with a pathetic smile of shame.

Everyone was coming together in Wenceslas Square. There were so many students there now, debating, making jokes against the enemy, and chanting: Dubček, Svoboda, Dubček, Svoboda.

The first real bad moment came when he realized that they had ringed the square with tanks. That was the only time *qu'il eût vraiment la trouille. Pas d'issue.* Up by the Museum, which had been badly knocked about by gunfire, the tanks formed a perfect wall, gun barrels pointing into the huge crowd. Yes, it was a Winter Palace kind of feeling. Occasionally, one of the tank turrets would swivel round like a, well, like a Dalek, as if looking for a target. The faces of the commanders were hard and unemotional. It was strange to be standing so close to the enemy you could see the stubble on their chins. If you touched the side of a tank, you would burn your hand. It was the heat of the engines, he remarked, that made you realize the enemy was not some, how should he say, *fantasme.*

The tension in the square grew. Reports came in: a demonstration was planned for five. Milena was saying that at last there would be a real confrontation. Yes, he was scared. Everyone was scared *vraiment*.

But nothing happened. That was typical of those days. At five o'clock the crowd began to break up. The tension went down. In a few minutes the place was empty. Nothing was left except paper, bottles and tin cans, and the Czech tricolour draped hopelessly over the good King.

That night Milena stayed in his apartment. The curfew made it impossible for her to go home. Apparently, she spent the time making posters, listening to the radio as she worked. The radio, it was an obsession during those days. Míša said he slept badly; his rest was interrupted by bursts of night-firing, spectacular but pointless demonstrations of Soviet strength.

What else could he remember now? Milena moved on before he was up next morning, leaving a mess of paint and paper in the kitchen. His cold was better and he felt less lethargic, but he didn't feel inclined to go out. He spent the day with the record-player, listening to Procul Harum and Jimi Hendrix.

Occasionally he tuned into the radio for news, but it was always more of the same, announcements from the Fourteenth Congress which had just met in secret at the ČKD-Praha heavy-machinery factory. *There is hope again. Keep listening to the radio and stay calm. It is our only weapon.* At midday there were sirens again outside and much hooting. The radio said it was a one-hour strike. Everyone was off the streets and there was more shooting from the Rusáci, probably out of frustration.

When Milena returned in the evening she was struggling with a street sign, wrenched from the wall a few blocks away. This was the latest protest. Overnight, Prague became an anonymous city without names or places as every form of identification was torn down in a great collective act of disfigurement. Oh yes, she was jubilant. Now the Rusáci would be totally lost. The Czechs were winning. The soldiers were losing their nerve, she said. She had talked to them. Many of them knew what they were doing was wrong. There was a report of a young trooper who'd committed suicide. It was only a matter of time, she said; oh yes, time was on their side.

That night there was a meeting across the river in the Malá Strana, in a crowded apartment on one of the streets leading up the hill to the castle. Míša went along too; he wanted to try to prove something to Milena. Because of the curfew, they stayed all night drinking and talking. It was like being back at college: everyone was having a good time plotting resistance to authority. Milena's group was planning a distribution network for protest literature. Míša said he stayed silent over his drink; when he listened to the patriotic talk he was afraid. What was he afraid of? His isolation, of course. Here was the pain of being invaded and yet he felt nothing. Christopher could sense a man accusing himself of a dreadful weakness.

On Saturday morning, they were on the street again. He could see it all so clearly. Everywhere there are posters. Dubček is on every wall. Many of the people who've come out to see what's happening are wearing national colours. The weather is still poor: it seems to have been raining on and off since the invasion.

Little scenes come to mind when he talks about those days: a clapped-out Škoda is passing a food queue. A bundle of illegal leaflets is thrown out. The queue surges forward and suddenly everyone is reading. Overhead, there are helicopters, rotors beating monotonously, thumpa-thumpa-thumpa, buzzing backwards and forwards, looking for trouble spots. From time to time they drop propaganda, but no one pays much attention. Besides, it's printed in Slovak not Czech! Typical Rusáci! He's never seen so much paper in the street.

Despite the extraordinary calm, a sort of heroic passivity that might also have been Švejkism there was fear at every corner. You looked over your shoulder whenever you heard someone behind you. Quite soon you learned to distinguish the sound of a Russian jeep from a Czech truck. If you were a sensible, law-abiding citizen, you learnt *le système D*, as they say.

Milena was not like that. Crossing the Palacký Bridge, they passed close to one of the tanks. Suddenly, to his horror, she started to argue with the tank crew. Why have you come? What do you want? The officer tried to reply reasonably. He was wearing glasses, Míša recalled; perhaps he was a university kid doing his national service. We were sent, he says. Your government invited us. This was not the government of the people, Milena replied, that was only a handful of traitors like Indra.

There was a heap of flowers nearby. This is what you have done, she went on, pointing to the place. You have blood on your conscience, she said. One of the other soldiers sitting on the tank waved her on with a jerk of his automatic. Míša said he stared in terror as she defied him. Would he dare shoot another innocent bystander? At this point, Míša said, he simply grabbed her and pulled her away. In the next street, they had this *grosse bagarre*. She accused him of being a *collaborateur* and slapped him across the face. Then she ran away, leaving him stunned and frightened. After that, he said, he only saw her once more.

Now he asked the waitress for more coffee. His hand was shaking as he brought the fresh cup to his lips.

All that night, he went on, there was a steady, relentless downpour, but on the Sunday morning, the first weekend of the occupation, the sun shone for the first time in days. Life and colour returned to the woods behind the castle, the river sparkled and the buildings of Prague were once again gilded with light. People came out of their houses, as if enjoying a visit to the city for the first time, seeing things new, and turning their faces to the sun. It was nature's ceasefire, he observed.

Everyone found their own recreation. He himself had gone for a walk by the river and lost his thoughts in the ceaseless movement of the water in the sunshine. The wind had flurried over the surface of the Vltava for thousands of years, tanks or no tanks. But it was hard to be distracted from the present for long. There was still the occasional burst of rifle fire and the helicopters buzzing over the rooftops.

In his walk he reached Jungmann Square. There was a student surrounded by a group of eager spectators. He went over to listen. The young man was reading the news, hurriedly and without emphasis, concentrating on the information, as if he feared interruption. There had been rumours of State Security police infiltrating the crowds and making lightning arrests. The speaker had the same sallow, exhausted look of the occupying troops. There were deep bruises under his eyes and a shadow on his chin. Míša said he recognized him as a friend of Milena's.

When the reading was over and the student had jumped down from his box, Míša came over to introduce himself. For a moment, he saw fear in the boy's eyes, the fear that this was a plain-clothes snatch. But when he asked where Milena Hamplová was, the newsreader relaxed. He didn't know, he said. He'd seen her last night, no, Friday night . . . but Míša had been there too. He was sorry he couldn't be more help. Soon they were talking *comme de vieux copains*. For the first time he felt the sense of brotherhood that all the others enjoyed in those days, and it made him feel all the more the odd man out, he observed bitterly.

So they began to walk, discussing the events and worrying about Milena's behaviour. Míša said he explained his fear that she was going a bit crazy. The student agreed. They say she does not care, he said. They say she has left her lover in England and does not think about her safety.

Yes, said Míša, pausing for Iles to take in what he had said, that was what he told me.

It was such a strange, quiet day. People in their Sunday best were out strolling with their families. Some were even pushing prams. Small children played soldiers, imitating the Rusáci. Childish machine-gunning echoed across the square, *der-der-der-der-der*. A poignant game: there were stern notices at every street corner urging citizens to report the dead and wounded to the nearest hospital.

But Czechs cannot let things get depressing for long. There were jokes scribbled over walls everywhere. IVAN. COME HOME QUICKLY! NATASHA IS GOING OUT WITH KOLYA. LOVE MUM. CZECHS, WE HAVE LOST FIVE ALLIES – BUT THE WORLD IS WITH US. THE SOVIET UNION IS OUR MODEL. LET'S INVADE MOSCOW! That sort of thing. Political humour, Míša noted, is always so heavy-handed.

He and the student talked for hours. The boy told him many things about the growing protest movement. He was quite pragmatic about it – a job to be done. Míša was impressed. Perhaps he could help after all. They exchanged addresses and phone numbers; he wondered what he had let himself in for.

The quiet of the evening was interrupted by gunfire. The curfew was due. They said goodbye and Míša walked quickly home with the sun setting in a clear sky. When he climbed the four flights to his apartment, he found Milena slumped against his door, asleep.

She was exhausted; he had to shake her awake. She was furious to have been discovered this way. When he offered her tea, a meal, a drink, she refused proudly, saying she could not stay, she had to be elsewhere before the curfew. She had come, she said, to say she was not sorry for anything. She had meant to hit him. She wanted him to know how much she despised him.

Yes, he reiterated, facing Iles across the table, that was what she said.

'And you?' More than ever, he felt a stirring of sympathy for the hapless actor.

Míša's expression was all regret. For a few weeks there had been a relationship. Now, *finis*. He had tried to catch hold of her as she spoke, but she pulled back.

'That was it,' he said. She was gone. The door slammed and the sound of her feet pattered down the stairwell. He had thrown open the window and had watched her moving, almost skipping, away down the littered pavement until the street turned and she was out of sight.

Iles asked what happened next. He could not help himself.

Míša flinched and looked over his shoulder as if afraid to be overheard. There was an elderly couple sipping tea at a table by the door; otherwise, they were still alone.

It was a simple tragic story. Even now, the sense of waste haunted him every day.

Iles made a murmur of encouragement.

Each day, said Míša, was the same. As dawn came, and the curfew ended, the people returned to the streets and repossessed their city. At night the Rusáci have power, they can move and shoot freely. In the daytime, they are helpless, trapped among the hostile crowds. But, as time passed and tiredness took over, night and day sometimes became confused, especially at dawn and at dusk.

Monday morning began with a huge protest, *une cacophonie insupportable*. Sirens, car horns, and the heavy tolling of church bells. Everyone, *tout le monde*, was protesting. It was lucky, he reckoned, that Dubček and the rest reached an agreement with the Kremlin that day. Much longer and there would have been an explosion. The Rusáci in Prague must have been very nervous. They sat in their tanks, cold, hungry, tired and uncertain. You could see it in their faces. They'd come with rations for three days, expecting a welcome from the people. Instead, even when they asked for water, they were told it had been poisoned. By Monday they were getting to the end of their tether, Míša reckoned.

The news came through much later. The moment he heard the familiar voice at his door, he knew something was wrong. It was the student newsreader with the late special, he said ironically. He had come, he said, because he knew Míša would want to know. He had just come from the hospital.

Milena had been walking home. Eye-witnesses said she was alone. A boy of about fifteen was painting a slogan on the wall:

RUSÁCI GO ... There was an armoured car passing by. It stopped, of course. A soldier pointed his machine-gun at the boy who bravely finished his work. HOME, he wrote. Ragged white letters dripping on a stone wall. He did not run, he did not even move. Perhaps he was paralysed with fear. There was some confused shouting from the armoured car, threats and commands, he supposed. Apparently, Milena had calmly walked over and stood next to the boy. You cannot shoot us both, she said. I am innocent.

The machine-gunner cut them down with a single burst. The boy was critically wounded. Milena was killed instantly.

Seven

[1]

'Sometimes,' Míša was speaking in French, with a touch of the viola in his voice, 'I lie awake in my bed and think: at least I have been part of something that people will talk about forever. History has touched my life with its wingtips and in a terrible way that has given it meaning.'

They were sitting on a spongy wooden bench under an apple tree on one of the hills overlooking the city. Sheer to the left, the jagged outline of the castle; at their feet, the old river moving slowly under the five bridges; around them the twittering woods, and high overhead the muted jets of a silver plane.

Míša had finished. Suddenly numb with introspection, he stared at the shining churches in the distance while the wind toyed absently with his wispy hair. Nearby, the Stars and Stripes fluttering in the grounds of the American Embassy caught his attention. 'The Rusáci were so hungry,' he said, with a last pulse of recollection, 'that they stole the pears from the trees there. We are forgetting so much,' he concluded sadly.

After a while, Iles repeated his thanks. His gratitude was all the stronger for knowing how hard at first it had been for Míša to speak of these things. In the end, the actor had become strangely eager to share all he knew, offering to take Iles to Milena's grave, to the place where she had died, the hospital and so on. But Iles had refused. He hoped it was a compliment to suggest that Míša's words were sufficient. Sensing there was more to hear, he proposed a bit of a walk from the little gallery. And so together they had crossed the Charles Bridge and up the hill into the woods, while Míša talked on about the years since the invasion, the troubles of finding interesting work, the restrictions and difficulties of life in Prague.

Now it was time to go. Instinctively, they knew they should exchange addresses. When Iles pulled a scrap of paper from his wallet a photograph fell out.

'My wife,' he explained.

Míša studied it like a jeweller. 'Beautiful,' he said.

'She still is.' He spoke with sad longing.

Míša shook his head. 'I understand.'

'Thank you.' He felt a shudder of friendship. 'I'm sorry to be going.' He wasn't able to find more words. They shook hands.

'You thank Hana please.'

'I will.' Was it simply *politesse*? Or did he know about their date? 'Hana has been very good to me.'

Míša seemed happier. 'She is beauty – and sometimes she does not seem to know it.'

Iles was spelling out his address. The actor wanted to know if Wandsworth was by Thames River.

'It is pronounced Tems,' he said.

'Tems.' Míša smiled foolishly, like one used to failure and correction. 'Thank you, Mr Iles.' He folded away the note and patted his pocket briskly. 'One day we will rendezvous.'

He said he very much hoped so. They shook hands again, repeating their goodbyes, and then Míša simply walked away down the hill, stooping slightly, merging into the green shadows of the summer woods.

For a few minutes, with Míša's words on his mind, he stayed on, seated in a kind of trance, unable to move.

It was late afternoon when he walked back into the city. Crossing the river, he watched the fishermen in rowing boats casting their lines onto the still water. A few bathers were splashing lazily in the late sunshine. He passed under an archway and into the vacant labyrinth of the Staré Město.

There is, he says, a sadness about the city and its people that is quite haunting; this evening there was laughter in the square, children's voices echoing in the empty spaces. It was impossible to imagine what it had been like when Míša's wings of history had been beating overhead.

He looked up at the façade of the National Museum. No sign of any damage. Míša was right. People would forget, the texts would be rewritten, and the fading memories eroded by the slow passing of time in an occupied land.

There was a field-green policeman in front of him as he turned into the street leading to the Hotel Palace. Calmly he produced his passport. The officer turned its pages.

'You?' He looked at the contemporary Iles and then down at the prototype, seeming to find in the fading dissident snapshot an amusing confirmation of the radical follies of the decadent West.

'I know.' His expression sparkled with ironic sympathy. 'It's dreadfully misleading. They shouldn't do it to you. Perfidious Albion, you know.'

The policeman returned the passport with a puzzled 'Děkuji', and walked on with the brutal saunter of authority.

The episode reminded Iles that he had made no plans for his return home. He found that the ice-cool receptionist was familiar with the timetables. It would have to be by train. He watched her long, exotic fingers work through the pages of the rail guide. Tomorrow morning he must buy his ticket at Čedok office in Na Příkopě. She would write it all down for him. He took the note and felt the dry thrill of her skin, but he could not hold her gaze. Perhaps his cheapness told against him.

He went to his room climbing up the threadbare staircase past the dusty ferns, weary after his long day. It was nearly seven. He wanted a shave and a bath. Hana would be here soon.

She came at eight, naïve with anticipation, and smartly dressed in a style that was ever so slightly out of date. How new she was! He kissed her without thinking, London-style, and she blushed. More deliberately, he complimented her evening wear and her lips parted with surprise. Oh, but she wanted to know how it had gone with Míša. 'He is so funny, don't you find?' Her artless enthusiasm was very much Milena's. 'So gloomy.'

'I liked him. We had a lot in common.'

She studied him disconcertingly. 'Yesterday,' she went on, 'you had such a sad face. Now I can see a different Christopher.'

'For years I have not dared come here. Now I know everything. Perhaps I have been set free.'

For Míša also, she said, it was good to talk. It was ridiculous, but he still blamed himself for what had happened. Nothing had gone right for him since. He was an unhappy man with unhappy memories. He had this plan to get out and go to the West, but it was very hard. There had been a chance to go to Vienna in the spring . . . Her free talk had betrayed her. 'Yes,' she admitted. 'That was the train. You were to meet. He would know you. And he would tell you everything. That was what we decided.'

Míša had talked all day and had still held this back: a few days ago Iles would have been hurt. Now he understood that this was how people had to live here. 'What went wrong?'

'Those things are difficult to arrange.' She sounded older then. There was a problem with the necessary papers, a last-minute hitch. No way to get a message to London before he left. 'Honestly,' she became suddenly practical, 'we thought we never hear from you any more.'

Iles became facetious. 'I'm sorry I won't fade away.' But she did not really understand, and he suggested a move.

They walked out on to the street: there are some conversations that breathe better with walking. Silly with happiness, he broke off to buy her a carnation. Shyly she let him fix it on her dress and then insisted that he have one for himself.

After he has come home, he will look back on this evening, the soft brown warmth of the city, Hana's dancing footsteps, his pleasure and her excitement at the brief, unrestricted sharing of these hours. These are the souvenirs – for all their final melancholy – which fill him with longing for Prague, the place where somehow he touched the seat of his feelings. It is a longing which, once these words become public property, he can never satisfy in his life again.

Of course, he could go to the Czech consulate in Kensington Park Gardens, hand over his passport, and watch the cabbage-faced stooge at the desk take it into the back office to check his name against her lists. But in a very few minutes she would come back, sternly refusing his visa with a non-negotiable 'Ne'.

Iles loves the mild flirtatiousness of such an evening. As they took their table in the restaurant (Hana's choice), he remarked seriously that the more he knew her the more he was struck by her likeness to her half-sister. 'In so many ways,' he said.

She accepted the compliment, but became momentarily guarded, as if unsure of its intention.

'But I've talked about Milena all day,' he continued, stepping up his direct attack. 'I want to know about you.'

'There is nothing to know. I am too young to be interesting.'

That was Milena all over: statements of ice-cold candour breaking like mountain peaks through the clouds of friendship.

He put on his ironic face: 'When you're as old as me, youth has its own special fascination. No, it does.'

'That is nostalgia,' she pronounced, icy mountains again. 'That is nothing. It is false consciousness.'

'Fantasy perhaps. But that's what people live by. Is that false?'

She considered the point carefully. 'Here, in this country, where there is so much they do not want us to remember, memory is a palace, Not Open to the Public. With you, memory is a prison. Just now, you said to me, perhaps I have been set free. That is what I am talking about.'

Her sudden eloquence prompted a question that has dogged him throughout his visit. 'I don't understand,' he confessed, probing again. 'Why is it you are such a different person with your mother?'

'Am I?' But her expression gave her away. 'You see, I love her, and I do not want to give her pain. She has one big fear, that I will be like Milena and she does not want to lose me. So . . .' Her smile of self-mockery was sad but so charming, he says. 'I try to be what you call a good girl.'

Half-teasing, he replied, 'Isn't that false consciousness?'

Hana's eyes became full and round; he says he wishes he had kept his thoughts back. She said: 'My feelings about my mother . . . I cannot tell you what pain I have. Especially now that my father is no longer between us.'

'How's that?'

'He had his faults, but he was a good man, you know. He accepted what had happened. He would tell my mother: Olga, let your daughter be. She is not Milena.'

She broke off to deal efficiently with the waiter and when the familiar negotiations were over, she returned voluntarily to herself. 'When I am with someone like you, I know I am a different person. Yes, perhaps I should leave. But I cannot.'

'I know what you're saying,' he replied. 'You pretend something is so, and you live that way. Then one day something happens – or perhaps it does not happen – but anyway you find you have no choice. You have to change.'

'I have this dream. There is this green field. Meadow?'

'Yes, a meadow.'

'In the meadow is a white coffin. I am so afraid that my mother is in it, but when I lift the lid I find it is not my mother but me, and I am happy. Strange.'

Iles, interpreting to himself, was disturbed. 'That's not a good dream,' he commented.

She put her hand across her breast. 'Here,' she replied, 'I know it. But here,' touching her high white forehead in another pidgin gesture, 'it is more complicated.' She sighed deeply. 'Oh it is so much more complicated. You see my mother misses my father so much. I have to try to make her happy.'

'You are very . . .' But he could not say what he really wanted and ended lamely '. . . very strong.' Then he said, 'I think I'll make a prediction.'

She was amused, curious. 'What's that?'

He was captivated by her youthful egotism. 'Three guesses.'

'No . . . please. I can't. You must tell me.'

She was leaning across, both hands pressed on the edge of the table. He bent towards her himself and pinned her wrist with a strong, clairvoyant finger. 'Despite Milena, you will come to London quite soon.'

'Oh no . . . that's not possible.'

'I'm not sure. There are some things you cannot know.' He cast his spell deliberately. 'And when you come, I shall look after you.'

Her anxiety softened and she laughed teasingly again. 'Well then, Christopher, I shall have to be good.'

They toasted his prediction, both half-serious, she admitting a strong streak of superstition.

The talk of England was apparently a reminder: Hana began fumbling for her bag under the table. Now she put it on her lap and pulled out a familiar black binder, bulging with onion-skin pages. It was Peter Císař's bibliography. 'Here. My mother said. You must take it. It is not finished. But perhaps in London you will find . . .' Her voice faded. She was repeating a message that made no sense to her. 'Please, Christopher, please take it. My mother wants it to be yours.'

He knew he looked discouraging; he has always hated these situations. 'Thank you.' He paused, leafing through the pages. 'I'm very . . . touched. I will see that it is not forgotten.' He laid it reverently under his chair. (He now admits he half-hoped he might leave it behind.)

They ate well; wine flowed. He told her funny stories and made her happy in the way that is his special gift. Other diners at nearby tables probably took them for lovers. What did he say? It's a fair assumption that he produced all the magic of his mind, and wove it round her like a charm. To put it his way, there are no cold black words on a page that can bring those moments back to life. We can only guess at the anecdotes, fables, jokes and inventions that he used, slowly drawing out the hidden parts of Hana's heart.

The waiter brought coffee, tart Slovakian liqueurs, and then more coffee. Even late, the restaurant was noisy and crowded in a way that is unusual for Prague. It was obviously the 'in' place to be. There was a string quintet vamping the slow sad music of Central Europe in the background. The musicians were old and tired. They chatted to each other as they played, nodding to familiar faces among the tables. Moved by the music, and by the imminence of departure, Hana and Iles toasted each other again, his visit, her future, his prediction, her hospitality . . .

'To you, Hana.'

'To you, Christopher.'

Sometimes the clink of glasses is a kiss. Just when the evening seemed to be almost over, Hana said impetuously, 'But I forgot. The dancing. Would you like?'

Of course he would like. Soon he was escorting her to the door with a more than faint suggestion of intimacy undiminished by her reminder to bring her father's bibliography.

The disco was on the first floor of a tourist hotel in Wenceslas Square, and crowded with teenagers. For a moment, Iles felt out of place, but she led him swiftly on to the dance floor and swept him up in the rhythm. They were both laughing and happy and slightly drunk. When the music went slower, he took her in his arms and they danced together, feeling each other's warmth. He closed his eyes and felt dizzy. When the last chords came, they kissed.

Something went wrong in her mind. She had to go home, she said. All at once they were downstairs again, looking for a taxi. He was begging her to come to England soon. But how could she? She had no money.

He pulled off his watch. 'Here. Take this.' Afterwards he hated himself for that imperializing gesture. 'This will pay for your ticket.'

She shook her head, almost scornful. 'It's not quite as simple as that!'

'Will you write? You have my address.' There was panic in his voice. 'I will come back.'

'Yes,' she said. 'I will write.'

He knew she was lying.

They walked hopelessly down the square. There was a line of taxis under the trees, and a few soldiers lounging at the top of the subway, looking on.

'Here is your watch,' she said.

'You have it, please.' He pushed her hand away, almost as offended as she. It slipped; the face smashed.

'Oh.' She was horrified. 'I am so sorry.'

'It doesn't matter. It was my fault.' Everything was a mistake. He picked it up. The hands had stopped. He wrapped it glassless and silent in his handkerchief. 'Not to worry. I expect I'll get it mended in England.'

'In England, in England,' she mimicked. 'Everything happens in England, doesn't it?' Too late, she realized what she was saying and tried to apologize.

'No, please,' he said. 'It's best to say goodbye and go home.'

They stopped by the taxis. 'You will go back to your wife tomorrow?'

He looked down. 'Of course.'

'Have a good trip, Christopher.' She kissed him quickly and they said goodbye.

Then she was inside the car, giving directions. He waved half-heartedly, watched the lights disappear into the surrounding summer darkness, and then turned away towards the Hotel Palace.

When he was alone in the room, he sat on the narrow, well-made bed with the bibliography on his knee, shrunken into his shell by a sense of hopelessness and defeat. His children will tell you he can often be moved to tears by a poem, or a film, or even the witness of a TV documentary; now, for the first time in years, his emotions were released by his own vulnerability: he cried for himself.

Eight

[1]

Sometimes, Christopher will remark with a sigh (lounging back with that characteristic weariness), he thinks he has known so many people he wonders who the hell he is. Faces in the street or at parties, names in the newspapers, reputations mulched in his mind by rumour and gossip: he can find himself running after a total stranger, but walking past an old friend.

Strangers, friends and acquaintances, even relations, all have participated in the making of this story. They have answered phone calls, patiently endured long interviews, sent me letters and cuttings, looked out photographs, suggested in their turn other contacts to contact.

Thanks to them there has been an *embarras de richesse*. So much has, perforce, been left out. Christopher and I have had long, agonizing sessions on that point. But if this collage has any hue or splendour then it is to these collaborators that much is owed.

Most of all, I want to thank the people who have appeared in these pages, the *dramatis personae*: Helen and her three daughters; Hal Strachan and his colleagues; Lizzy; and above all Mrs Rosemary Iles, who interrupted her tour of the United States (where she was lecturing to the luncheon circuit on 'Coping') in order to provide invaluable material in time to meet the publisher's deadline.

It has been a Boswellian credo with me that every fact has to be checked at source. To re-emphasize my opening words, everything in this book is real – every episode, scene, weather reference, conversation and name (with one exception: Dr Jaroslav

Novák is necessarily a pseudonym; I could not guarantee his safety without it).

And then there is Dr Augustus Kuhn (or Siegmund Dukatenzeiler, if you prefer). I imagine that it will be many months, even years, before Christopher gets to the bottom of that story, as he surely wants to. (At the moment of writing, Kuhn's trail has gone rather cold; he has ignored at least three letters addressed simultaneously to his club and his place in Vienna.)

The cutting from *The Times* remains in Christopher's wallet, a nagging reminder. He tells me he's determined, now that his own story has been committed to print, to have a really serious go at tracking down the slippery entrepreneur. Christopher – bless him – simply cannot resist the temptations offered by the bizarre. His enthusiasm for novelty has always been one of his finest qualities, but also something of a weakness. He admits that.

A special thank-you, of course, must go to my partner himself. This has been, quite frankly, the most absorbing project of my short literary career. The most successful passages owe everything to his guiding hand; he has, so to speak, played something of a Stevenson to my Lloyd Osbourne.

Now that our work is almost over, what of Christopher Iles himself? What is his mood? His future? He says, very gratifyingly, that he has been inspired by his work with me on this manuscript. It has, he announces, changed his life. This is true; but there is a part of him that will never change. Oddly enough, there's a passage in Kafka's Diary which gives a sort of apt expression to this:

> Anyone who cannot come to terms with his own life while he is alive needs one hand to ward off a little of his despair over his fate – he has little success in this – but with his other hand he can note down what he sees among the ruins, for he sees different (and more) things than do the others; after all, dead as he is in his lifetime, he is the real survivor.

So he will continue to watch and take notes. He will worry

about himself and the world about him. With that ironic smile of his, he will say that there are only three questions that matter: Where are we coming from? Where are we going? And why are we here?

Only those who know him well can decide if he is joking or not.

Finally, there is my boundless gratitude to my wife, Jane, who says that Christopher and I were made for each other.

[2]

Iles says that when you return from a place like Prague you experience an ill-defined relief which, although he admits it sounds trite, has to do with a sense of freedom and familiarity. I think that he, who is so proud of his loyal, unmilitant opposition to so many norms, surprised himself with his reaction. How scornful he can be about his society! And yet he confessed to finding renewal in the speed, the thoughtlessness and the blatancy of the West. Even he, who often sees a darker picture, found that the railway's summer bazaar – backpacking students at Ostend, holiday-makers on the pier at Dover, schoolboys playing cricket among the hopfields of the Weald – made him affectionate for the world he knew, not forgetting its restrictions and frustrations. When you have been to Prague, he says, you have an experience against which to mark the value of what you know. Perhaps, he will add, these confusions explain why he got so drunk on the train coming home.

His departure went badly from the first. Oversleeping, he missed the early morning express. It was raining hard when he woke; there was no incentive to move. If the maid hadn't come to strip the bed and tidy up, he might have missed the next train too. As it was, he struggled into the railway station to catch the eleven o'clock with just ten minutes to spare.

He walked across the high-tech underground concourse and climbed up a broken escalator to the station itself, a draughty, single-arched iron-and-glass vault with red muslin flags hanging damply from the rusty stanchions. The place had the emptiness of a film set. There were some peasant travellers with dogs and straw baskets queueing for hamburgers and synthetic ice-cream. They might have been extras. When a line of heavy green carriages pulled toweringly alongside the nearest platform, stirring life into the waiting crowd with a long imperious hoot, he imagined a Lenin or a Trotsky stepping down to begin a revolution.

His train was in already and preparing to depart; it was not full. He chose a carriage near the restaurant car and went to get a drink. But the barman was gossiping with two soldiers and would not serve him until they left Prague. He returned to his compartment and discovered that he had been joined by an elderly couple with two battered suitcases, Germans returning home after a short visit. He exchanged evasive noises of politeness, sat down by the window and stared self-accusingly at his reflection.

He was ashamed – there was no other word for it – of the scene with Hana. Of course she was not Milena: he had bewildered her with his clumsiness and had lost her. It was hard to accept there was no more hope, only memory. Some people's lives look back; others look forward. He knows he should be a forward-looker, but there is a part of him that will always be turning back, turning to salt.

Outside on the platform last-minute passengers were joining the train. They had the look of people going home. There was none of the expectation of starting out in their faces, just the contented tiredness of travellers coming to the end of a journey. He feels the weariness but none of the satisfaction. He is confused in his mind. Part of him, as he told Hana, will always be left behind here.

A young woman pulled the door open, glanced nervously at Iles, made a polite inquiry of the old couple and took a seat. There was a bit of shouting outside, the couplings clanked and they jolted forward. Soon they were coasting slowly through the city suburbs and into the Bohemian countryside, open grazing and a leafy river.

The old people were discussing a map, already transforming their visit into anecdotes. The girl was reading. She looked up and caught his curious eye. He deflected his glance, annoyed that, preoccupied and slow-witted, he should be found out in this way. One day this would be the experience of his daughters, bored men on trains translating looks into amorous fantasy. His sense of shame redoubled, he stood up and pulled his suitcase off the rack, unearthing a safer distraction.

He took Císař's black binder into the corridor. There was a half-open window and he leaned out. The cold air whipped the hair back from his forehead, massaging his face. The rain had stopped but the air was still heavy with water and the land was sodden. Three farm children, a boy and two girls, were dancing by a white fence. The boy carried a transistor and the girls were moving to its music. As the train passed their dumb-show they waved, and Iles waved back. The pleasure he felt at this exchange was interrupted by a tap on his shoulder. It was the guard. Leaning out of the window was *verboten*. Iles said 'English' with a hopeless vague smile and, turning away, carried the bibliography off to the restaurant.

The soldiers had gone. Several passengers were already tucking into plates of veal or chicken loaded with overcooked vegetables. There were long glasses of yellow Pilsner beer on every table. Two businessmen with meaty, post-prandial expressions were talking contracts at the far end. Iles ordered a bottle of Slovakian wine and a salami sandwich and sat down nearby. When he had finished the sandwich and two-thirds of the wine he felt better, warmer, more cheerful.

The train stopped at a station. Doors banged and a few more passengers climbed on. Local people stood watching, immobilized spectators. There was a distant whistle and the train jerked forward again, knocking over his wine. But the bottle was empty. He ordered another. Refilling his glass, he raised it to the two

businessmen who seemed slightly astonished by his mad, ingratiating smile.

The barman brought his change. 'You can tell them,' said Iles,
speaking slowly in his English-as-a-foreign-language, 'that if
they think I'm pissed I'm going to get pisseder.' He noticed one of
the businessmen murmur, 'Englander', to his partner, and raised
his voice above the rattling train. 'Have some wine, friends.' But
they refused, joking uneasily together. 'No, really,' he went on.
'I've got something to celebrate. I have.' He leaned towards them
confidentially. 'Everyone knows my agent was a son of a bitch, but
I've no regrets. That's what he was paid to be. There's only one
place to have a shit and that's behind you.' This seemed to strike a
chord: one of the Germans said, 'God save the Queen,' and
applauded ironically. Iles gave them a confused sketch of his
glittering future (taking my name in vain, I'm afraid to say), and
then he was on his feet, the last of his wine in his hand. '*Guten Tag*,
gentlemen. You may forget this meeting. But I shall not. From
now on, everything is fiction.'

He stood in the corridor, leaning against the window, Císař's
bibliography tucked under his arm. The atmosphere seemed
close, oppressive. He yawned. The express, still travelling at a
stately 35 m.p.h., trundled into a tunnel. The lights did not work
and he stood in darkness, feeling the rush of sooty wind. When
he poked his nose illegally into the roaring blackness he could
see a prick of light in the distance. Soon they would be at the
frontier.

Anxiety returned. Císař's typescript looked like *samizdat*: he
imagined guards, a search, interrogations. Suddenly he very
much wanted to be with his wife and children again. He wanted a
life without sorrows, a release from the old bookseller's spell.

How often have we talked about this moment! He still worries
that he does not feel guilty. I say that some emotions can only find
their right expression in action. We do things for reasons we only
half understand. It is only in retrospect that we know we are right.
He accepts this. I say you cannot have your life mortgaged to the

past for ever. He listens. I'm proud to say that though I began as a collaborator, in the end I've become his guide and interpreter, as much to himself as to others.

So there he was by the window. The paper fluttered in his hand like a white bird; he released the spring and the bird flew away broken-feathered. When the train came back into the watery midday sunshine with a triumphant whistle the black binder was empty. Iles threw it on to the embankment without a qualm and danced back from the window, sick with wine and joy and originality. He was almost laughing.

They were running between thickets of sickly green trees. Bindweed and cow parsley, soaked with rain, crowded high on both sides of the narrow track. Through the forest clearings beyond he could occasionally glimpse signs of military activity, tank compounds, entanglements of barbed wire and pillboxes.

When they began to slow down the grinding of the brakes sent a metallic shudder through the train. Iles found a young American standing outside his compartment. In his elation he had to say more than 'Hi'.

'This must be the frontier.'

'I guess so.' The boy's smile had perfect athlete's teeth. His skin was lightly ski-tanned and his casual clothes, grey flannels and a navy blazer, hung well on his body. He spoke with the assurance of the naturally wealthy and successful. 'It's always a great feeling to cross over.'

'I've not done this trip before.'

The American had a junior post in the Embassy, commuting between Prague and Bonn. Sometimes he would take the train for variety's sake. 'The border – it's a pretty impressive business. I mean,' he searched for the right word, 'it's serious.'

'It's meant to be.'

'I once saw them take a man off this train. As long as I live I'll not forget the look on his face.'

They stood and watched two guards with Alsatians peering under the wheels and bogies of a goods train in the adjacent siding. A solo engine went past in a cloud of diesel fumes and disappeared up the track.

'They change the locomotives here,' the American explained, and pointed out a prosperous-looking West German ticket inspector with the stub of a cigar gripped between his lips.

It was beginning to rain again and the light was almost painfully white; over the hills there was the suspicion of a rainbow.

Iles asked his companion the time, and found they had been stationary for nearly three-quarters of an hour already. Once again he wondered vaguely what he should do about his file of letters.

The carriage was strangely quiet. They could hear orders shouted in the distance and the thump of military boots. Then the connecting door swung open and two passport controllers, stern-faced women in badly-fitting uniforms reminding Iles of traffic wardens, began to work their way down the corridor guarded by soldiers with sub-machine-guns.

Iles returned restlessly to his seat and waited. The soldier at the door was wearing a lot of leather and metal, like a horse. The elderly couple and the girl sat very still, not talking any more.

One of the women appeared and asked for their passports and visas. Everything was in order. The soldiers began to search the luggage, and Iles saw the girl blush as their coarse military fists fingered through her bras and knickers. Then they turned their attention to his own bag. He felt swollen-headed with the wine and suddenly nervous of showing nervousness. Anxiety drummed in his ears; he thought his head would split. But there was no danger. They were not interested in his correspondence; they were not, apparently, interested in anything. 'Is that all?' Their English was thick but intelligible.

'Nothing to declare,' said Iles, using the ancient formula with relief.

The soldier's attention hardened with suspicion. 'Please?'

Iles shook his head, and repeated a phrase he had found in his Nagel. '*Nemám nic k proclení*,' he said.

The guard nodded woodenly, bent down briefly to search under the seat and moved on. The long wait continued. Iles watched a row of birds twittering on the fence outside, an inane chorus.

Eventually the train gave a premonitory hoot, the birds rose in the air, the couplings creaked and in a minute the checkpoint was slipping away.

Christopher Iles settled back in the musty plush seat and watched the landscape gather speed outside. For a while his thoughts raced with the train: Helen, his children, old Císař, Dukat/Kuhn . . . But quite soon his hangover had the better of his anticipations and dreams. He dozed; he slept. And the train, moving like an express at last and breathing a cool reviving wind from the German plains, thundered through the afternoon towards the West.